D0315353

GODZILLA

—— *and* ——

GODZILLA
RAIDS AGAIN

SHIGERU KAYAMA

Translated and with an Afterword by Jeffrey Angles

UNIVERSITY OF MINNESOTA PRESS
MINNEAPOLIS
LONDON

JAPANFOUNDATION
国際交流基金

The University of Minnesota Press gratefully acknowledges financial support
for the production of this book from the Japan Foundation.

Godzilla, by Shigeru Kayama, copyright Yoshihiro Yamaguchi, 2004. All rights
reserved. English translation rights arranged with Chikumashobo Ltd., through
Bureau des Copyrights Français, Tokyo. Both novellas were published in
a single volume in 1955 as *Gojira* and *Gojira no gyakushū*; this was the first
volume in a series for young adult readers titled Shōnen Bunko (Youth Library)
published by Shimamura Shuppan, Ltd.

Translation copyright 2023 by Jeffrey Angles

All rights reserved. No part of this publication may be reproduced, stored in
a retrieval system, or transmitted, in any form or by any means, electronic,
mechanical, photocopying, recording, or otherwise, without the prior written
permission of the publisher.

Published by the University of Minnesota Press
111 Third Avenue South, Suite 290
Minneapolis, MN 55401-2520
http://www.upress.umn.edu

ISBN 978-1-5179-1523-0 (pb)

Library of Congress record available at https://lccn.loc.gov/2023019309

Printed in the United States of America on acid-free paper

The University of Minnesota is an equal-opportunity educator and employer.

30 29 28 27 26 25 24 23   10 9 8 7 6 5 4 3

Contents

Godzilla: Godzilla in Tokyo

Godzilla Raids Again: Godzilla in Osaka

Note on Japanese Names

All Japanese names in this book are presented in the Western order (given name followed by surname), instead of the order ordinarily used in Japan (surname followed by given name). The author of *Godzilla* and *Godzilla Raids Again* is known in Japan as Kayama Shigeru, but the Kayama estate prefers that his name in this book appears in the English-language order, Shigeru Kayama.

GODZILLA

Godzilla in Tokyo

As you readers already know, the main character of this tale, Godzilla, is an enormous, imaginary kaiju—a creature that doesn't actually exist anywhere here on the planet. However, atomic and hydrogen bombs, which have taken on the form of Godzilla in this story, do exist. They are being produced and could be used for war at any moment.

If that were to happen, it wouldn't just be big metropolises like Tokyo and Osaka that would be destroyed. The entire Earth would likely be laid waste. To prevent something so frightening and tragic from coming to pass, people all over the world are pouring their energy into a new movement opposing the use of atomic and hydrogen bombs.

As one small member of that movement, I have tried to do my part by writing a novel—the tale you now hold in your hands. Reading this book in that context will make it all the more informative and interesting.

JULY 1955

A Strange Bright Light from the Ocean Floor

"I was totally terrified when the sea down there in Okinawa got so rough. One minute, *whoosh*, we were lifted up to what felt like the top of a mountain, then before we knew it, *whoosh*, we were dragged down into the valley on the other side. When I caught a glimpse of the ocean, it was folded up like an accordion, and right in front of us was another huge wave, about to crash down on the ship. I thought we were completely done for."

Takeo laughed. "What a wimp! I remember that day. You grabbed onto the handrail, quaking with fear. Just because the seas were a little rough!" He stuck out his chest boldly and made a serious face. "I practically grew up on rough, choppy water—a little weather doesn't scare me!" He brought his pointer finger close to his thumb to indicate how small the waves had been.

"What the hell are you talking about? You were green from seasickness, Takeo. Don't you remember? You mistakenly grabbed my leg and clung to me like you were holding on for dear life!"

Takeo gave a hearty laugh. "Give me a break. I felt so sorry for you, Saburō, that I was just trying to save you."

"Whatever . . . Hey, we ought to be able to see the mainland before long."

Still smiling, the two of them turned their gazes to the wide-open plain of the sea. It looked like it stretched on forever.

That year, both Takeo and Saburō had graduated from high school and taken jobs as sailors on the *Eikō-maru*, a cargo vessel designed for short ocean voyages. They had left Yokohama in mid-June for Okinawa, meaning they had been at sea for more than a month. They were the youngest crew members on board—white faces surrounded by suntanned adults with skin of reddish bronze. They worked hard and had become best friends, second to none.

Fortunately, there had been no hitches on the return trip, and the *Eikō-maru* was proceeding steadily toward Yokohama, sliding across the quiet ocean.

The two were leaning against the bow as they looked out over the surface of the water. A handful of sailors—three over here, two more over there—were also on deck, smoking and relaxing. They were all wearing shirts with horizontal stripes and round necks without collars. As the boat pressed forward, the bow left trails of pure white on the blue-black surface of the Pacific. The sun shone brightly as it sank, and its light had started to turn the tall, multi-layered clouds on the horizon a pleasant, warm red.

"Nice." Takeo looked up at the sky and filled his lungs with the salty sea air. The two stood still, gazing steadily at the horizon. They were still greenhorns, just barely out of high school when they left their parents, and now, there they were with only a single board under their feet separating them from the rough sea—a place that would have struck many people as worse than hell itself. What thoughts were running through the minds of the two young men? What could they be thinking about?

It was early summer, and evening darkness settled quickly over the plain of the sea. Before long, the last vestiges of light were floating over the horizon by the mainland.

After years, I return home and see
Flowers blooming, birds singing, breezes blowing
The whispers of the stream by the gate do not differ

From those of the past I know so well
Yet not a single soul lives in the abandoned ruins
Of the place I once called home

Saburō sung these words quietly as the evening darkness crept in slowly like a descending fog. The sea breeze stirred his hair, which moved freely. At some point, Takeo snuck his hand into his pocket, pulled out a harmonica, and began quietly accompanying him. His breathing suited the melody perfectly, and as he played, the music crossed the darkening swell and disappeared into the darkness of night.

A sailor named Tetsu who was standing near the bow teased him, "Geeeee, look at that! You're not half bad."

Someone else laughed and added, "For a kid, that is."

Everyone was relaxed. Since the most important part of their voyage was over, it was only appropriate that everyone should take it easy on the return trip.

That's when it happened. *Flash!* A strange light suddenly illuminated the entire boat.

"Oh, my god!"

Some of the sailors dove into the captain's cabin, while others dropped to the deck, face down . . . For a moment, an eerie silence washed over the boat.

Takeo was lying flat against the deck. "How weird!" he whispered as he fearfully raised his head.

Saburō, who was lying flat next to him, also lifted his head and exclaimed in wonder, "Couldn't have been lightning. There're no clouds out . . ."

Hearing this, several of the other, older sailors scattered across the bow lifted their heads.

"Look! In the water," said Takeda, the captain.

Hearing this, the sailors who had hidden themselves in the cabin ran out to the deck and leaned over the railing to look.

"My goodness! What's that? . . ."

At precisely that moment, they heard an earsplitting roar that sounded like an avalanche. *Rrrrrrrr* . . . The ocean began to churn, forming a massive whirlpool that must have been ten meters in diameter. Right before their astonished eyes, the whirlpool seemed to rise up when suddenly, *flash!* An intense burst of white-hot light illuminated the surface of the water.

"My god!" The sailors let out a shout as they covered their eyes and fell to the ground. At almost the same moment, *BAM!* The boat tilted precariously as if it had run into something.

Fingers of flame immediately began to crackle, rising from the stacked boxes of cargo on deck. In just moments, the bright red flames were crawling toward the captain's cabin.

The flames surrounded the radio room. Matsubara, the communications officer, was already sending a desperate series of distress calls to the mainland. *Click-click-click* . . . *Click* . . . *Click* . . . *Click* . . . , *Click-click-click* . . . *Click* . . . *Click* . . .

SOS, SOS . . . The *Eikō-maru* cast its sad cries across the sea, hoping for rescue . . .

As the sweat rose to his forehead, Matsubara frantically clicked the telegraph key. Smoke was already billowing through the window.

SOS, SOS . . . He continued to strike the telegraph key as if his life depended on it. Please, they need to know . . . Someone has to be listening somewhere on the Japanese mainland . . . If they hear us, they could help . . . The sooner, the more chance we've got . . . The radio waves from the *Eikō-maru* stretched across the plain of the sea, carrying the sailors' anxious prayers through the nighttime sky.

▶

Right about then, the neon lights of the main boulevard of the Ginza were flickering on. The street was bustling with throngs of men and women eagerly going home from work.

Emiko—the daughter of Professor Yamane, the best paleontologist in Japan—had promised her friend Shinkichi that they would go to a concert together at the Hibiya Public Hall that evening. It had been years since they had seen each another. Emiko had met him when she was evacuated to the mountainous region of Shinshū in central Japan. Shinkichi had also been evacuated there from Ōdo Island out in the Pacific, and since they were about the same age, they quickly became friends. Shinkichi had now finished high school—he had just graduated earlier that spring.

Emiko was headed toward Tokyo Bay Rescue and Salvage, where Shinkichi was now working. All the buildings along the shore, where the wind blew in strong from the ocean, looked nice and sturdy. Emiko knocked. The sound reverberated through the building, and the thick wooden door opened. The room inside was big and nearly empty. The only person there was a darkly tanned elderly man who seemed to be the custodian. He had been walking about the office with a big tray, collecting empty teacups from desks when Emiko knocked.

"Who is it?" His voice was that of an elderly man, and he had a strong accent from the northeast of the country. "Today's Saturday so everyone's gone home. If you're here for business, you should come back Monday."

"No, I'm not here for that. I promised Shinkichi Morita I'd meet him here."

"Oh, Shinkichi? He's still here. I'll go get him."

"I appreciate it." Emiko held the pleats at the top of her pastel-colored dress and smiled pleasantly as she thanked him.

The custodian placed the tray on the desk in front of him and plodded toward the back, hardly lifting his feet and dragging his sandals along the floor. She heard a glass door open somewhere in back, then a surprisingly loud *"Shinkichiiiii!"* He looked like such an old man—who would have imagined his voice was so loud? Emiko smiled to herself.

"Back here! I'll be right out!" Shinkichi's voice, also full of energy, rang out in the distance. However, his voice wasn't the familiar voice of the boy she'd befriended as an elementary-school student. His was the powerful voice of an adult seasoned in the salty sea breeze.

Emiko began to worry. "Goodness, is that the same Shinkichi I knew? Maybe not, maybe just someone with the same name." She thought about calling the old man to double-check.

But right then, she heard the heavy footfalls of someone running toward her. For some reason, he had come around the building to the front door she had just come through.

The door swung open. "Why, hello! So good to see you!"

Standing in the entrance was Shinkichi Morita—no doubt about it. His hands were glistening with jet-black oil, suggesting he'd been working in an engine room or something.

"Look at you, Shinkichi!"

"It's been forever. Wow, you're so grown up and pretty, Emiko! For a moment, I almost didn't recognize you."

"Goodness, I could say the same about you. When I heard your voice just now . . . Well, I got worried."

"Worried? Why's that?"

"Well . . ." She chuckled quietly.

"Funny . . . In any case, let me wash my hands and get ready. Do you mind sitting and waiting a few minutes?" He pulled a chair from one of the nearby desks and offered it to her. Meanwhile, the elderly custodian walked between the desks toward the entrance a few meters away.

Right then—*brrrring, brrrring, brrrring*—the phone on the company president's desk began to ring. The loud, shrill ring carried across the room.

"Hello, Tokyo Bay Rescue and Salvage . . . Wha? . . . What?! You've got to be kidding!!"

The telephone receiver Shinkichi was holding between his black, glistening thumb and pointer finger began to tremble, and all the color drained from his round, red cheeks.

Although she had just sat down, Emiko quietly stood up and approached Shinkichi worriedly. Clearly, something had happened.

"Alright, got it. I'll be there straight away!" He clanged down the receiver and abruptly turned to face her. Large drops of nervous sweat were gathering on his pale forehead. "Emiko, I appreciate you coming, but I'm really sorry. Would you mind going by yourself tonight? . . ."

"Why? Was there an accident or something?"

"Yeah, we got a distress signal from one of our company's ships."

"Oh my . . . Really?"

◣

The *Eikō-maru* had turned into a ball of fire on the dark waters of the Pacific and was leaning dramatically to the starboard side. The larger waves crashed halfway up the deck, and each time they struck, the entire boat shook precipitously. Some sailors had grabbed fire extinguishers but had been thrown overboard, leaving the fire to spread to the radio room. There, with a face distorted by anguish, Matsubara was using his left hand to dispel the sparks and smoke as he continued to strike frantically at the telegraph key.

Click-click-click, Click . . . Click . . .

But no one answered. A succession of gut-wrenching groans rang out from the steam whistle, announcing the end was near— *Whoooo, whoooo, whoooo . . .*

Almost immediately, a deafening *CREEEEEEAK* sounded

throughout the boat, as if something or someone had been lying in wait. The bow of the ship lifted toward the night sky while the stern plunged deep into the ocean water.

The froth and bubbles, which had been rising from the churning water with tremendous force, stopped almost completely. Now, the only bubbles were extra large ones that occasionally floated to the surface of the water, then vanished as if trying to dispel their resentment into the sea.

Just moments before, the sailors on the *Eikō-maru* had been talking excitedly, thinking of their mothers and yearning to go home, but now the ship had disappeared completely from the world. A silent curtain of darkness descended over the spot, and gentle moonlight illuminated the glittering ocean surface as if nothing at all had happened.

◢

The Maritime Safety Agency did hear the *Eikō-maru*'s calls for help and immediately convened an emergency meeting. A large map of the sea filled the wall in front of everyone, and on it, someone had carefully placed a red marker to indicate the spot from which the calls seemed to originate.

A communications officer from the agency sat next to a machine just down the hallway from the entrance, holding a receiver to his ear. Through the wireless, he was sending out shrill orders in all directions. "At 19:05 today, the *Eikō-maru*, a 7,500-ton cargo vessel belonging to South Sea Steamships, began sending a distress call from near 24° N, 141°2′ E. The SOS continued for some time, then suddenly stopped for unknown reasons. Rescue vessels from the third and fourth regions, finish your preparations so you can set out immediately . . ."

"I'm so sorry . . . Thank you so much for all your help. I hate to put you to so much trouble." The president of South Sea Steamships noisily entered the room, accompanied by a chubby gentleman who seemed to be one of his executive officers, and a second gentleman, who was thin and tall. Behind them was Shinkichi with his powerful, muscular build. The Maritime Safety Agency had immediately contacted the president and his chief officers, who then rushed to the spot.

The president asked worriedly, "What on earth could've been the cause?" His face was far paler than usual.

"No idea," said the officer, removing the receiver from his ear. "The whole thing's just like the explosions that took place at Myōjin-shō. Suddenly there was an SOS, then the distress call stopped . . ."

"But my goodness. Out there?"

"You're right. If we look at the maps, we see the SOS came from a place where nothing's ever happened before."

"Right before we came here, Shinkichi here . . ." The president looked back over his shoulder to indicate Shinkichi behind him. "Shinkichi here called the Central Meteorological Observatory to ask if anything unusual had happened. But they said that with today's conditions, there shouldn't have been any sudden winds . . . That made me wonder if there could have been some sort of mechanical breakdown, but I don't know . . ." The president spoke slowly, as if he were carefully weighing each word. "It doesn't make sense that something happened to that ship. It was newly built last year; in fact, it was one of the best in our fleet. And the crew that was on it were among the *very best sailors working for our company* . . ." As he emphasized those final words, he hung his head.

The sailors had been close to him—so close, in fact, that they ordinarily referred to him as *oyaji*, a playful term meaning "old man" or "Dad." The president was a tender soul and treated his employees with as much affection as if they were his own children. As he spoke, their faces appeared before his mind's eye one after the other.

Words deserted him, and he sighed quietly. The feelings that he had silently been holding back until that moment burst through, and large tears began to fall onto the floor by his feet.

The officer felt sorry for him and quietly looked away. "Our ship the *Bingo-maru* is headed out there on a rescue mission right now. Surely, they'll come up with a clue." He pointed to the map on the wall.

The president looked up at the map with teary eyes. The officer placed a pin shaped like a boat near the marker indicating where the distress call had originated.

Whoooo, whoooo, whoooo . . . The *Bingo-maru* sounded its emergency whistle as it rushed with incredible speed across the nighttime water toward the spot where the *Eikō-maru* had last been detected.

The searchlights on the mast tore through the darkness, illuminating vast swaths of sea before them. The agents on deck were all wearing protective helmets, strapped on with neat bands around their chins. Their eyes were focused on the sea before them so as not to miss even the smallest scrap of wood floating between the waves.

The emergency whistle rang out from time to time with a small, piercing cry—*toot, toot* . . . In between was the pleasant sound of the engines churning, slicing through the waves, propelling the *Bingo-maru* toward its destination.

To the agents on deck, the other long, low sound from the emergency whistle—*whoooo, whoooo*—sounded like the boat whispering across the water to the survivors that might still be out there somewhere, "Hold on . . . You're still alive . . . Hang on a little bit longer until we reach you . . ." The thought weighed heavily on the crewmen's hearts.

Hoisted high on the mast was the warmly familiar, old military flag showing a red sun surrounded by red, radiating rays. It flapped back and forth in the salty air.

The moon appeared between the clouds. As its face peeked out, it suddenly illuminated everything. The waves undulating below glittered in its light.

The entire boat was nervous, feeling as if something was amiss. Finally, two young shipmates, unable to stand it any longer, began whispering in low voices.

"Hmmmmm . . . Strange that something happened on such a quiet night . . ."

"I know, hard to believe."

"Whatcha think? What could've caused a boat like the one we're on to sink so suddenly?"

"Come on, don't talk like that. It's one thing to talk about things like that on land, but we're out in the water now. We're not just playing around."

"I don't mean anything. I'm just speculating. We left port with orders to get to the bottom of the mystery, right? Maybe we can come up with a theory or something."

"Well, I guess. If their machinery broke down, the boat would still be afloat. And it's not that easy for a fuel tank to blow up. Maybe something else was involved?"

"Yeah, the same thought occurred to me. Maybe a mine? Or maybe the ship was suddenly attacked—maybe an airplane or a Soviet submarine."

"But when the problem with the *Eikō-maru* started, it wasn't really dark yet. None of the crew would've been so reckless as to miss a mine. It would've taken longer for the ship to go down if it'd been attacked by air or submarine. Of course, it'd be a whole different story if throngs of enemy forces were attacking . . ."

"Yeah, I don't know. Something about this makes me uneasy."

The sailor reached up to pull the neck of his shirt tight against his throat as if to keep warm. He looked out at the sea. Clouds had hidden the moon, and the waves that had been glittering until just a moment ago had been plunged into pitch darkness. The waves swelled up, making the unsettling sound of rushing water, then retreated behind the boat into the distance.

The searchlights were the only thing now illuminating the pitch-black sea. They continued to rush busily over its surface, making the situation all the creepier.

The emergency whistle sounded again, this time with a low tone that split the darkness. *Whoooo, whoooo, whoooo . . .*

Right as the third whistle ended, there was a sudden *flash!* A tremendous burst of white-hot light illuminated the surface of the sea.

Whoosh! The seawater began to turn, forming a massive whirlpool. "My god!" thought the crew. But no sooner had they reacted than the entire boat was bathed in a strange light, and the enormous *Bingo-maru* began to tilt.

The crew screamed and rushed toward the cabin. It was as if the ship was doing its best to throw the sailors overboard as it started its descent into the deep water.

The Kaiju of Ōdo Island

"Hello, this is the *New Japan News,* right? This is Hagiwara from the Society section calling. We've got a huge emergency on our hands. Could you connect me with the editor-in-chief of the Society section?"

Hagiwara was in the press office of the Maritime Safety Agency with several other reporters from different agencies. All were tightly gripping the phone receivers in their hands as they called their home offices.

"Is this the editor-in-chief? Yes, I'm out gathering information. You know the *Bingo-maru* from the Maritime Safety Agency? Something happened to it . . . That's right. In exactly the same spot in the ocean . . . The *Eikō-maru,* the cargo vessel with South Sea Steamships, was the first to go down . . . The cause? Who knows? No one's got a clue what happened to either boat. Everything seemed just fine as of 2:35 a.m., but suddenly the captain of the *Bingo-maru* started sending out an SOS, and within two minutes, the message went dead. That means . . . What? Oh, I see . . . So then . . ."

Forty or fifty of the crews' family members had already gathered at the reception desk and were weeping loudly as they tried to find out what had happened to their sons and husbands.

"You'll have to wait until morning. Helicopters have been dispatched to investigate . . ." The agency representative raised his voice nervously, but the uproar from the families drowned him out, rendering his voice nearly inaudible. "We've sent out the *Kōzu*

17

and the *Shikine*—they're rushing to the spot as we speak. We won't be able to give you any updates until they get there."

Through her tears, one of the wives demanded in a shrill voice, "Aren't you even going to tell us if there were any survivors?!"

"I'm afraid I don't have any news," said the representative. His tone made it clear that he felt sorry for her.

"Why's the agency just messing around?"

"Say! Why don't you dispatch more ships to go out and search? Two ships are all you can spare? Just think how you'd feel if you were in our shoes!"

"No, it's not just two ships out there. We're investigating with all we've got."

One mother with disheveled hair shouted, "My son's daddy . . . Bring his daddy back! We want him back!" She shouted like a madwoman through her tears while clinging to a little boy who was only two or three.

Startled, the boy in her arms began to wail plaintively. *Waaaaaaaa, waaaaaaaa . . . .* It was as if he had suddenly burst into flames.

A twelve- or thirteen-year-old girl who had been clinging to her mother behind the representative leaped up, her face drenched with tears. Before anyone knew it, she had slammed the door shut and was running toward the beach. "Takeo! Takeo! Where are you, brother?" Takeo on the *Eikō-maru* was her older brother. She shouted his name to the nighttime sky.

The president of South Sea Steamships sat down on a sofa in the corner of the room and looked at everyone. "I'm sorry. I'm truly, deeply sorry for all your suffering. Please forgive us. I hope you can forgive us somehow . . ." He leaned forward and put his head in his hands like he was ready to tear out his gray hair.

"Sir." With a sad expression, Shinkichi walked over to the company president and wrapped his arms around the older man's shoulders. "Hold yourself together. We don't know the cause yet, so it's too early to dwell on it. Grief should come later." His words embraced the president like a firm hug, giving him emotional strength.

"Thanks, Shinkichi . . . But, you know, I . . ."

"You can't help it. This was a natural disaster. A natural disaster!"

"But two ships, right in the same spot? . . . I can't imagine what might've happened." The president was whispering these words mostly to himself. He was leaning so far forward that he was almost rubbing his face, twisted with grief, on the fabric of the couch.

In the next room, an operator was turning the radio dials. He had removed his shirt and bared his chest, and he'd tied a towel around his head with the knot facing forward.

Clickety-clack, clickety-clack. The sound of a teletype. It sounded like something from a battlefield.

Suddenly, the agent who had been receiving the message dropped the receiver from his ear and ran up to the representative who had been fielding the families' questions. He handed him a small scrap of paper with one hand.

The representative acting as spokesperson practically ripped it out of the radio operator's fingers. "What? . . . Oh, oh . . . Good . . . I see!"

This time he spoke to everyone in a completely different tone of voice—far more confident. "Everyone, we just received confirmation over the wireless from our helicopters. Three survivors were rescued by fishermen. There'll be more details momentarily, I'm sure, so just be patient for a few more minutes."

Until just a moment ago, the families had been riled up and bloodthirsty, but with this announcement, an expectant look rose to their faces, even though they still didn't know who the survivors were.

Right about then, the fishermen who had rescued the three survivors were speeding like an arrow over the ocean surface. Dawn still hadn't arrived.

"Hang in there! We'll reach port soon."

The fishermen were each taking care of the rescued men in their own way—one was taking off a rescued man's shirt, stained dark with oil, to wipe him clean, while another fisherman was taking off his own shirt to give it to another survivor.

One of the survivors was no longer able to see any more. Another one was having trouble breathing—a loud wheeze was audible each time he took a breath. The third one—Saburō—had burns over half his face, but he seemed to be in surprisingly good shape.

"What the hell do you think happened?" The fishermen had been out to sea and didn't have a clue what had transpired.

"I don't really know how to explain it. The sea just exploded all of a sudden . . ."

"Exploded!?" The astounded fishermen looked at one another in confusion.

◀━━━

Back in the Maritime Safety Agency, an uncomfortable silence settled over the room for a moment. However, the silence wouldn't last long, not with so many families worried about losing their beloved fathers and brothers.

"Which crew got rescued? The one from the *Eikō-maru* or from the *Bingo-maru*? Don't you know?"

"Three men were rescued by fishermen and are now being taken to Ōdo Island. We immediately dispatched the *Hatsushima* to go out there, so we should know more shortly."

Hagiwara, the reporter, was seated in a chair near the sofa as he asked, "Ōdo Island? Where's that?"

Shinkichi, who was standing beside him, pointed to a map of the Pacific and responded simply, "Here."

"I'm glad there were three survivors! We should be able to find out the cause of the accident . . ." A more relaxed expression came over the president's face. "What a relief. This'll help us avoid future accidents. We don't want to lose anyone the same way."

Another agent burst into the room and whispered something into the ear of the representative who had been speaking with the families. Quickly, the two of them left the room. Without thinking too much, Hagiwara, the president, Shinkichi, and the families followed.

"Please! Wait here!!" The second agent held out his arms to block the doorway. He looked deadly serious as he stopped everyone from passing through. However, the president, Shinkichi, and Hagiwara managed to push their way through his blockade.

Approaching the spokesperson, Hagiwara asked, "Can you tell us what happened?" The reporter took off the cap on his head and wiped the sweat from his brow with a few quick movements.

"I can't believe it. I simply can't believe it!" The spokesperson shook his head from side to side, then whispered, "The fishermen from Ōdo Island met the same fate . . ."

"What?!" The three of them were taken aback.

▶

Drifting mine?
Underwater volcanic explosion?
Another unexplained sinking ship in the Pacific
No hope for additional survivors

The next morning, news of the incident crowded everything else from the papers and the radio waves.

When Shinkichi, a native of Ōdo Island, heard that the fishing boat had met the same fate, he became anxious. *Was it my family?* . . . He got permission from the president of the company, then hastily set out to return home to the island.

Cream-colored evening primroses were blooming profusely on the familiar sandy beach where he had spent his youth. Shinkichi was in such a rush, however, that he didn't even see the lovely flowers. He didn't care that he was getting lots of white sand in his brand-new shoes as he sprinted home. All his attention was focused on getting home where his mother would be.

"Mom!" He flung open the wooden door and shouted, "Is brother here?"

Startled, a rooster began to crow loudly as it dashed across the yard.

"My goodness! Shinkichi, is that you?" His mother appeared. "Why're you home so suddenly? Did something happen?" She must have just been doing the washing at the back well, since she was clutching her dripping hands, surprise clearly visible on her face.

"Um, is brother here?"

"I asked you what's going on."

"I'll tell you later. Where's brother?"

"Don't you get it? Your brother Masaji went out fishing last night."

"Oh, my god. Just as I thought."

"Come on, tell me what's going on."

Shinkichi answered impatiently. "Mom, surely you heard about what happened last night."

"I did. A boat from the island disappeared . . ."

"I can't believe you're so calm, Mom."

"Wait, you don't think? . . ."

Shinkichi didn't say anything as he slammed the door and ran back down to the beach. He began to pant as he ran, all the while imagining the sad sight of the weeping families who had lost their fathers.

The evening darkness was settling over the shore. The villagers were lighting small campfires with gloomy expressions as they gazed anxiously out to sea.

The pitch-black waves pushed inland, sending up white sprays of water as they crashed onto the sandy beach before pulling back into the dark ocean.

The villagers were staring at the sea when they noticed a comet streaking across the sky near the horizon where the sky met the deep water. It felt like an eerie sign.

The evening primroses popped out of the darkness at their feet. Nothing could be heard other than the sound of the waves.

One of the elderly fishermen who was gazing at the ocean mumbled, "Nothing good ever happens when a comet appears. That's what the old-timers used to say."

The young folk who had gathered around him looked quietly at the old man's expression for a moment, then dropped their gloomy eyes to the ground.

"Wait!" Shinkichi dropped to the ground and stared hard at the black water as if he had spotted something.

"What is it, Shinkichi?" The old man turned his anxious gaze to rest on him.

"Look, a raft!" He pointed to a spot around a hundred meters out to sea.

"Where? Where?" The old man sat down on the ground and gazed in the direction Shinkichi had pointed. "Oh!" He stood up quickly as if he'd seen something. "He's right. A raft out there!! The currents must have carried it here!" He looked around at the faces of the people gathered there.

Astounded, the younger folks all peered out to sea. One of the campfires in front of them made sputtering noises and blazed up. Shinkichi started running toward the water.

"Hey! Hold on! We'll go with you . . ." The others trailed behind.

They could hear the faint sound of the waves against the raft as it became visible in the large swells of the dark sea. It was being carried toward them.

Shinkichi quickly tore off his clothes and splashed toward it, sending up sprays of water.

"Brother, it's you!! Masaji . . ."

Shinkichi's older brother Masaji was lying face down, seemingly unconscious, on a raft fashioned out of the wreckage of his ship. Shinkichi desperately pulled the raft toward shore.

"Masaji! Wake up!!" The old man gave him a rough smack across the cheek.

"Uhhhhhhhhh . . ." Masaji groaned, and his eyes popped open. He looked around at everyone in confusion, then as he realized where he was, he shouted, "It got us, the whole ship." Just saying that much exhausted him, and he closed his eyes again.

Shinkichi shouted sharply, "Masaji! Stay with us!!"

The old man grabbed Masaji's arm and shook it. "What was it?! Masaji! What got you?!"

Maybe he was losing consciousness again, but Masaji didn't move a muscle.

The Eerie Island of Ōdo

The white waves of the tide were rising onto the shores of Ōdo Island. Groups of children and wives were waiting for the boats to return at different locations at the water's edge—one here, one there. Everyone seemed to be on edge, talking about the strange events that had unfolded the previous night.

"The newspaper said two big ships went down last night. Must've been the same thing that downed Masaji's boat too."

"My brother said he thought it was a submarine."

"Maybe. If it'd been an airplane, there should've been lots of American boats there to stop it."

"I wonder if there's going to be another war."

"But if there was a war, seems like the enemy would go after big American battleships, not Japanese boats."

"Yeah, certainly not little fishing boats like ours . . ."

"The whole thing is really creepy." The lead fisherwoman uneasily pulled together the sides of her padded jacket tightly around her neck as she sighed and looked over her shoulder at the ocean.

A fishing boat that had been no bigger than a grain of millet appeared between the waves. Eventually, it floated into shore and slid up onto the sandy beach. Breaking from their parents, the children ran up to greet the boat, followed by some of the slower-moving wives.

A deeply tanned fisherman, wearing a twisted towel tied around his forehead, tossed out his net with a heavy *thunk*. The only things

25

in it were scraps of kelp and some messy, muddy clumps drawn from the bottom of the sea.

The wives sighed, "Oh, well."

In an exasperated tone, the fisherman said, "I haven't seen waves that high for decades." He jumped down from the stern of the boat into the water, then groaned as he pushed the boat farther onto shore.

"I'm just glad you came home alive, dear."

"What?"

"You were out at sea, honey, so you probably didn't hear, but last night, Magobei's boat sank."

"What? Magobei's boat?" The fisherman stopped pushing his boat and looked in astonishment at his wife.

"The same thing happened to it—same as those big boats."

"Oh my. What about Magobei?"

"Masaji was the only one who managed to make it back to shore on a raft. The rest of the crew was lost."

"Goodness . . ."

"I'm just glad you're alive."

Another of the ladies on shore nodded, "Us too, Shinzō!"

The old man from the previous night quietly walked up to the boat. "How was the catch?"

"We didn't catch a thing—not even any small fish. I'm not sure what happened."

"I see . . . Like I thought . . ." The old man stopped in his tracks. He looked at Shinzō as he set the tools in his hands down, then his eyes turned to the ground. "Might be Godzilla," he said quietly.

A young girl near him frowned and said, "Oh no! Gramps is going on about Godzilla again. You think monsters really exist in this day and age?!" She spat these words out and quickly turned to face the other way.

"Don't be stupid . . . Spoiled little girls like you who make fun of the old stories will get fed to Godzilla next time he comes around. You'll get eaten alive!" The old man glared at the little girl. All the local girls had grown up hearing their mothers shout, "Watch out or Godzilla's gonna get you!" whenever they misbehaved. The threat still maintained its effect, even after years of use. Everyone clammed up, looked at one another, and pitched in a hand to help them work.

Right then, the villagers heard a helicopter grazing the treetops on the promontory. The helicopter approached and set down on solid land. On the tail of the helicopter was the symbol of the *New Japan News*.

One of the passengers pulled a handkerchief from his pocket and held it over his eyes with both hands to keep out the dust as he disembarked. It was Hagiwara. The children ran to gather around the helicopter—an unusual sight for them. Hagiwara asked them something, then took a large manila envelope from the passenger's seat and began plodding across the sandy beach to where the homes were.

They heard the gentle mooing of cows. On Ōdo Island, people allowed their cows to wander around the island, eating freely from the pastures.

A while later, Shinkichi led Masaji and Hagiwara through the grassy field to the top of a high hill. Masaji had undergone a miraculous recovery, thanks to his mother's and Shinkichi's care. His head was wrapped in a white bandage. Sometimes when Masaji looked back, Shinkichi felt sorry for him, thinking how bad his wound looked.

"I'm not kidding. It was a living creature, no doubt about it. Whatever it was, it's still out there causing havoc in the water somewhere. It's why we didn't catch anything, not even any small fish . . ." Masaji sat down on the soft, young grass and rubbed the bandage on his head. He looked at Hagiwara with a frightened expression as if he was remembering how frightened he'd been the night before. "It's hard to believe . . . Such a big creature . . . Could something like that really . . . ?"

A slight smile rose to Hagiwara's lips. "You think something like that actually exists? . . . Don't be silly." He didn't say it, but he was under the impression Masaji wasn't thinking straight because of his head wound.

This ticked Masaji off, and his face flushed. "That's exactly why I didn't want to tell you."

As Shinkichi caught a glimpse of his brother's expression, he also noticed Hagiwara smirking. He had become acquainted with Hagiwara in Tokyo, but now he felt his anger rise. What an insufferable man!

Masaji spat, "No one'll believe me, even if I am telling the truth." He nodded at his little brother and abruptly stood up. "Shinkichi, let's get out of here."

"Come on, you guys!" Hagiwara shouted in exasperation. He held out his right hand to stop them, but Shinkichi glared back with glittering eyes, and a despondent look came over Hagiwara's face. Shinkichi and Masaji didn't even bother to look back at him as they walked back along the path.

"Darn it! I can't make a story out this." Hagiwara scratched his head with a pencil and flicked out his tongue to lick his lips.

◄━

During the day, it's possible to forget all sorts of things because of work, but when nighttime comes and wraps all distractions in darkness, forgetting isn't quite so easy. The rumors began as soon as the neighborhood children got together.

"So, the other day I was out in rough water fishing when farther out to sea, I saw a big white wave roll by really fast. I thought, 'Over there, over there!' but no matter how hard I looked, I couldn't get a clear glimpse of it . . . The whole thing shook me up."

"Wow, that's creepy."

"I thought a lot about it after I got home. It realized it was probably a submarine. Come to think of it, I seem to recall something dark peeking out over the tops of the waves . . . a periscope or something . . ."

"Oh, no! We're not going to be able to go out in the deep water anymore. Who knows when whatever it is will resurface and get us?"

The children were out in front of the cigarette shop talking when Bunsuke, one of the old men from the village, joined in. "It's got to be Godzilla. When I was a little boy, the old folks used to say that whenever Godzilla came along, you couldn't catch anything. Just like now. My dad told me Godzilla has rough skin like a crocodile all over, tough as iron. When it stands up . . ." Bunsuke turned his head to look in all directions, then pointed to an enormous thirty-meter-tall cypress in the woods surrounding the village shrine. "It's much bigger than that tree over there. A monster . . . a kaiju . . ."

The village had begun to recall the things he was speaking of, and they were overcome by fear, making it impossible to just stay quietly indoors. No one had given them instructions to do so, but the villagers gathered in the woods around the village shrine and started lighting bonfires to hold a kagura ritual to drive away misfortune.

The village chief was in front of the main hall of the shrine. His assistants from city hall were there too. There were so many people gathered that it looked like the whole village might have come out.

The branches of the cypress trees stirred in the wind. The fires flickered up, illuminating the pale faces of the frightened villagers.

Too-toot, too-toot, too-toot, too-too-tum . . . As the warbling of the flute grew faster and faster in the darkness of the woods, the dancers in the lion costume shook the costume's thick black hair and pounded their feet on the ground as if the lion were breaking into a run. *Stomp, stomp, stomp*—the sound was as loud as a railway car taking off. Then suddenly, with a high, ear-splitting note from the flute, the dancers stopped in their tracks. The black hair danced up into the air, and the downward-facing lion head lifted so its bright-red mouth opened from ear to ear. The lion's glittering eyes glared at everyone, and before they knew it, the villagers were trembling in their shoes.

Suddenly, "Heh, heh, heh." The crowd heard a disconcerting chuckle behind them. The surprised villagers turned to look. "Heh, heh . . ." The person who had been unable to contain his laughter was Hagiwara, the newspaper reporter. He turned hurriedly to hide his reaction from the villagers.

The villagers were so tense that even his meaningless laughter was enough to set them on edge. The blood had drained from their faces, but as they realized where the laughter was coming from, the color began to return. Their faces immediately registered their irritation.

Tooooot, whump-whump, toot-toot . . . The flute and drums started up again as if they were possessed, continuing the ritual dance. The villagers turned back to watch, and serious looks came over their faces as if they were trying to hold onto the dancing lion with their gaze.

Seeing this, Hagiwara let down his guard. He whispered to the elderly fisherman right in front of him, "So, who is this Godzilla, anyway?"

"Huh? A big, scary monster. They say that when he's eaten all the fish in the sea, he comes onto land and eats people. A long time ago, when the fishermen couldn't catch anything for weeks on end, they'd sacrifice a young girl to Godzilla by sending her out on a boat to sea . . . But now this ritual is the only thing we've got left to chase away evil and keep us safe."

"Really? Keep you safe from Godzilla, eh?" Hagiwara stuck his hands lazily into his pockets and kicked at the sand with his shoe. The strange dance and the seriousness with which the fishermen were praying reminded him of the Indians he'd seen in Westerns. Everything seemed so ridiculous that he couldn't stand it.

From somewhere came the faint voice of an old lady chanting what seemed like a spell. "Oh, gods in heaven above, please grant Ōdo Island your divine protection."

The dance continued in an increasing frenzy. The villagers put their palms together in front of them and looked up hesitantly at the old woman as they prayed.

Again, the old lady's voice: "Oh, gods in heaven above . . ." But this time, nobody looked. There wasn't any need to look. Everyone was repeating the same prayer in their own hearts. All the villagers were filled with fear of that terrible Godzilla smashing everything in his path. Some of the villagers prayed so fervently that they leaned forward and pressed their foreheads against the dirt.

The more serious the villagers became, however, the stranger they looked to Hagiwara. He began to chuckle again and quickly raised his hand to cover his mouth.

Right then, there was a loud shout, "You idiot!!" Everyone tensed up.

In between the old men who had prostrated themselves on the earth, Shinkichi stood up. Then someone stood next to him—Masaji, his head still bandaged. The young folks rolled up their sleeves and stood up too, two of them in back, three in front.

Right then, one of the old men who had been gazing at the youngsters raised his head to the sky and let out a gut-wrenching shout. "*Look!* The comet's gone!"

The startled villagers all looked up at the sky. A gust of wind blew through the trees, sending sparks from the bonfires crackling through the air.

"This is terrible! Something awful's going to happen!!" Bunsuke, the old man who had been talking in front of the cigarette shop that afternoon, had jumped to his feet, shouting, "This is terrible, terrible!!"

By this point the commotion had spread. There is an old proverb: even if just one dog howls for no reason, ten thousand dogs will follow. Everyone gathered by the shrine dedicated to the village's protective deity was soon in an uproar.

"Ken . . . Where are you?"

"Mom! . . . Mommy . . ."

"I'm frightened, sis."

Children cried and called out for their parents. Parents shouted plaintively for their children. Fear ran through the crowd like a dog with its tail on fire. Everyone was suddenly afraid.

Whoooooosh . . . Whoosh, whoooooosh . . . The wind was growing steadily stronger. The cypresses were so large that a man's outstretched arms couldn't reach around them, but even so, they were starting to bow their tall heads. The trees let out such a terrifying creak that they seemed ready to snap.

Perhaps it was better that no one could see what was going on in the darkness, but it seemed as if a pitch-black whirlwind was whipping wildly through the forest, doing whatever it liked . . . They could hear an eerie howling that seemed to shudder up from nowhere—*Whooooooooo-hooooooooo . . .*

Crack! Then a rustling noise . . .

Right before the eyes of the fleeing villagers, one of the really big trees—twice as big as the ones that were bowing their heads before—snapped off right in the middle and fell to the ground with a loud *THUD.*

Shinkichi and the others dashed home so quickly that they hardly remembered how they got there. They continued to huff and puff for so long it seemed like their breath might never return to normal.

"Masaji, do you think something's really going to happen? I can't stand it . . . My heart's beating so fast."

"Shinkichi, you don't think!? . . ."

"Don't think what?!"

"That . . . That, *he* might have climbed ashore."

"'He'?"

"Yeah, that wind just now was like the wind I felt the other day. It was really strong—so strong you thought it might blow you over—but it was warm, too, and strangely sticky on your skin . . ."

"But here on the island . . . Really?"

"I don't know! How should I know?! Godzilla needs something to eat. If he did come ashore, we're in trouble! Anything could happen!!"

Their mother sat in the middle, sprawled on the floor, with Shinkichi at her right and Masaji at her left. Masaji had folded his knees in front of his chest and wrapped his arms around them. His sad eyes seemed to be quaking.

"Damn it!! We were praying with all our might when that stupid Hagiwara starting making fun of us and ruined the whole thing . . ."

The boy's mother looked anxiously at both boys' faces, then quickly stood up to offer a votive candle at the Buddhist altar on the wall. "*Namu Amida Butsu, Namu Amida . . .*" Her fervent prayers rose into the air, but inside, she was praying that her irreplaceable, precious sons would be safe from disaster.

"Darn it!! No way I'll let us go down like this!! Even if I have to stake all my honor as an employee of Tokyo Bay Rescue and Salvage on it!!" Shinkichi was young and hotheaded. "Masaji, we'll be fine. It's not like we're in a war where we don't know how many people we're up against. If this monster is a living thing, it doesn't matter if he's as big as a mountain. A single artillery shell will bring him down!"

"Shinkichi, it'd be easy if that was all there was to it. When he moves, you get a super strong wind like this . . ." Masaji stopped, looked at the front door, and pricked up his ears. "Strong wind that whooshes around just like this . . ."

His expression grew deadly serious, and he looked at Shinkichi.

"What?!"

"Shhhhhh!"

No one made a sound.

"Shinkichi!! Do you hear something strange?!"

"Yes! What is it? Like big, heavy footsteps . . . Oh, my god! It's coming!! It's coming this way!!"

The two terrified boys looked at one another.

"Masaji! Shinkichi!!" Their mother, Omine, had stopped praying to run over and hold her two sons close, but once she took them in her arms, she burst into tears, not knowing what to do next.

Meanwhile, the sounds seemed to be getting closer and closer. With each step, the house shook.

Then with a *whoosh*, the wind blew through. The sound of cracking wood, then *crash!!* A tree had been knocked down.

From outside in the darkness, they heard intermittent screams. It was as if the bowels of hell had opened and they were hearing the sorrowful screams of sinners begging for help . . .

Shinkichi couldn't stand it anymore. He grabbed a knife from a desk drawer, looked around, and dashed toward the exit.

"No, Shinkichi! Don't go out!!" Omine frantically tried to stop him, but Shinkichi rushed outside into the roaring wind.

"Shinkichi!!"

Masaji pushed his mother aside and opened the door to follow, but right then, "*Aaaaaargh!!*" A scream from Shinkichi pierced the roaring darkness. It wasn't exactly a scream of surprise, nor a scream of terror.

"What is it?!" Masaji flew outside, thinking of nothing but his brother. Who knows exactly what he saw right then, but he let out a shriek, turned around, and flew back into the room as quickly if he had been tossed back in.

"Mom! Look out!!" Right as he threw himself on her to protect her, there was a deafening sound of wood breaking, and the ceiling caved in . . .

Lying outside on the ground, Shinkichi raised his blood-covered face into the howling wind and screamed, *"Mother!!! Masaji!!!"* He kept screaming as he struggled to crawl little by little toward the crushed ruins of his house.

Godzilla Appears

An emergency public hearing had been convened in the National Diet, and numerous witnesses were called to testify. The mayor of Ōdo Island was there, standing formally at the speaker's platform, explaining what had happened to the rows of representatives from the various political parties that made up the committee.

"Thirty-two buildings were completely destroyed. Thirteen buildings were partially ruined, and forty people were fatally injured. It was a dark night, and to make matters worse, the wind was so strong you couldn't even keep your eyes open . . . That made things worse."

The committee members silently stared at the mayor as he spoke. The head of the committee quietly raised his eyes from the documents before him. "How many domesticated animals were killed?"

"Ah, I forgot to mention that. Twelve head of cattle, eight pigs."

The head of the committee nodded and wrote something down. "Yes, that'll be enough for now. Could we have the next speaker come to the stand?"

The mayor quietly returned to the witness seats. The speaker stood up. It was Shinkichi, and he was covered in bandages. He had clearly been through a lot recently.

He wasn't intimidated by the formality of the surroundings, and when the committee started asking him questions, he responded in a confident tone. "No, sir, I'm telling the truth. It was dark, and so I couldn't see clearly, but there's no doubt it was a living creature that attacked us. My older brother . . ." With the thought of Masaji, his words trailed off, and his eyes filled with tears. He started over. "My older brother was killed that night . . . But even before that, he had been attacked by the same creature while out at sea . . . He told me before he died . . . He said it was the same monster . . ." He choked up with tears, rendering what came afterward inaudible.

Several members of the committee let out sympathetic sighs. One could hear someone choking back tears in the spectator seats at the side of the room. It was Kiyo, the younger sister of Takeo, the young sailor who had died when the *Eikō-maru* went down.

The next person to take the stand was Hagiwara, the reporter. "The day before the incident took place, I went to the island to investigate. As a newspaper reporter, of course, I didn't believe the old stories about Godzilla they've got on the island, but what I witnessed makes me doubt common sense. I don't know how to explain it, but something left giant footprints—no question about that. Whatever it was smashed entire houses and flattened the helicopter . . . Judging from that . . ."

All the witnesses claimed the disasters had been the work of a living creature. During the testimonies, the color drained from the faces of the committee members.

"Finally, we'd like to call the paleontologist Professor Kyōhei Yamane to share his opinion." The announcement from the head of the committee brought a smattering of applause.

Professor Yamane, a gray-haired, elderly gentleman, stood up. "Ladies and gentlemen, I must admit that I feel strange presenting my thoughts without actually going to Ōdo Island to investigate, but I'm unable to definitively state one way or the other whether such a creature might actually exist. As you know, people have found footprints in the Himalayas that seem to belong to some sort of snow creature—a yeti—and no one can explain that yet. So who knows what sorts of unimaginable mysteries might be lurk-ing at the bottom of the deep seas? That's why people sometimes refer to the ocean floor as the 'the closed pocket of the world' . . ."

Was he right? Could such gigantic, mysterious monsters actu-ally exist in the world?

The eyes of the nation and of the entire world were on Japan, so the government finally decided to dispatch a survey ship, the *Seagull*, to investigate. Professor Yamane, the paleontologist, was selected as the head of the expedition, and the courageous, quick-witted young Shinkichi, who worked at Tokyo Bay Rescue and Salvage and already had such valuable knowledge of the island, was selected as part of the expedition team. When Emiko learned this, she pressured her father to take her along too. Eventually, he agreed to take her along as his assistant.

Shinkichi, however, didn't know Professor Yamane was Emiko's father—in fact, there wasn't any reason he might have known. When Shinkichi saw her on board, he shouted, "Emiko! What are you doing on such a dangerous trip?"

She laughed. "I heard you'd be coming, so I asked Papa."

"'Papa'? So, Professor Yamane's your dad?"

"Uh-huh . . . Say, the boat's about to leave." Emiko took a handkerchief in her right hand and waved it in the air to the people who had come to see them off. With her left hand, she let a paper stream unroll. Holding onto the other end was Daisuke Serizawa, who was standing in the crowd of well-wishers on the pier. He waved silently as the boat started its journey.

Serizawa was a chemist and Professor Yamane's protégé. He had lost one eye during the war, and half his face was covered with painful-looking scars, giving him a cold, prickly look. Serizawa was aware of his own dark tendencies, and that's why he was so incred-ibly fond of his mentor's daughter, Emiko, who nature had given exactly the opposite personality—bright, cheerful, and lively.

Rip! The paper streamer in Emiko's hand tore. "Oh!" But

immediately, she started waving cheerfully. "Sayonara! We'll be back soon." Her energetic voice rang out over the water.

Had Serizawa heard? There was no change in his sad expression as he stared at the departing boat.

Whump, whump . . . The engine pounded as the ship sailed comfortably over the ocean. If they hadn't been heading toward the dangerous waters near Ōdo Island, no doubt it would have been a lovely trip.

"Papa, this is Shinkichi, the friend I made when I was in Shinshū."

"Oh, this is the fellow you mentioned. It's good to meet you, Shinkichi. I'm Emiko's father."

"Pleased to meet you, sir. I'm Shinkichi Morita."

"How are your wounds?"

"Healing, thanks."

"So for you, this is the beginning of a battle for revenge, eh? Well, I wish you the best." He clapped his hand down on Shinkichi's shoulder in encouragement.

All the passengers put on their life jackets. Professor Yamane glimpsed at Emiko and said, "I hadn't expected Serizawa to see us off today . . . He hardly ever leaves his laboratory . . ."

Without taking any time to reflect, Emiko turned to look at her father. "Maybe he thought this'd be the last time he'd ever see us . . ."

"Why do you say that?"

"We're going to go around the most dangerous waters, of course, but you never know what might happen." She instinctively looked at the sea. The undulations of the larger waves that everyone had been expecting were growing more ominous. She gazed at the water for a moment, then looked up anxiously and asked, "Do you think it's really out here somewhere? I mean, such a huge creature . . ."

Professor Yamane answered, "I can't really say."

Emiko continued to stare at the ocean.

Shinkichi's cheek twitched as he gazed steadily through a pair of binoculars.

After a few hours, Ōdo Island appeared in front of the *Seagull*. It looked like a dream, floating there above the water.

Shinkichi's mind filled with sad thoughts. However, almost immediately, they turned into anger at the gigantic monster who hadn't yet dared to show himself clearly.

"My god! How awful!!"

"Wow . . ."

The passengers had landed quietly on the island, but as they caught their first glimpses of the horrific destruction, they couldn't hold back their surprise. Things were even worse than they had imagined. The place was a mess—thick pillars had been snapped in two, and wooden doors had been ripped right off their hinges.

The mayor led them to the island graveyard, high on a hill overlooking the sea. Brand-new markers had been erected all over for the casualties, and the purple smoke of incense trembled sadly in the air.

Emiko and the others approached and placed their hands together, praying that the souls of the lost villagers would rest in peace.

"Say, where's Shinkichi?" Emiko had quickly raised her head and realized he wasn't at her side. She looked around and started to shout, "Oh, there he is," but the words stuck in her throat. She was struck by the realization that the graves he was looking at were those of his mother and older brother. She walked over quietly, gazing at him.

Perhaps Shinkichi didn't notice her. He didn't move—his

hands were pressed together, and his face was looking downward. An unbroken string of tears was falling onto his hands . . .

After leaving the cemetery, the group broke into two. Shinkichi and Hagiwara guided Professor Yamane to the flattened ruins of Shinkichi's home. With a serious expression, the professor observed the unusual damage and recorded it using his camera. Another researcher by the name of Professor Tabata went with his assistants to the communal well, where only half of the well walls were still standing. There, they pulled out some Geiger counters and busied themselves measuring radiation levels. The old ladies and children of the village watched anxiously from a distance.

"Wow, that's a lot." One of the assistants exchanged glances with Professor Tabata, then turned to the villagers and yelled, "Please don't use any water from this well for the time being. It's quite dangerous . . ."

The villagers let out a cry. "What're we supposed to do then?" They sounded distressed.

"How strange," Professor Tabata commented, cocking his head to the side with curiosity. "Why's this well the only place around here where we detect radiation?"

The assistant behind him said, "Sir, if it was radioactive fallout in rain that caused this, then it should show up in the well on the other side of the village too."

"Yeah, you're right." He was obviously puzzled.

Over by Shinkichi's house, Hagiwara stood up from the fallen palm tree he'd been sitting on and pointed to a large indentation in the road. He shouted, "Sir, this one over here is a little bit clearer."

Professor Yamane came from behind and recognized the indentation as the print of a gigantic foot. "Oh my!!" He stared hard at the print, then hopped inside. "Hagiwara, would you believe me if I were to tell you that this is the footprint of an animal?"

"Are you serious?!" Hagiwara's eyes glittered with surprise.

Shinkichi, who was standing next to him, glared at him as if to ask, "And you didn't believe us, did you?"

"Look here. If all this damage was from a landslide, we'd expect to see a pile of dirt and gravel somewhere over here." Shinkichi, Emiko, Hagiwara, and the others nodded and looked at a rock outcropping the professor was pointing to. Here and there, one could see bare earth. In the middle was a fallen tree and roof that had been squashed flat.

Professor Tabata's group arrived. The assistant holding the Geiger counter was leading the way, following the footsteps. Professor Yamane, Shinkichi, and the others were still looking up, puzzled by the exposed earth on the rocky precipice.

The assistant turned pale and shouted, "Professor! Watch out! Inside the indentations, the radiation's strongest!"

"What? Radiation in the footsteps? . . ." The surprise was visible in his face and from the perplexed way he tilted his head.

The assistant warned the villagers who had followed them, "Everyone, please don't come any closer. It's dangerous!"

"Did you hear that? Everyone go home. They said it's dangerous to get close . . ." The mayor and the other important villagers chased away the women and children, then immediately roped off the area.

"What's this now?" Professor Yamane picked up something carefully like he had found something valuable. It wasn't a shrimp or a crab but some sort of crustacean. He grew delirious with excitement. "Emiko, look at this! It's a trilobite. They're supposed to be extinct!!"

"My goodness . . ."

"Um, sir?" Professor Tabata called down from the top of the hole. "It's probably not a good idea to touch it directly with your hands." Professor Yamane didn't even turn. Instead, the assistant jumped into the hole with him and held out some rubber gloves. Not having much choice, the professor put the trilobite back on the ground, put on the rubber gloves, picked it up carefully once again, and put it into a small sack.

Hagiwara looked into the footprint. "What was it?"

Professor Yamane simply responded, "Something unbelievable," but nothing more. The entire group jostled against one another to peer into the sack.

Night fell. The expedition had already been far more successful than ever imagined. The investigators had set up camping tents. In front, a red fire blazed as a few people stood there, keeping careful watch.

Emiko and Shinkichi were walking around the camp.

"Has your father said anything?"

"He said it's not the right time yet—we shouldn't jump to conclusions. He takes this all very seriously. What do you think, Shinkichi?"

"He's right. It's not the right time yet—we shouldn't be jumping to any conclusions, I suppose."

"Sure."

"Common sense can't explain this. Suppose this 'Godzilla' is real, and he's bigger than a whale. How did he survive the incredible pressure at the bottom of the ocean? According to everything we know, that ought to be impossible, right?"

Emiko nodded vigorously. If she were talking to Hagiwara, she probably wouldn't have been talking about this so openly. She might have simply insisted to him that Godzilla was real.

Right then an alarm sounded in the darkness.

"The fire alarm!" shouted Shinkichi at almost the same instant Emiko grabbed onto him from behind.

"What is it? What happened?" The investigators rushed out of their tents.

The unsettling sound of the alarm rang across the night sky. Villagers ran out of their homes, up the sloping street carrying rifles, bamboo spears, swords, and any other weapons they could find. Rushing along behind them was Shinkichi, who led the two professors, Hagiwara, and the assistants. It was so dark out that they could hardly make out what was right in front of them.

Suddenly, Godzilla's head appeared from behind the ridge of the hill before them. It was unimaginably enormous. It floated up in the darkness, emitting a pale white light as if painted with fluorescent paint. What a terrifying face!! In his mouth was a cow, red with dripping blood.

"Aaahhh!!" Everyone screamed and began to shake in fear. The professors were shaking, too, even as they got their first clear look at the monster of the century.

Click! Hagiwara pressed the shutter button on his camera.

Godzilla was bent over, picking up a young girl, judging from the silhouette in his claws.

"Aaargh!!" People were screaming at the top of their lungs and running down the hill. It was utter chaos.

As Emiko ran for her life, her foot got caught on a tree root, and she stumbled. "Help!!" Godzilla saw her and opened his mouth.

Her life was in danger! Shrinking up in a ball and not moving wasn't an option, but she also found herself unable to make a sound. Godzilla's face got closer and closer.

"Aaaaaaahhh!"

Right at that moment, Shinkichi sped back to her as fast as the wind, grabbed her, and ran down the hill for dear life. At the bottom, they rolled under a rock outcropping.

Emiko was huffing and puffing wildly, trying to catch her breath again. Shinkichi protected her, rubbing her back and saying, "We'll be OK now, Emiko!"

He silently climbed out from the rock outcropping and looked around. There was no sign of Godzilla anywhere.

"You saved my life."

The tension drained away, and the two grabbed onto one another's hands, happy to be alive.

"Emiko! Emiko!" The professor's voice echoed across the darkness as he searched for his only daughter. His voice sounded like home, filling her with relief. She smiled and stood up.

"Emiko! Emiko!" Professor Yamane ran up to them, panting and out of breath.

The villagers shouted, "This way! Over here!!" Another group was running back up the hill. From the top, they looked out over the sea, dazed. Professor Tabata, Hagiwara, and some of the others also went back up, but by that time, Godzilla had already returned to the bottom of the ocean, leaving only his enormous footprints on the beach.

The Mysterious Trilobite

"Serizawa, I know I'm not saying anything new here, but you hate giving presentations about your research, don't you?"

"Huh? What're you trying to say?"

"If it begins to look like Godzilla's appearance has something to do with the hydrogen bomb tests out at sea, well, it might well create a precarious political problem for all countries involved."

"I'm well aware."

Seated in the Cadillac barreling down the national highway from Yokohama to Tokyo were Professor Yamane, Emiko, and Serizawa. Shinkichi was also there, sitting in the passenger's seat.

"That's why it's so important you make your research public now. A scholar's mission is to present the truth as it is, right?" Emiko's cheeks flushed with the passion of her words.

Leaning in from the passenger's seat, Shinkichi chimed in. "I'm of the same opinion. If scholars get preoccupied with every single political problem, then it'd be impossible to do any research at all. You know I'm right, Serizawa!"

Serizawa gazed at Shinkichi's expression for a moment, then nodded vigorously. "Yeah, maybe."

Professor Yamane shifted in his seat and chuckled. "Having allies like all of you gives me strength."

Serizawa looked out the window and said, "Well, Professor, it's time for me to take my leave." He started to lift himself up.

The brakes of the car let out a screech, and the car came to a halt in front of Serizawa's home.

"Serizawa, are you headed back into your lab?" The professor's tone of voice grew worried as he warned him. "The air in there's poison. Step out from time to time for a breath of fresh air!"

Serizawa laughed and climbed out of the car.

Emiko said, "Come again. Next time we'll have a nice meal waiting for you."

"Thanks, Emiko. See you later."

The car started up again.

Left all alone, Serizawa watched the car drive away. When it rounded a curve in the road and was no longer visible, he walked up to the front door and rang the doorbell.

His elderly maid came to the door to greet him. "Welcome home, sir."

The interior of the room was still—not a single sound to be heard—and had an antique quality about it. The room was quite big and contained several imposing, dignified pieces of furniture.

Serizawa went downstairs to his basement. There, behind a set of massive, heavy doors lay his laboratory. He switched on the light, revealing all kinds of chemistry equipment, reference books, a television, and other objects.

The room was as cold as death, but there seemed to be something moving around inside, ever so slightly. It was a group of attractive fish, fins stirring as they swam around and around their aquarium.

Serizawa quickly became absorbed in the research notes he'd been writing earlier.

After dropping off Serizawa, Professor Yamane and the others with him headed directly toward the National Diet. His goal was to share the findings of his recent survey with a group of specialists from each of the political parties.

Professor Yamane had a front-row seat, but he was standing as he spoke. Behind him Professor Tabata and the members of the expedition team sat waiting, while Emiko, who had come as her father's assistant, sat shoulder to shoulder with Shinkichi.

"Around two million years ago was the heyday of the dinosaurs, when creatures like the brontosaurus were alive and flourishing. Scientists refer to this as the Jurassic Period . . ." The slide projector advanced, showing a new image on the screen. "Starting then and continuing into the following Cretaceous Period, we see a process of evolutionary development in which an exceedingly small number of marine reptiles crawled out of the sea and developed into land creatures. I think it's safe to assume that there were intermediary creatures. However, there appears to have also been another creature, which for the time being I'll call 'Godzilla,' after the legend passed down on Ōdo Island."

The slide projector advanced to a new slide showing a photo of Godzilla's head taken on Ōdo Island. His mouth was wide-open, and he looked like he was about to jump out of the screen, sending ripples of terror through the astonished audience. All over the room, people involuntarily exclaimed, "My god!!"

"This is the head of Godzilla, the creature we encountered on Ōdo. Judging from this photo, I estimate he stands around fifty meters tall. So why did he appear on the shores of our nation so suddenly? . . . I imagine his kind probably used to live hidden away in underwater grottoes, living out their lives, keeping to themselves, and managing somehow to survive until this day . . . Recent hydrogen bomb tests must have destroyed Godzilla's habitat. Let me be clear. Damage from the H-bomb tests seems to be what drove him from the home where he had been living in relative peace up until now . . ."

Hearing this, the committee members representing the various political parties all burst into a great uproar.

Professor Yamane didn't ignore the disturbance passing

through the room, but he continued speaking. "I've got some strong evidence to back up my theory . . ."

Instantly, everyone in the room fell silent, as if a cold wave of water had washed over them. They stared at the screen to which the professor was pointing.

"I'll cut to the chase. First, we have this trilobite that we found in Godzilla's footprint . . ." On the screen was a large image of the creepy, crab-like marine creature. "Until recently, scientists believed trilobites were an extinct animal related to ancient crustaceans; however, this trilobite fell off Godzilla's body. Second, we discovered some pulverized volcanic rock on the trilobite's exoskeleton—sand, in other words." The projector clicked to the next slide. "Without a doubt, this reddish, claylike fragment is from the Bifurcatus Zone and shows characteristics we would expect from the Late Jurassic."

One of the committee members raised his hand. "Professor! What makes you so sure this has to do with hydrogen bomb testing?!"

The professor turned quietly to face him. "We tested this fragment for radiation using a Geiger counter. We found it had a certain amount of the radioactive element Strontium-90, which is created in a nuclear blast. My colleague Professor Tabata will give you a fuller explanation later, but the tests showed that in this fragment of rock that we found on the trilobite—a creature from two million years ago believed to have gone extinct—there was a large amount of radiation that could only have come from a hydrogen bomb!"

No sooner had he said this than the room once again exploded with clamoring voices.

The head of the committee banged on the table in warning. "Order, please! Order!"

Professor Yamane continued. "One more thing. Witnesses reported Godzilla emitted a strange, white light all over his body.

Perhaps he picked up some radioactivity from the hydrogen bomb tests."

As he completed his explanation, the room erupted in an even louder clamor than before.

"Order! Order, please!" The head of the committee pounded the table again.

A politician from one of the major political parties suddenly jumped to his feet. "Mr. Chairman, Mr. Chairman!!"

The head of the committee turned and acknowledged him in a quiet voice. "You may have the floor, Representative Ōyama."

"Professor Yamane's report just now is of grave national importance. In my opinion, we should proceed with caution. I don't think we should be hasty and make this public knowledge yet."

There was a great commotion in the room as people began to heckle and boo. "What're you talking about? It's precisely *because* this information is so important that we ought to let the world know about it!"

Representative Ōyama looked around the room. "Be quiet!! The idea this Godzilla creature is somehow the unintended offspring of experiments with the H-bomb is dangerous . . ."

"But he is! That's what the scientist was just saying!"

"But if we share that information with the public, we won't just have the public to deal with. The whole international community will be in an uproar. Who on earth knows what'll happen?!"

"But the truth is the truth!"

"And that's why this is so important! If we're too rash and make this public, the nation will be plunged into fear, and we'll have all sorts of trouble—political problems, economic problems, diplomatic problems . . ."

"Idiot! You're being ridiculous!"

"'Idiot'? Who are you calling an idiot? I demand an apology!"

The entire room devolved into loud confusion.

"Don't make this public! Absolutely not!"

"We've got to make this public! We've got to! We've got to be brave and honest."

In the middle of all this, Professor Yamane stood there, unmoving with shut eyes. Emiko and Shinkichi gazed at him from behind with tears sparkling in their eyes.

Things were bad. In fact, rumors about Godzilla were already spreading throughout the country. His name was on everyone's lips, everywhere you went.

A crowded train on the Keihin Line had just left Ueno Station in Tokyo and was heading north toward Ōmiya. In it, two male students who appeared to be in middle school were chatting with a cute female student who had dimples on her cheeks and a gentle curl in her bangs.

She said, "How awful! First we had radioactive tuna and radioactive rain, now Godzilla . . . What on earth do you think will happen if he makes his way up to Tokyo Bay?"

"He'd gobble you up in a single bite. First thing!"

The girl shot back, "You're such a jerk. I finally managed to recover from the atomic blast in Nagasaki, so I'm going to take care of myself . . ."

"I imagine we'll have to start thinking about evacuating. We'll have to think about where to go."

"Evacuating? You mean going to the countryside?"

"What choice is there? All of us young people are going to waste our youth out in the boonies . . ."

The girl started laughing. "Listen to you whining about your youth. I was evacuated last time around."

"No way. I didn't mean to be rude. Do you remember?"

"Boy, you are rude!" She gave the student to her right a gentle slug on the shoulder.

"Gosh, evacuation, eh? What an irritating world we live in."

In the downtown commercial district of the Ginza, two students were chatting underneath an umbrella as they waited for the street-car. Both were wearing high school uniforms with caps sporting two stripes around the brim.

The short, squat student cocked his head at an angle as he spoke to the taller student beside him. "I wonder . . . Isn't there any way to destroy him?"

"There doesn't seem to be. Whatever happens, it's like we Japanese are sitting ducks, waiting for a death sentence." He gazed up at the sky with a lonely look on his face.

A continuous rain was falling. It wasn't falling hard, but the drops were big, and it covered the entire Ginza in a thick haze.

Suddenly, they heard three loud beeps from a loudspeaker installed at the entrance of the street. The sound was unfamiliar, like nothing that they had ever heard before. An excited announcer started speaking over the loudspeaker.

"Breaking news! Today at four o'clock, *Sakae-maru*, a fifty-three-ton oil tanker owned by Far Eastern Commerce went down at sea, sinking at approximately XX° N and XX° E.[1] A fleet of frigates has been dispatched to that region of the sea to carry out a torpedo attack against Godzilla. All shipping vessels and other boats in that area should proceed with caution . . ."

---

1. In Japanese literature, when authors, for whatever reason, do not want to be specific about a particular place or name, they often substitute the letters X or O as placeholders. In other words, it is clear Kayama didn't want to specify exactly where in the Pacific Ocean this is. One might argue that by doing that, Kayama makes the entire Pacific Ocean seem more ominous.

The two students waiting for the streetcar listened with uneasy expressions on their faces.

▸

Shinkichi started going to the Yamane home so often that he felt like a member of the family, able to act freely around them. That day, he went there with his employer, Hideto Ogata, the president of Tokyo Bay Rescue and Salvage. He was seated with the professor and Emiko in the parlor talking excitedly about Ōdo Island when Okimi, the maid, came running into the room. She was pale as she told them the most recent breaking news.

"What? Again?"

Everyone turned to look at one another. "Damn it!!"

Professor Yamane had his eyes closed. His cheeks, which were drained of color, twitched nervously.

Shinkichi stood up and flipped on the television sitting on the mantle. Ten frigates were rushing through the ocean, kicking up white waves. Each one had a flag depicting the rising sun.

Kaboom! Kaboom! Here and there, tremendous sprays of water exploded into the air. The ships were releasing a round of torpedoes.

"Wow! Look at that!" Ogata clapped happily.

"How awful. It makes me remember the war . . ."

"Sure, but this might be what it takes to defeat Godzilla . . ."

"Yeah, Shinkichi, this could be how you get revenge for your mother and brother."

"Damn it! I wish I was out on those frigates with those guys."

Professor Yamane, who had been seated there with eyes closed, quickly rose to his feet and went into his laboratory.

The three of them stopped talking and glanced at one another.

"Papa! . . . Papa!" Emiko stood up and followed her father as Shinkichi looked at Ogata with an uneasy expression.

"Did I do something wrong?"

"Ummmm . . ." Ogata turned to Shinkichi and said, "The professor studies animals, so he doesn't want Godzilla to get killed."

Shinkichi was stunned. That wasn't the answer he was expecting. "But Ogata, that shouldn't matter, should it? If we just sit around and don't do anything, what'll happen to us humans?"

"Shhhh." Ogata raised his right hand and interrupted him. Emiko was knocking on the laboratory door.

"Papa, Papa . . ."

But the room returned to silence. Professor Yamane didn't respond.

Emiko summoned up her courage and opened the door. It was pitch black inside.

"Papa . . ."

When she flipped the light switch, the light illuminated the back of her father's head. He was seated deeply in his armchair, facing away from her, surrounded by fossils and piles of books.

"Papa?"

She saw the back of his head move. "Emiko, would you mind leaving me alone for a bit?"

She didn't know how to respond.

His voice was quiet and seemed to sink into the silence. Emiko loved her father deeply and was immediately able to detect what he was feeling. As she started to leave, she heard her father call out.

"Yes?"

"Turn off the lights on the way out."

"Sure, Papa . . ."

She flipped the switch with a small *click*, then closed the door quietly. The professor sat without moving in the darkness, just like before.

The Underground Laboratory

The leisure boat *Tachibana-maru* was enveloped in a pleasant melody. It slid quickly over the quiet nighttime bay as it sailed toward Ōshima out in the Izu Islands. In the distance, the passengers could see the neon signs of the Ginza, glittering in all the colors of the rainbow.

Adults just do whatever they want without necessarily giving it a lot of thought. When the news had come about Godzilla's attack on Ōdo Island, everyone was so astonished that they trembled with fear, but some time had gone by since then. People wanted to have fun, so they banished fear from their minds.

A group of men and women wearing brightly colored outfits were dancing wildly on deck. They were so caught up in the music that they gazed at one another as if they were dreaming.

The five members of the band were on a platform in the middle of the deck, dressed in matching snow-white uniforms with bright-red sashes, reminiscent of some country in the south. They were playing the gentle tune "Saint Louis Blues."

A group of heavy drinkers had gathered by the bow and were busy talking nonsense, even as the beer still clung to their lips. On the table was a line of large beer mugs.

"Say, just look. The sea's so beautiful at night, don't you think?"

"It sure is. Look, we can't really see the lights of Tokyo anymore."

"You're right! We must be a long way out. Seems that way, anyway."

"Look, the noctiluca in the water are glowing."

"Oh, how pretty!"

The young man and woman who were having this conversation leaned against the railing at the edge of the boat.

"Look, they're glowing from here to all the way out there in the distance, like they're following in the wake of the boat. Say . . . What do you think that is?"

"What? Oh, wow!"

"So pretty! But wait, that's odd . . ."

"You're right . . . The water seems to be bubbling up out there . . ."

Anxiously, the two pulled one another close. The bluish-white bubbling water made a loud gurgle and formed a tornado-like whirlpool. Just as the couple realized the water had started to swell upward, Godzilla's gigantic head appeared above the surface of the sea.

"Oh, my god!!"

As the woman screamed, the dancers stopped in their tracks and turned to look.

"My god!!"

"Godzilla!"

High-pitched screams of fear burst out all over the boat.

Back in Tokyo, an Anti-Godzilla Task Force was immediately mobilized in response to the radio call from the *Tachibana-maru*, and by the time dawn broke, the hallway was already clamoring with advocates and people with questions. A familiar black Cadillac stopped in front of the main entrance. In it was Professor Yamane. He was dressed in light clothing—a white open-collar shirt with tea-green slacks.

He pushed his way through the chaotic corridor and opened

the door at the end of the hall. The leader of the task force hurriedly came over to greet him and lead him inside.

Waiting on the large, imposing sofa were Commandant Satō and Vice-Commandant Itō, the heads of the Japanese Maritime Safety Agency.

"We're in a terrible mess. Professor . . . if this continues, we're going to have to suspend all international ship routes in the vicinity. Is there anything we can do? Right now, we'd welcome even the slightest hint . . ."

"I need to think . . ." The professor looked hard at the commandant without the slightest hint of a smile on his face.

At his side, Vice-Commandant Itō took a hurried drag on his cigarette and said, "Professor Yamane! Let me speak frankly. How can we kill Godzilla? That's what I want to know!"

Professor Yamane grew agitated, and the color drained from his face. "It can't be done! Even though he was baptized by the hydrogen bomb, he didn't die! He's tenacious! And you want to kill him somehow? That's not what we should be doing. The first order of business is to study his unbelievably tenacious vitality . . . For all humanity everywhere in the world! This is a unique chance, one given to us in Japan, to us alone . . ."

It was Saturday, which ordinarily is the most pleasant day of the week for public employees.[2] When the afternoon siren went off, Shinkichi bounded outside and headed toward the Yamane household.

Naturally, people who worked in open-water rescue and salvage—people like Shinkichi—caught wind of what Professor Yamane had said earlier that morning to the Maritime Safety Agency. After all, it affected their work.

Not long before, Shinkichi had overheard his boss Ogata saying, "The professor studies animals . . . It only makes sense he'd

_____

2. Public employees would typically work only a half day on Saturdays.

say that." It was clear he didn't quite trust the professor's opinion. Now that the professor had made his opinion publicly known, there was even more distrust. If someone else had expressed the same opinion, Shinkichi would've probably become furious, but he'd been through a lot with the professor and now trusted him like a father. Together, he and the professor had confronted the terrifying monster and faced down death.

Shinkichi was overcome with unbearable sadness. "Godzilla killed my mother and brother. No matter how much I hate him, it's still not enough." Even so, the professor, who ought to understand everything Shinkichi was feeling, was telling people, "Killing Godzilla is out of the question!!"

"The professor . . . I respect him, but he doesn't seem to be paying any attention to me at all! Godzilla left me an orphan." Shinkichi was so preoccupied that before he knew it, he had arrived at the front gate of the Yamane home, barely remembering how he'd got there.

He went around the house to the kitchen entrance and found Okimi, the maid, doing the wash. When she caught sight of the unexpected visitor, she grew slightly pale for a moment, then gasped, "Oh, it's you, Shinkichi!"

"Hello. Is the professor in?"

"Yes, in the dining room."

Shinkichi headed straight there. The windows were open all the way. The professor was wearing his reading glasses, and his head was tilted slightly upward as he read the newspaper.

"Hello, sir."

"Well, hello, Shinkichi. Come on in. My goodness, you look pale. Is something wrong?"

He was always thoughtful and kind when he spoke to Shinkichi, but for some reason, that day the professor's words lay heavily on Shinkichi's heart.

Shinkichi felt as if he might burst into tears if he held back a second longer. To dispel the tears welling up in his eyes, he adopted a firm tone and spoke his mind. "Professor, I came here today because there's something I've got to ask you! I came even though I'd made up my mind I didn't want to come here ever again . . ."

For a few seconds, the professor remained silent as he looked at the boy's expression, then he removed his glasses. With his deep wrinkles, his face seemed full of love and affection. "I was expecting you, Shinkichi. I thought you might show up before long. I'm glad you came."

"What's that, you say?" he said, raising his head. There was a part of Shinkichi that wanted to lash out and use strong, less polite language.

"This morning, I made that statement. I suspected you'd be the very first person to come speak your mind to me . . ."

"Huh?" Shinkichi was surprised—so surprised, in fact, that he could have jumped into the air. He had come thinking that things would be awkward—he'd have to break off all further relations with the professor, and all his brooding had made him terribly sad. It would have been much easier if the professor had barked at him, "Darn kid!" but he hadn't.

Wordlessly, Shinkichi thought to himself, "My goodness . . . You mean you were concerned for me all this time? And I was ready to call you a traitor, to say that you weren't thinking about me in the slightest . . . Professor! Can you forgive me?"

Big tears began to run down his flushing cheeks.

"Oh my! It's Shinkichi . . ." Right then, Emiko entered the room and spoke in her cheerful voice. "How naughty of you not to let me know you were coming!"

Shinkichi hurriedly rubbed his eyes and blinked a couple of times to hide his tears. "Gosh, I've gotten so sleepy."

"My goodness. Have you already been here that long?"

"No, not really, but I heard you playing the piano, and it didn't seem like you were close to finishing anytime soon . . ."

"Oh, sorry about that . . . Gosh, I'm terrible anyways. You must be upset with me."

He chuckled. "No, not at all."

"Well, good then."

They exchanged smiles.

Everyone was still cheerful when Okimi walked in, carrying a tray with teacups filled with black tea.

"Miss, a gentleman by the name of Mr. Hagiwara has come to see you. He's at the front entrance."

As she took a cup of the tea, garnished with a slice of orange, in her hands, she asked, "To see me? How strange. I'd understand if he was here to see you, Papa, or Shinkichi maybe." She shot a quizzical look at Shinkichi, and he gave a grin. "Must be Hagiwara from the *New Japan News,* right?" She was still suspicious.

"I'm not sure, miss. He didn't tell me that much."

"In any case, show him in."

Okimi left, and a moment later, sure enough, Hagiwara from the *New Japan News* came in. In his right hand, he was clutching his usual cap.

"Hello there. Oh, look! Shinkichi's here too."

"It's been a while."

It was just an exchange of simple words, but since their time together on Ōdo, Hagiwara had been unable to face Shinkichi. He seemed to have come for some different, more complicated purpose today. As he stalled, he avoided looking Professor Yamane and Shinkichi in the eyes.

Emiko was quick to detect this and said, "Mr. Hagiwara, let's step into the living room." She stood up and led the way.

"I'm sorry to bother you, but I've come with a request."

"What is it? If I can help you somehow . . ."

"So, here's the situation. I went over to Dr. Serizawa's place, but I didn't get past the gate. Ogata was his classmate from school, so I presumed upon him for an introduction, but then I got to thinking and realized that if you came too, Emiko, I'd probably have more luck getting to see him . . . Of course, I'll tell you everything you need to know, but this is urgent. I'm sorry to bother you. I'll owe you big . . ."

Brrrring, brrrring. The telephone on the table began to ring.

"Excuse me for a second." The phone made a click as she picked up the receiver.

"Let's see, today? . . . Yes, he's here right now. I don't have any idea, but is it really that important? . . . Sure, I won't tell my father. Well then . . . Good-bye." She hung up.

"It was Ogata. He said you should go see Serizawa."

Hagiwara smiled, "Really? Ogata's a good guy. I'll definitely take him up on his introduction." As if he was trying to hide his joy, he bowed so low that his face practically bumped into the table. He grabbed his briefcase.

Emiko gave some excuses to her father and Shinkichi in the dining room, then accompanied Hagiwara to Serizawa's place.

Serizawa reluctantly came to meet them on the terrace.

His long hair hung down over the scarred half of his face. The only thing with any light in his gloomy face were his glittering eyes. If someone were meeting him for the first time, a shiver would have gone down their spine.

"There must be some kind of mistake . . ." Serizawa started.

A quizzical expression came over Hagiwara's face. "You think? . . . That's strange. Before coming, I confirmed that you were the person I need to talk to . . ."

"Let me say this right off the bat. My research is in a completely different arena."

"Hmmm, I see . . . A special reporter in Switzerland spoke directly to a researcher in Germany. He said that if you, Dr. Serizawa, were to complete your research, we might make a breakthrough that would help us combat Godzilla. That's what I heard, anyway . . ." As Hagiwara spoke, he stared suspiciously at Serizawa.

"I don't have a single friend in Germany."

Hagiwara paused for a moment. "Is that so? I guess there must be some mistake. I've just been so preoccupied with all this Godzilla fever." He chuckled, then scratched his head. "So, just out of curiosity, what have you been working on these days?"

"Nothing important."

"Well then, I'm sorry to have bothered you."

"No worries. I'm sorry that I couldn't be of more help."

"Well then, we'll be off."

Hagiwara looked at Emiko, who took the chance to speak up. "It's been so long since I've seen Dr. Serizawa. Would you mind if I stayed a few moments longer to catch up?"

"Sure. Well then, I'll say goodbye to the two of you." Hagiwara set off, with Emiko walking him to the front door.

Once Serizawa was alone, a dark cloud quickly came over his face, and he fell into deep thought. As Emiko returned, she saw this and right away realized something was up.

When Serizawa noticed her, he apologized. "I'm sorry. It's been so long since I've seen you, Emiko. What a surprise to have you stop in . . ."

"No, don't worry. Ogata said he was busy, so I came instead . . . There wasn't any reason you should have expected me." She gave an innocent smile. "Say, you haven't visited us at the house recently. Will you level with me about your research? What are you working on?"

Serizawa quickly looked away from Emiko's flowerlike smile. Two sparrows chirped at one another in the hedge. A moment passed before Serizawa made a serious expression and asked, "Would you like me to show you, Emiko?"

She was stunned. "What? . . . Yes, of course. Show me . . ."

"But you've got to promise me something in return. I want you to promise to keep this top secret."

"Sure."

He paused for a moment. "I didn't want to show this to anyone. I'm not done yet, but I've staked my entire life on this project . . . You're just about the only one I can trust with this, Emiko . . . All right then. I'll show you!" Serizawa's cheeks were flushed.

Emiko remained silent, not entirely sure what to say next.

"Just to be sure, you'll keep this secret, right?! I've put my whole being, everything, into this project . . ."

She nodded. "Yes, absolutely."

"Good! Now, come!" He walked down the stairs to the basement.

The stairwell was gloomy, illuminated only by a few rays of light seeping in from the top. Serizawa stood in front of her as he pulled out a key and with a loud *gachunk* unlocked and pushed open the heavy door at the bottom of the stairs.

Emiko quietly peeked in, but the room was pitch black. She could smell something medicinal, and she felt a chill pass over her.

There was the sound of rustling and—*click*—the lights went on.

The small room was crowded with all sorts of equipment for experiments. It was everywhere. Facing the wall were several aquariums, each filled with fish gliding through the water inside.

"Wow!" Emiko went close to look, not giving it a second thought.

Meanwhile, there was another *gachunk*. Serizawa had locked the door from the inside. *Creeeeeak* . . . He drew the curtains even more firmly shut, and the room was plunged into an even more eerie silence.

From the back of a case, he drew a small, important-looking metal box and walked over to the aquariums.

Emiko watched him quietly.

He prepared the wiring and other equipment with a practiced hand. The wire ran from the small box to some apparatus made of a light metal.

She just held her breath and watched.

Serizawa made a sign to her with his eyes, then dropped the small apparatus into the tank full of swimming fish. It quietly sank to the bottom.

Emiko instinctively leaned in to look, but he shouted, "No! Step back!!" His voice was unexpectedly forceful. Surprised, she shrank back.

Serizawa flipped the switch, and the box began to rumble with a creepy noise. *Rrrrrrrrrr*. His eyes moved back and forth between the aquarium and the meter in front of him. The meter began to tremble slightly.

Emiko was now staring at the aquarium intently. And right then, a look of astonished horror came over her face, and suddenly she let out a terrible, piercing shriek. *"My god!!"*

We Mustn't Kill

Wobbly on her feet, Emiko stumbled and grabbed onto a pillar for support. She was terribly pale. Worried, Serizawa ran up to her.

Trying to suppress the frantic beating of her heart, she started to bound up the stairs, but he chased after her. "Emiko, I only showed this to you because you wanted to know . . . Please, don't forget that!"

"I know, I'll keep your secret." The shock seemed to have affected her greatly. She leaned on the banister as she climbed the stairs on unsteady feet.

Serizawa stayed in the gloomy basement, watching her leave. Complicated emotions were visible in his expression—he was glad he had cleared his conscience by revealing his important secret, but he was also overcome with regret.

After Emiko had set out for Serizawa's place, Shinkichi had calmed down from all his ramped-up excitement. He and the professor were back to their usual selves as they conversed.

"Professor, I still don't entirely see where you're coming from."

"You probably don't, but, Shinkichi, try to think about this from a higher perspective. During the war, the atomic bomb dropped on Hiroshima blew away an enormous city in a single instant. However, the hydrogen bombs they're now testing in the South Pacific are many hundreds of times more terrible than the atomic bombs dropped on Japan. They say it's dangerous for people even to eat the tuna irradiated by the hydrogen bombs, but just think—Godzilla was able to take all that radiation. If anything, it was because of the bomb's influence he's as strong as he is. When I say that's not all that makes him so frightening, I'm not exaggerating. He's survived for millions for years—think about that kind of vitality! The hydrogen bombs didn't even faze him. Where on earth could such a powerful life force possibly come from? If humans could have only just a small fraction of that vitality . . ."

As Shinkichi listened to the professor's explanation with its well-ordered line of reasoning, he wanted to interject. He felt sure that he if said the right thing, the professor's arguments would crumble. "You're completely right, Professor, but . . ."

"Fortunately, this amazing chance . . ." Professor Yamane's explanation was so passionate and grandiose that Shinkichi could barely get a word in edgewise. "Has been given to Japan. We Japanese have caused a great deal of trouble to people throughout the world. Carrying out this research is our one and only chance to make reparations for all that. Can't you see where I'm coming from, Shinkichi?"

That was the first time he'd stopped to ask the boy's opinion. Shinkichi had hung his head as he listened. He felt embarrassed as he realized that brooding over the past wasn't the only way to think about the problem. The professor's line of reasoning hadn't occurred to him.

Even so, somewhere in his heart, he still had a never-give-up spirit that he couldn't extinguish even if he tried. That spirit crackled, rose up, and burst into flame, engulfing his entire heart.

"I understand what you're saying. If I were in your position, I'd probably feel the same way. But Professor! My mother and older brother were killed by this monster . . . You yourself ought to understand how frightening Godzilla is from your own experiences on Ōdo. Emiko was almost killed by him too . . ." Shinkichi looked hard at the professor's face. "Just imagine if he had gotten to Emiko . . ."

The professor hung his head.

Realizing he was close to scoring a point, Shinkichi summoned up all his might. "How would *you* have felt if he had killed your precious one-and-only daughter!?"

Tears welled up in the elderly professor's eyes, but he didn't beat around the bush. "I'd be in mourning, the same as you. However, as a paleontologist, I'm not likely to change my opinion."

Shinkichi had poured out his heart hoping there might be some way of changing things, but he'd hit a brick wall. He was upset. If he couldn't even convince the professor, Godzilla had already won. Shinkichi was incredibly frustrated—could he have given up too quickly and withdrawn at the critical moment? He wanted to explode, releasing all his pent-up energy.

Ding-dong. Right then, the front doorbell rang. As if giving an outlet to his irritation, Shinkichi bounded to his feet.

Emiko was standing on the cobblestones by the front entrance. She looked miserable.

"You're home," Shinkichi said, unlocking the door.

"Oh, you're still here?"

She was lightly dressed and carried only her purse, but her feet seemed terribly heavy as they stepped over the threshold.

"What's going on, Emiko?"

"Nothing. Why?"

"No reason. Glad you're OK."

"I suppose I could ask you the same question. Anything happen?"

"No."

"Your forehead is covered in oily sweat, like you're upset or something."

He hurriedly pulled a handkerchief from his pocket and wiped his brow. "Your father's in the dining room." He spun around and walked with heavy footsteps in the professor's direction.

She was hardly in the house as she forced a smile and said, "Papa, I'm home."

"Welcome back." The professor's words were barely a whisper.

From just those few words alone, Emiko immediately detected the gloomy, awkward atmosphere pervading the room. Placing her purse on the tea cabinet, she said, "Gosh, I'm wiped out. I think I'd like something sweet." She stood up straight, as if nothing were the matter. Something must have happened while she was away, and she wondered what she could do to dispel the gloom.

And what should happen right then? Sirens suddenly started going off—some nearby, some off in the distance. They screeched through the air, their unsettling sound trailing on and on . . . Just like the air-raid warnings from the war.

At the same time, a sharp buzzing sound came from the radio, and they heard a loud voice start repeating, "This is the emergency broadcast system, this is the emergency broadcast system . . ."

Even before the radio had the chance to complete the announcement, the professor jumped out of his chair and shouted, "Emiko, it must be Godzilla! Godzilla's back!!"

Shinkichi and Emiko stood up, stunned.

The professor dashed through the hallway and flew outside.

Astonished, Shinko and Emiko followed. As they spilled out of the house, Shinkichi caught a glimpse of the professor's back as he ran at full speed toward the bay. Cupping his hands around his mouth like a megaphone, Shinkichi screamed at the top of his lungs, "Professor! Professor! . . ."

When the professor heard Shinkichi's voice, he looked back over his shoulder, and for a moment, a pained expression rose to his face. "Shinkichi, let's each do the best we can! We'll deal with this!" He shouted with full force, as if trying to convince himself too. There was no trace of any harsh feelings.

Shinkichi contemplated these unexpected words. *Let's each do the best we can! We'll deal with this!* He imagined this meant the professor would pursue the path he thought was right, and Shinkichi should pursue the path he thought was right. They would each do their very best and put up a good fight. The professor was saying that even though their two hearts were full of conflicting emotions, each had to follow his own path—one leading right, one diverging to the left—now that Godzilla had reappeared.

Not sure what to do, Shinkichi felt his heart pound.

The professor set off running again. Shinkichi started running too. The people from the neighborhood poured into the streets, screaming and dashing in every direction.

The high-pitched shouting from the radio wove its way through the waves of people running like mad through the streets. "Just now, Godzilla has appeared in the water near Shinagawa and seems ready to come on land at the No. 2 Battery. All boats in the area should immediately evacuate. All people in the coastal areas should also evacuate immediately. An evacuation order has been put into effect for Minato Ward, Shinagawa Ward, Ōta Ward, and the other coastal wards. We repeat, there is an emergency evacuation order in effect, there is an emergency evacuation order in effect . . ."

The radios were still blaring as the rooftop police station and city hall sirens also started going off. Some of you readers probably know how weird and unsettling it can be when terrified people are running around in a panic as sirens wail overhead, high and low, their trailing notes reverberating across the landscape . . . The continuous, drawn-out sounds of the sirens coming from every direction sounded like sobbing.

All the wards where there was an evacuation order in place— Minato, Shinagawa, and Ōta, plus the other wards along the coast— were thrown into complete chaos. People piled chests, bedding, and other important belongings high in trucks and three-wheeled motorbikes, then fled toward Yamanote, the central part of the city located on higher ground. Others had filled small trailers—the kind usually pulled by cars or bikes—with household goods and were struggling to pull them along as fast as they could. They didn't even stop to wipe off the sweat, even when they grew so wet that they looked like they'd been doused with water. One mother wearing a large, stuffed backpack dragged along two hysterically crying children, one hanging from each of her two hands, as she dashed into a train station. Such sights were everywhere . . .

And all this happened within just the first ten minutes of the evacuation orders.

The entire sky quickly became overcast. *Whoosh*—a great gust of wind began sweeping in from the coast, whipping dirt and dust up into the air. The sudden blast of wind whooshed past the refugees as if trying to topple them.

Twilight had fallen over the No. 2 Battery in Shinagawa—the place where the authorities were expecting Godzilla to come on land. The bay beside it suddenly began to bubble wildly, and a gigantic surge like that of a tsunami came crashing against the coastal embankments.

What was that? The reverberations of the turbulent water? The roar of the wild wind? No, a loud rumbling rising from the earth. Everyone's hair stood on end. It felt as if the ground was suddenly starting to collapse.

Waaaaaaahhhhhh, waaaaaaahhhhhh, waaaaaaahhhhhh . . . The sharp wailing of the sirens continued to reverberate through the air. Trucks filled with stern-looking police wearing military gear and steel helmets began arriving one after another on the coast.

Screeech . . . The trucks slammed on their brakes. At the same moment, someone shouted the sharp order, "To your places!!" The policemen scattered.

Suddenly, *BOOM!* An earsplitting crash echoed through the entire landscape, shaking everything in sight. A blinding white-hot light bounded up from the turgid, overlapping waves.

"Whoa!!" The force was so great that even the policemen couldn't help lowering their heads to shield their faces under their metal helmets.

"Wow!!"

One of the policemen screamed, "Godzilla!!" His cry pierced the darkness.

Splash! A massive spray of water rose from the turbulent, tsunami-like wave. And there, in the middle of it, was Godzilla's upper body sticking out of the sea!

Bluish-white light was emerging from every part of his body, and with a huge roar—*GRAAWRR!!*—he opened his red mouth and moved to attack the lighthouse right in front of him.

The policemen who had taken their positions along the coast opened fire with machine guns. *Rat-tat-tat, rat-tat-tat . . .*

By that point, the refugees had grown even more frantic and were besieging the train stations. However, there was one elderly gentleman who was doing the opposite. He was going against the flow, pushing and trying to make his way through the throngs of people. His bloodshot eyes were turned toward the coast. It was Professor Yamane.

About one hundred meters from the shore, he came to an intersection. The police had erected a cordon to keep people out.

The professor's shirt was soaked from sweat, and he was huffing and puffing loudly as he tried to catch his breath after running there. He didn't pay the barrier any mind and started to climb over.

"Stop! Stop! We can't let you inside!!" A pale police officer came rushing over.

Shinkichi had also found it impossible to get to the shore along the other roads. At that very moment, he came running up from the left and caught sight of the professor arguing with the officer. The professor was beside himself, screaming, "But I'm Professor Yamane! Professor Kyōhei Yamane!!"

The policeman took an even firmer tone. "There's no entry!! It doesn't matter who you are!! You can't come in!!" He clutched the front of the professor's shirt and pushed him back.

Shinkichi gave up. "Professor! Let's go up to that high ground over there." He took the professor's hand and started running. The professor followed, but he kept casting quick, repeated glances over his shoulder as if he wasn't entirely ready to give up just yet.

Right then, the police began to fall back, forming what seemed like an avalanche rushing through the streets. They were retreating.

The ominous machine guns that had been placed here and there on either side of the highway suddenly started firing all at once. *Rat-tat-tat, rat-tat-tat* . . . Great puffs of purplish smoke rose from them as they continued their mad noise.

Moments later, Godzilla showed his full form! He was so gigantic that everyone lifted their heads to see him.

The machine gun fire raining down on him didn't seem to have any effect whatsoever. With a single kick—*BOOM!*—he smashed a huge concrete, steel-girded warehouse to bits and squashed the fence surrounding it. Without even pausing, he pushed his way toward Shinagawa Station.

At that moment, an express train, unaware of what was going on, passed through Ōimachi Station and headed into Shinagawa. *Fweet! Fweee-fweeet!* The conductor sounded his whistle.

Those of you readers who live in Tokyo know this already, but express trains leaving Yokohama do not stop at all the stations along the way. Instead, they speed along, not stopping until Tokyo Station. That meant that by the time the train was passing through Ōimachi and Shinagawa Stations, the passengers were just beginning to make their preparations to get off, even though the train was still moving at full speed. Of course, there was no way the conductor or train attendants could have known what was going on, much less the general passengers!

Godzilla stomped his way into the grounds of the station.

With just his toes, he sent rows of freight trains flying into the air. It was as easy as smashing eggshells. *Crash, crunch . . .*

At that moment, a frightening sound reverberated through the air. *Fweet! Fweee-fweeet!* The express was rapidly approaching . . .

Kaboom! Crash, crunch! The monster pushed a freight train with dozens of cars right up onto the platform. *CRASH!*

The express had rounded a curve and pulled into sight.

"My god!" screamed the conductor in the railway engine. He had a clear view of what lay ahead, and he jumped into the air.

Squeeeeeeech!! He slammed on the brakes, but the train continued to slide forward anyway. The sound of metal upon metal was so loud that you would have thought the train rails themselves were ripping apart.

Kaboom!! Crash, crash . . . The tail of the locomotive flew into the air like a great serpent lifting its tail, and a moment later it collapsed, slamming back to the ground in a gigantic cloud of dust and dirt.

GRAAWRR!! The enraged monster grabbed the train, which was now lying on its side, and—*crunch!!*—bit down upon it, then—*crunch! crash!*—he shook it back and forth with the force of his enormous body. The back cars of the train groaned and were thrown all the way to the water's edge.

The coupling mechanisms between the cars snapped, and the train engine fell to the ground. With a huge *CRUNCH!!*, Godzilla smashed it underfoot.

GRAAAAAAAWRRRR!!!! The sound he made was ferocious.

The police were scrambling to get to the nearest high ground. Like all the refugees, they were trembling in fear as they watched the disaster unfold. Among the people who had fled there were Professor Yamane, Ogata, and Shinkichi. Reflexively, the professor clutched the open collar of his button-down shirt and watched in amazement. He was pale, and his shining eyes were wide-open like marbles.

"My god! What terrifying strength! Unbelievable . . ." said the professor in a voice that was little more than a whisper, then he fell silent.

Godzilla smashed the Yatsuyama Bridge underfoot and stepped onto the National Highway. He surveyed his surroundings, and with another unsettling *grrrrrrrrr*, he stepped back and retreated into the sea.

The Tokyo Godzilla Society

That evening, the radio waves flew all over the world, carrying the headline "Godzilla appears in Japan!"

It was only natural that scholars everywhere looked at the news in wide-eyed astonishment. Even though no one had believed it possible, a terrifying kaiju from two million years ago had appeared in Tokyo.

The next morning, the silver wings of Pan American, Northwest, and other international carriers, filled with researchers from all over the world, started landing one after the next at Haneda Airport. A fleet of luxury cars ran back and forth continuously along the road from the airport to Anti-Godzilla Task Force headquarters.

Shinkichi was so exhausted from the night before that his head still wasn't clear, even after coming to work. He leaned against his desk as the gigantic form of the monster rose once again in his mind's eye.

"What a powerful body!" he thought. "No matter how many rounds of machine gun fire were let loose on him, the bullets just ricocheted off. If machine guns won't do the trick, would a cannon? Aerial bombardment maybe? . . . No, wait a sec. Godzilla managed to withstand the radiation of a hydrogen bomb without dying . . . That's what the professor said, right? So what then?"

It didn't matter how much he sat at his desk and thought. Someone had to try something . . . Shinkichi's thoughts were consumed with the monster. He wasn't a scientist, so he couldn't come up with a better plan, no matter how hard he tried.

"It's no good! We can't kill him even if we try. Our only option, I suppose, is to make the professor reconsider and help the people of Japan. We're all completely terrified . . . But even so, the professor . . ."

These thoughts were circling around in his head when he heard a *knock, knock* . . . Someone was quietly rapping at the door behind his chair, off to his left.

He turned and called out, "Come in!" The person at the door hesitantly opened the door a sliver, then peeked inside. She was a cute girl of around fourteen or fifteen, and her braided hair hung down from near her ears all the way to her chest, but her face was as pale as a wax doll.

"She looks familiar," Shinkichi thought to himself.

"Can I help you with something?"

She walked over to a desk at the end of the aisle and asked timidly, "Are you Shinkichi Morita?" Her head was turned down slightly, with only her eyes looking up at him.

Shinkichi was just about to say something when he looked at the girl again and recognized the dimple in her right cheek. "Oh, I know you," he thought. It was Mitsuko, the younger sister of Saburō, the young, healthy sailor who was unlucky enough to be on the *Eikō-maru*. "I'm sorry it's been so long, but the day after your brother was hurt, I caught a glimpse of you at the Maritime Safety Agency . . . My condolences. I didn't want to disturb you . . ."

"Oh, really?" Her response was feeble, but her eyes were darting around. They seemed to be searching for something.

Thinking how strange she was acting, Shinkichi asked, "Is there something I can help you with?" He spoke quietly, as if he was the one peeking in.

She looked at the doors nervously and spoke in a quiet, quick voice. "There's something I'd like to discuss with you!" This time she looked around the room at the windows as she said, "But it has to be somewhere private . . . I, I, I'm frightened!!" No sooner did she mutter these words than she began to tremble.

Shinkichi's eyes brightened despite himself. "Well, let's go outside then!"

When talking about things that no one else should hear, the safest spot is outdoors on the coastal embankments. There's nothing to get in the way, and one can talk while gazing at the wide-open sea.

The strong sunlight glittered on the quiet undulations of the water. Farther out in the water, no boats were visible, not even a small one.

"Um, it's about this letter . . ." She took a small, folded letter from the chest pocket of her dress. She held it tight for a moment against her body, but then she quickly extended her hand to Shinkichi.

He took it with a puzzled look, then following Mitsuko's lead, he held it close to his body so no one could see as he read it.

He felt as if all the blood in his body had let out a roar and started flowing backward through his veins. Reflexively, he gasped. "Oh, my! This is really something!!" He was about to add something else when—*Sssshh!*—Mitsuko shushed him.

Shinkichi also felt a chill go down his spine, and he glanced around nervously.

▶

At the Anti-Godzilla Task Force headquarters, the commander-in-charge was standing in front of a large map on the wall, presenting the newest strategic response. The investigative teams arriving from all over the world were rushing in from the airport and flowing into the room, filling it with people.

The chairs had been placed in a U-shape with the map at the

top center, and the commander was standing in front of a conference table as he puffed out his chest and spoke. "We estimate that if we line the entire coast with a thirty-meter-tall, five-meter-thick barrier of barbed wire, then run fifty thousand volts of electricity through it, that should kill Godzilla. He's an animal, so there's no way he could withstand such a strong electrical current. We'll have all the residents living within five hundred meters of the barbed-wire perimeter evacuate. Of course, I'm not just talking about the people who live in the fenced-off zone, but also the people who live outside of it as well. Based on the warning plan that you see on this other sheet, the Japan Ground Self-Defense Force, together with the Maritime Safety Agency, have rapidly carried out . . ."

The speaker's cheeks were red, but he spoke with obvious conviction. Seated next to him in a haughty posture was Dr. Hopman from the country of A—.[3] He was the one who had suggested the plan.

There's an expression in Japanese, "When the demons are away, that's when the washing gets done." Now that Godzilla was out of sight, all the folks in the parts of town that had witnessed his ferocious strength the day before were hurriedly packing up their things to flee. The whole area was in an uproar, and people were thronging the streets. Three-wheeled motorbikes, piled high with household goods, were heading toward Yamanote.

Passing them on the way to the coastline were giant trucks from the Japan Ground Self-Defense Force, piled high with barbed-wire fencing.

---

3. In Japanese literature, when an author does not want to specify exactly who or what he or she means, it is common to use only the capital letter of the name. Although the use of the letter A could stand for any country whose name starts with the letter A, it seems obvious that Kayama was thinking of America since the United States was so intimately involved with Japan's defense and scientific establishments in the postwar period.

Clouds of dust swirled in the air. The coastline felt as solemn and imposing as a battlefield. The soldiers were working together as fast as they could to complete the defenses.

Now that Tokyo was in danger, crowds of refugees were fleeing the city and spreading out and into the countryside. They flowed in a continuous stream westward along the Ōme Kaidō.

"Little Katsu . . . Katsu, darling . . . Where are you?"

"Mommy! Where are you, Mommy? . . . I can't find you."

"Where's my brother? Brooooother . . ."

The air was full of the heart-rending cries of people seeking their loved ones. Unused to such a difficult forced march, some of them sat down, listless, on the side of the road, not knowing what to do. For them, this was a living hell.

Shinkichi brought Mitsuko with him as he went to see Professor Yamane about the terrifying letter. It was written on thin, traditional paper in handwriting that wasn't very good. The niceness of the paper, however, didn't disguise the threat that it contained.

To Mitsuko,

Godzilla killed your older brother. However, that was not without reason. If you hate Godzilla for killing your brother and you want Godzilla to die too, then you'll likely befall the same fate as your brother.

What do you say? Are you prepared for that?

Our leader, the Great Lord Godzilla, will probably be back tomorrow night to stir up the weak-kneed, cowardly people of our nation.

Signed,
The Tokyo Godzilla Society

Sinking down deep into his couch, the professor stared hard at the letter. It was so strange that he instinctively shook his head. "Hmmm . . . This doesn't make any sense!!"

Shinkichi stared hard at the professor as if trying to see what was going on inside.

"Incomprehensible, really! After reading this letter, I'm not sure any longer if Godzilla is an animal or a machine under human control." The professor shook his head, put both hands on the back of his head, and quietly closed his eyes. He'd gone completely pale.

"What's this Tokyo Godzilla Society, Professor? Who are they?"

"No clue!!"

"I can't help feeling like they've got some terrible plan afoot."

"I've got no idea, of course!!" Clearly, the letter had put him in a foul mood.

"In any case, if any of this is true, then that means Godzilla's going to appear again tonight!! The letter was postmarked yesterday."

The professor remained silent.

It was two in the afternoon. Thanks to the diligent efforts of the Japan Ground Self-Defense Force, many of the preparations had been put in place. By this point, heavy field artillery, armored vehicles, first-aid ambulances, antiaircraft cannons, and so on were being dispatched one after the other.

On the coastline, everyone was working with dizzying speed, finishing up the barbed-wire perimeter.

Suddenly a loud, shrill voice resounded from the megaphones. "This announcement is from the Emergency Broadcast Service. I repeat, this announcement is from the Emergency Broadcast Service. Just now, at 16:30 on the twentieth, Godzilla was spotted in the sea several nautical miles north of Kannonzaki. He is presently moving along a northwestern trajectory. People in the coastal areas between Tokyo and Yokohama should exercise extreme caution."

Preparations had been completed at the electrical transformer station, and the Self-Defense Force was about to test the power lines. A buzzer went off, and a light marked "Area Three" switched on. The men threw a few switches—*click, click.*

"Area Four!"

"Ready, sir!"

"Area Five!"

"Ready, sir!"

They were still in the process of double-checking their equipment when they heard a loud *beep, beep* . . . It was the unsettling sound of the emergency broadcast system. The entire room fell silent for a moment as everyone pricked up their ears.

"This announcement is from the Emergency Broadcast Service. Repeat, this announcement is from the Emergency Broadcast Service. As of 17:40, an urgent warning has been issued. We have reports that Godzilla has shifted his course and seems to be moving north-northwest. A complete evacuation order has been issued for Minato, Shinagawa, Ōta, and the other coastal wards. Repeat, this emergency announcement is from the Emergency Broadcast Service . . ."

Back at the Yamane household, Shinkichi had no sooner left than someone rang the front doorbell. Emiko went and found Ogata there wearing navy slacks and a light aqua-colored open-necked shirt. In his hand, he had a navy hat with a wide brim.

"Is the professor in?" His question was friendly, but there was something in his look that was different from usual.

"He's here, but Ogata, I wish you could've been here earlier . . . Shinkichi was here until just a moment or two ago."

"What business did he have?"

"It doesn't matter. Please come in. I'll call my father right away . . ."

Emiko led him into the living room. Ogata put his hand on the window and started gazing outside at the searchlights lighting up the nighttime sky. There was a worried look in his eyes.

Creeaaaak. A door opened, and the professor charged in busily with heavy footsteps. He was shaking with rage.

Worried, Emiko followed him in from behind and quietly asked, "Papa! What's the matter?" She peered into his face as she whispered this question.

"They're wasting a one-in-a-million chance! Wanting to catch the king of the Jurassic in a giant electric chair is sheer madness!" He wasn't speaking to anyone in particular, just flinging out words angrily.

Ogata had been standing by the window watching the night sky. His facial muscles tensed as he turned. "Professor, I'm of the opposite opinion."

The conversation was off to a bad start. How long would this continue? . . . Emiko was worried.

"Ogata, I've given this a lot of thought. No scholar in the world has ever seen a creature like Godzilla before, but here he is, right here in Japan. He's a living fossil—priceless!"

Ogata's response was also emphatic. "But Professor! We can't let that berserk offspring of the H-bomb just run around wild! If anything, Godzilla himself is the hydrogen bomb hanging over Japan right now!"

"He absorbed all the radiation from the hydrogen bomb and still survived. Why aren't you interested in trying to figure out the secrets of his incredible vitality?!"

Ogata bit his lip and stared so hard at the professor that he could have practically bored a hole in him.

"You, too, are arguing we ought to exterminate him? Get out of here! Just leave! Go!!" Perhaps the professor was speaking rashly, but he gestured to shoo Ogata from the room.

"Please, Professor! Just hold on a minute!" Ogata quickly moved in front of him to block the way. "Don't you understand how terrified everyone in Japan is right now because of Godzilla?"

The muscles in Ogata's face began to twitch, no doubt from the mental anguish of standing up to the professor to whom he was so indebted. He took out a letter from his left breast pocket. It crinkled as he opened it and stuck it in front of the professor.

"Oh!" The professor almost cried out in surprise. It was the same as the letter Shinkichi had shown him just a moment ago. "You got one of those letters too?"

"What? . . . You already know about this?"

"Yeah, Shinkichi came here just now to show me a letter like this."

"I see. But Shinkichi and I weren't the only ones to get a letter like this. As far as I know, there've been around twenty so far. All the people who got them were involved with the Godzilla problem somehow . . . Let me be clear. People all over Tokyo right now are trembling because of this letter. They're even saying that the leader of the Tokyo Godzilla Society must be you, Professor Yamane!"

"What?!" Emiko let out a cry of surprise.

All the color drained from the professor's face, and he slumped into the sofa.

"It makes sense people would think that. 'We shouldn't kill Godzilla!'—that's what you were saying, Professor, and that seems to be the intent of this letter too. I don't think it's a stretch to say that you and the letters seem to be saying more or less the same thing . . ."

Emiko couldn't stand it any longer and burst out, "Ogata, this is too much! Simply too much! It's ridiculous to insinuate that Papa . . ." She began to sob, rendering the remainder of her words inaudible.

Ogata spoke up clearly in support. "But we believe in you!!"

Right then—*beep, beep*—they heard the gloomy sound of the radio emergency broadcast system. They drew in their breath sharply as they pricked up their ears.

"This announcement is from the Emergency Broadcast Service. Repeat, this emergency announcement is from the Emergency Broadcast Service. Just now, at 19:30, aerial surveillance discovered Godzilla headed toward the coast somewhere in the Tokyo, Kawasaki, and Yokohama region. As soon as he reaches land for the first attack, the coastal perimeter of that region will be electrified with high voltage. All people within the vicinity are to exercise extreme caution . . ."

Godzilla's movements had begun. He was once again headed toward the coast.

At one of the houses, a canary hanging in a cage from the eave suspiciously cocked its head and twittered. *Pipipipirrrrrrrrr . . . Pipipipirrrrrrr . . .*

Godzilla Attacks the Metropolitan Center

There hadn't been much foggy weather recently, but as evening fell, a fog settled over the city. It was hot and muggy, making the city residents feel as if they were in a steam bath.

Like the previous day, a strong wind began to roar. An enormous swell of wind came through the Shibaura area.

Flash! A bluish-white light illuminated the surface of the water, and Godzilla's neck extended upward from between the waves. As he looked around, he quietly, noiselessly crept toward the coast.

The tanks had fallen silent as well, but their gun towers quietly followed his movements with the whirring of metal gears. On the higher ground behind them was a long row of heavy field artillery. Their reddish-black muzzles also slowly shifted, never letting the target out of their crosshairs. How effective would these modern weapons be against the seemingly invincible Godzilla?

Godzilla versus modern weaponry! Once the battle started, no doubt the fireworks would fly!

Floating above the waves, his neck quietly approached the barbed-wire fence.

Ogata and Shinkichi were standing on a rooftop, holding their breath as they watched. The rumor had been going around that the monster who had appeared there, rising over the waves and pressing in toward the shore, was a robot controlled by the Tokyo

Godzilla Society, with Professor Yamane at its lead. As Ogata looked at Godzilla, however, the thought struck him as entirely ridiculous.

A loud buzzer went off in the electrical control room, and a foreboding red light for Area Three switched on. With a sudden movement, the person in charge flipped a switch. Fifty thousand volts of strong current flowed through the barbed-wire perimeter of Area Three. That ought to be enough to kill the monster with a single touch, right?

Godzilla approached the breakwaters near the Tokyo Bay Ocean Liner Piers. Suddenly, he let out a ferocious *GRAAAAAAAWRRRR!!*

Even though the concrete breakwater was two meters thick, he shattered it in an instant with a single kick. He leaped onto land and placed his paw on the barbed wire.

Crackle, crackle . . . For a moment, there was a tremendous shower of sparks flying in every direction, and an ear-splitting *GRAAAAAAAWRRRR!!* pierced the night sky over Tokyo. It wasn't exactly a battle cry, nor was it a shriek of sadness or pain. In the middle of a great cloud of white smoke, Godzilla shook his head and lifted his tail. With bloodshot eyes fixed on the defense forces, he began to flail wildly around.

Ka-boom!! Ka-boom!! Thinking that this was their chance, the heavy field artillery on the hill began firing all at once.

But as soon as the white smoke cleared, Godzilla was still standing there, right before the barbed-wire perimeter!! He glared at the soldiers on the hill with a terrifying look.

Godzilla was enraged. With each violent, angry breath, he set a cloud of dirt flying into the air. Opening his mouth wide, he looked around.

Everyone reflexively put their hands to their heads in terror. Ducking down, they ran into the streets.

"Shinkichi! The defenses won't hold! Run!!" Ogata wrapped his arms around Shinkichi's chest as he started to run.

"Ahhh!!" Instinctively, Shinkichi screamed.

Whoosh! A couple of dark shadows dashed down the fire escape from the roof!

"Ogata!!"

"Here I am!!" The two started running for all they were worth. Just as they reached the fire escape, they spied a snow-white half sheet of paper that had apparently just been posted by the railing. On it were printed big, black letters.

LOOK! GAZE UPON OUR LORD!!
The Tokyo Godzilla Society!!

"My god! What weirdos!!" With angry eyes, Shinkichi and Ogata followed the dark shadows fleeing down the stairs in front of them.

"Let's catch 'em!!"

Clackety-clack . . . The two ran down the stairs so quickly that they almost tumbled down.

In his rage, Godzilla shook his entire body, and a strange, white light shot out from his back. He opened his mouth to let out a roar. *GRRRAAAAAWWWWR!!* And with it, a white-hot beam of light shot out from inside his bright-red mouth.

How terrifying!! Everywhere the white-hot ray touched was instantaneously engulfed in a sea of flame.

Ogata and Shinkichi were still chasing after the dark shadows. They ran down from the rooftop and were about to turn into a narrow street when they glanced back over their shoulders. What they saw made their blood run cold.

The same building that they had just escaped from, the very same building that ought to be towering up right behind them, was collapsing into nothingness!! Godzilla's white-hot beam was responsible.

Four or five homes went up in flames.

A group of firemen, still completely astounded, were rushing down the crowded, confused streets, sirens on. The fire trucks raised a loud racket as they sped through the streets.

Godzilla grew even more enraged. He spat out another strong, white-hot beam as he pushed forward, trampling every building in his path. He was headed toward the Ginza.

Dear readers, I imagine you must be familiar with the weapon known as a flamethrower. You've probably seen them in newsreels at the cinema, in American movies, and so on. Soldiers use it when they suspect the enemy is hidden away in a building or some such place. The soldier aims what looks like a rifle, and a great stream of fire shoots out from the mouth, incinerating everything for fifteen or sixteen meters!! That's the terrifying weapon I mean.

The white-hot column of fire shooting out of Godzilla's mouth was hundreds of times stronger than any flamethrower. It shot out of his mouth—*Whoosh!*—piercing the night sky like a searchlight.

The firemen tried desperately to escape. Right behind them, Godzilla, who was as big as a small mountain, stomped along, smashing all the stores and businesses in his path. Each time he caught sight of a slightly taller building, he breathed out another white-hot beam—*whoosh!*—completely incinerating it.

Before long, Godzilla was standing on the national highway connecting Tokyo and Yokohama.

Ten tanks rushed to the spot and formed a diagonal column. All at once, they started firing large, rapid-fire cannons—the pride of the military—from the tops of the tanks.

But what should happen? Just moments before, Godzilla had smashed through barbed wire charged with fifty thousand volts of electrical current, but that didn't even faze him. Not surprisingly, the cannon fire didn't affect him either.

The Japan Ground Self-Defense Force had poured all their hopes into their preparations, but even this last line of defense was completely crushed underfoot by the monster.

Earlier, the Anti-Godzilla Task Force command had called yet another emergency meeting. They had spread out a large map on a table, and as the news rolled in, they quickly wrote it down on the map.

The leaders leaned into look. All color had drained from their faces.

The marks that they had made on the map were all leading closer and closer to the Ginza. Their hearts were pounding loudly, like alarm bells going off. Nonetheless, not a single person said a word. They had tried everything and didn't know what to do next.

"The fires around Shibaura are growing more and more intense. No prospects for putting them out . . ."

"Car No. 167 reports that over here, near Tamachi Station, fire has broken out in three more spots."

"A report came in from Car Number 405! The fires near Mitadai Station are spreading to Minami Teramachi and Isarako-machi."

"Car Number 215 reporting! The warning post at the Fudanotsuji Interchange has been destroyed, and all the tanks of the Forty-Ninth Division have been wiped out. Further engagement is impossible!"

"Task Force Command, this is Car No. 129, Talk Force Command, this is Car No. 129 . . ."

Information was flowing in from all directions. The policemen near Shinbashi had heard the news from the front lines and had lost all will to fight. They had gathered around their police cars and were awaiting further instruction.

"All units should leave their offensive positions and work with all their might to extinguish the fires! At the same time, do everything you can to help the wounded!"

The fight against Godzilla had already sunk into desperation.

"My god! This is terrible!!" One of the policemen let out a sigh of grief and lifted his head. But there was no time to scream before a beam of white-hot light showered down from above, turning the police car into a ball of flame, which careened wildly across the road.

Godzilla had entered the Ginza, leaving a massive trail of flames in his wake.

Following the tracks of the city rails, he plodded along, reaching the Owarichō intersection. Suddenly, he breathed his white-hot beam at the large department store building there.

The armored doors of the department store were down, so a little fire wouldn't have caused any trouble, but almost immediately, the entire building was engulfed in a red flower of flame.

Whooooo, whooooo . . . The high-pitched squeal of the sirens echoed over the city as the firemen regrouped. Godzilla peered down at them with his gigantic eyes. There was nothing the firemen could do. All they could do was watch helplessly from a distance.

Fire was spewing from the windows on the upper floors. Far beneath that, a mother huddled with her children by the ground-floor entrance.

She held her three children tight by her side and whispered quietly as the sparks rained down all around them. She sounded as if she was praying. "We're going to be with Daddy soon . . . We'll be with Daddy soon enough . . ."

Standing in the middle of the intersection, Godzilla raised the upper part of his body and looked around with a sharp light in his eyes.

The clock tower on the top of a building on the other side of the street began to chime like usual. *Ding-dong, ding-dong* . . . It sounded clear and refreshing in all the chaos.

Godzilla made a confused face as he looked at it and let out a single, sharp *WRRRAWR!* Then—*crunch!*—he suddenly grabbed hold of it.

He wrenched off the clock tower with his teeth and spit out the wreckage, which clattered back to earth.

On the roof of the TV broadcasting corporation, an announcer was shouting into his mike in a determined, heroic voice. "Unbelievable! Absolutely unbelievable! But yes, unbelievable events are unfolding right before our very eyes! Godzilla has left a sea of flame in his wake. As I look around, from Owarichō in the Ginza out toward Shinbashi, Tamachi, and Shibaura, everything is a sea of fire! Just now, Godzilla has started moving again. He appears to be headed in the direction of Sukiya Bridge. All you who are watching right now, this is not a play or a movie. This is real! One of the strangest events in all history! Has our world been dragged two million years back into the past in a mere instant?"

Godzilla turned right at the Owarichō intersection and headed toward Hibiya Park. He crushed Sukiya Bridge underfoot. A train that was just sliding into Yūrakuchō Station, right next door, was crushed under falling girders, making a sickening crunching sound. Godzilla spewed out another white-hot beam and pushed forward.

At the Anti-Godzilla Task Force headquarters, they had already sensed the enormity of the danger pressing down upon them. Some people were carrying out important documents, while others were taking out their own belongings. The entire place was in chaos.

Then suddenly, a voice started screaming like crazy over the speaker. "Everyone, take shelter in the basement! Everyone, take shelter in the basement! Run as fast as you can! Members of the Anti-Godzilla Task Force should regroup in Room 306 of the basement . . ."

Right then, CRASH!! Half of the building collapsed with an ear-splitting crunch.

Godzilla continued to spit out his strange, white-hot beam as he trudged heavily through the city. The National Diet Building showed up nice and white in the darkness. As he showered his angry white beam upon it, the building began to groan and rip apart with a sound that was enough to make a person's blood run cold. Then, crushing part of the building underfoot, he continued on his way.

The next thing to catch his eyes was a tall television tower. *Crack!!* He broke it off with a single paw, then—*crunch, crunch!!*—he bent it nearly double with his ferocious strength, leaving it a twisted mess.

He let out a ferocious *GRAAAAWRR!!* that echoed high across the night sky. Then, as if he pleased with his victory, he began to retreat toward Tsukiji, which neighbors the bay.

As he jumped into the water, *splash!!*—he sent up a huge spray of water. With the force of his entire body, he started to push over Kachidoki Bridge.

A raging swell of water crashed like a tsunami against the shores on either side of the bridge. The metal of the bridge began to let out a long metallic *creeeeeeeek,* and then *CRASH!*—it collapsed into the water below.

The bridge sent up a huge splash that came down like a waterfall. In the middle of this, Godzilla brazenly continued his march into Tokyo Bay.

The stunned onlookers could do nothing but watch in amazement. Some of the people had lost their homes to fire; some had lost their families, but still they stared dumbstruck, as if their minds were temporarily blank.

Then one of them began to shout, "Damn it!! Go to hell!!" It was a young man. He shook his right fist in the air, and his angry eyes flooded with tears. Shinkichi. His face looked especially miserable and dirty like a hobo's, probably because he had wiped the tears pouring down his dust-covered face with the back of his hand. Surrounding him were Emiko, Ogata, and Professor Yamane.

Shinkichi's despairing shouting and crying flowed through the crowd of stunned, standing onlookers, reverberating like a heart-rending echo. In no time at all, they all began to feel the same way.

Right then, an ear-splitting, metallic sound screeched through the northeastern sky. A squadron of jet fighters were headed to attack Godzilla.

Ka-bang!! Ka-bang!!

Great pillars of water rose into the air with a roar.

The planes entered into a nosedive one after the next, descending from an altitude of ten thousand meters. They were flying with such speed that they were hardly visible as they attacked Godzilla with their rockets.

The onlookers on the shores suddenly came to their senses. They gripped their sweaty hands tight and shouted for all they were worth.

"Come on! You can do it!!"

"Take revenge for us!!"

"That's it!! Shoot, shoot!!"

But the assault from the jets didn't seem to bother Godzilla in the least. He swatted two or three jets near him into the sea and let out a gigantic *WRAAAWR!!* like a battle cry. He howled into the nighttime sky and then began plodding into the deep water. The surface glittered like white silver, and it swelled up like a hill as he disappeared into the sea.

Shinkichi was so distraught that he couldn't cry anymore even if he wanted, so he ground his teeth together instead. The others stamped their feet in anger to vent their feelings. No one even noticed that in the meantime, Professor Yamane had slipped off, alone.

The face of the metropolis had changed so drastically in a single night that it was hardly recognizable. The sky that hung over it was thick with smoke. The fires hadn't yet been extinguished.

A temporary first-aid center had been set up at the Anti-Godzilla Task Force, but there were so many wounded that the sick rooms couldn't hold them all. The wounded spilled out into the halls and corridors. It was so crowded that there was hardly anywhere to step.

The moaning of the seriously wounded . . . The crying of children . . . The shouts of relatives searching for their loved ones . . . Amid all this tragedy and confusion, Emiko was hard at work.

She was holding an orphaned baby someone had brought. The baby had no way of knowing that her mother was dead, and she waved her sweet, red hand in the air innocently as she reached playfully for Emiko's chest.

Right then, Shinkichi came bounding up the stairs. He knitted his brow as he looked around the misery-filled room. He spotted Emiko and walked over.

The sweet little girl lying in front of Emiko had her head wrapped in bandages. She was undergoing a test for radiation. The Geiger counter let off an unsettling clicking sound; however, the girl was too far gone even to notice the machine's reaction.

Emiko couldn't take it any longer and instinctively averted her eyes. To her surprise, her gaze fell upon her father crouched in a corner of the room. His eyes were closed, and he seemed to be praying. Letting out a little gasp of surprise, she moved to stand up, but before she could, she felt a tap on the shoulder. With a little "Oh!" she turned to find Shinkichi standing there, looking at her worriedly.

"Shinkichi! I've got something important to tell you." Still holding the baby in her arms, she led him toward the back staircase. "After seeing all this, I can't stay silent any longer . . . Things are so bad that I don't care whose trust I break . . ."

"What's this about breaking trust?"

"Well, I'd be breaking the trust of my father, who's the person I respect most in the world. I'd also be breaking Dr. Serizawa's trust in an even bigger way."

"Dr. Serizawa?"

"Yeah, I made him a promise I wouldn't tell anyone."

Shinkichi wasn't sure how to respond.

"I even kept it a secret from you. But the time's come for me to break my promise . . . It's about that day—the day I visited him with Mr. Hagiwara . . ." She leaned her forehead against the window in the stairwell and closed her eyes. As she did, her memories came back so vividly that she could see them clearly in her mind's eye.

Serizawa dropped the small, metal box into the aquarium, and as Emiko instinctively leaned forward to watch, he shouted, "No! Step back!!" His voice was unexpectedly forceful.

As he flipped the switch, the electricity began to hum.

Serizawa stared at the tank with such intensity . . .

The small box in the aquarium broke in two, and immediately, the whole tank filled with bubbles. The boiling continued, and in an instant, the fish that were writhing around in anguish were reduced to nothing but bones. A moment later, even those had disappeared. What was going on!?

Emiko screamed and covered her face in her hands.

Serizawa looked at her with a mournful gaze, let out a deep sigh, and hung his head.

Once the frantic beating of Emiko's heart had calmed somewhat, she gasped, "What? What on earth? . . ."

A pained look came over Serizawa's face. "Let me tell you. In a single instant, I split all the oxygen in the water. That causes all living beings to suffocate, and then their bodies melt away . . . This is the 'Oxygen Destroyer'—it breaks apart the oxygen atoms contained in liquid water."

A fire rose in Emiko's eyes. She felt her criticisms mount inside.

"At first, my research was all about oxygen . . . But through my work, I discovered an unimaginable source of energy. When I tested it for the first time, it was so powerful that I even surprised myself. It made me shake uncontrollably. I couldn't eat for two or three days. If I made a single device about the size of a cannonball, it would be enough to wipe out everything in Tokyo Bay in an instant. The whole place would turn into an aquatic graveyard."

"My goodness! Why research such terrifying things?"

"Emiko, I'm just a scientist who takes his work seriously. All I was doing was testing the limits of this power . . ."

"But if—just supposing—what would happen if someone were to use this for some horrifying purpose?"

"You're right to be concerned. If this were used as a weapon, it would be more dreadful than a hydrogen bomb. It could very well lead humanity to extinction."

Emiko was so frightened that all the color drained from her face.

"When I show the world the Oxygen Destroyer, I'm going to be sure to present it as something useful. Until then, I'm not going to tell anyone about my discovery. That's why I didn't give anything away to the reporter you brought here. If someone forces me to use the Oxygen Destroyer in some capacity while it's still in this preliminary state, well . . . I've made up my mind to kill myself so my research dies along with me."

Serizawa's cheeks had become hollow and sunken from all the time and worry he had expended on his research. As Emiko looked at his gaunt face, she felt strong emotions stirring within.

"That's very noble of you . . . I promise I won't tell my father. No matter what."

As Emiko replayed the entire frightening scene in her imagination, she laid out the entire story step-by-step. None of the surprise from that day appeared on her face. If anything, she felt resolute strength. Nonetheless, when she finished, one could detect a trace of pain in her relieved expression.

"So . . . I'm breaking a promise . . ."

Shinkichi had been watching her facial movements carefully as if trying to read what was behind them. He clapped a strong hand on her shoulder and said, "Emiko, I'm glad you told me. If this information can help save us, I'm sure everyone will forgive you! Even Dr. Serizawa."

At some point, the two of them had grabbed one another's hands tightly, and tears of joy welled up in Shinkichi's eyes as he spoke.

The Oxygen Destroyer

The garden was overflowing with sunlight that made everyone feel like autumn had arrived. A canary was tweeting at the end of the eaves.

Since early in the morning, Serizawa had been cooped up in his laboratory, concentrating hard on his research. As he worked, he heard the faint sound of the front doorbell.

Ordinarily, not many people stopped by. Thinking it was odd to have visitors, he went to the door, where he found Shinkichi and Emiko.

"Oh, it's you . . ." A smile came over his pale face.

Shinkichi summoned up a forceful tone of voice. "Dr. Serizawa, I've put a lot of thought into this. I have something important to ask!!"

"You do?" Serizawa gave a quick glance at Emiko, and he led the two of them into his living room. Emiko followed, feeling guilty.

Serizawa sat down. "Have a seat," he suggested. However, Shinkichi remained standing with a tense look on his face.

"So, what do you want?"

In response to Serizawa's curt question, Shinkichi poured out his heart. "I want you to let us use the Oxygen Destroyer."

Serizawa immediately shot a surprised look at Emiko. She, however, didn't meet his eyes. Instead, she averted her gaze to Shinkichi's back.

Serizawa looked back at Shinkichi and said, "What's this

'Oxygen Destroyer' business? Never heard of it . . ." He turned his vexation at having been betrayed into mean-spirited sarcasm directed at Emiko.

Shinkichi couldn't take it and shouted, "Dr. Serizawa! Why are you lying!?"

"Lying? . . . What?"

"Please, Dr. Serizawa!" This time, it was Emiko. She began pleading with him as if her life depended on it. "I betrayed my promise to you. I felt like I had to tell Shinkichi . . . Please, I'm begging you. Let us use it!!"

Serizawa's expression was as firm and cold as glass.

Emiko couldn't take it and broke down in tears. "I'm so sorry. Please forgive me."

Shinkichi rushed to her aid. "You've got to forgive Emiko! It's just that she couldn't bear all the suffering she's witnessed. Coming to you for help is our only hope!"

For a moment, a pained expression came over Serizawa, but he answered coldly. "Shinkichi, if Emiko told you about my secret, then you probably also learned why I can't use it. I flat out refuse!!"

"Please?!"

"Absolutely not!"

Shinkichi insisted. "We're begging you!!"

"Get out of here!" Serizawa quickly turned his back to his guests and rushed down to his gloomy basement laboratory.

"Dr. Serizawa!!" Shinkichi and Emiko followed him down the stairs. However, a moment later, they heard the door slam. Serizawa locked the door with a *ga-chunk*.

"Please! Open the door!!"

"No!"

"Dr. Serizawa . . . Dr. Serizawa . . ."

No matter how much they called out his name, there was no response.

Shinkichi put his ear to the door. The laboratory was utterly quiet; however, he imagined that somewhere in the unsettling silence, he could sense Dr. Serizawa's heart pounding from the strain.

"Emiko, we have to do something!"

Pushing Emiko back to the staircase behind them, Shinkichi pushed hard against the door with his full body. The door gave a loud groan, then gave way, breaking under his weight.

But a moment later and it would have been too late!! In the lab, Serizawa had lifted an axe above the metal orb of the Oxygen Destroyer and was about to bring it crashing down.

"WAIT!!"

With ferocious energy, Shinkichi leaped at him.

As the two struggled, Shinkichi tried to protect the Oxygen Destroyer, but the axe Serizawa was swinging grazed against Shinkichi's head.

The blood began running from the wound, and—*thump!*—Shinkichi fell to the ground.

"Shinkichi!!" Emiko ran to him and wrapped a handkerchief around his head.

Serizawa saw the snow-white handkerchief she'd applied to his wound quickly turn red with blood, and in a flash, he returned to his senses. The axe dropped from his hand with a clatter.

"Shinkichi, I'm so sorry! Forgive me! If the Oxygen Destroyer is going to be of any use, I should be the one to bring it to the world's attention . . . But right now, in its current state, it's nothing but a weapon of mass destruction . . . You've got to understand . . ."

Still lying on the floor, Shinkichi opened his eyes weakly. "I get it . . . But right now, we've got to prevent another attack by Godzilla . . . If we don't, what on earth's going to become of us?"

"Shinkichi, if we do use the Oxygen Destroyer, there's no way the big shots of the world will just stand by watching silently. They'll rush to turn this technology into a weapon that will drive humanity to the brink of destruction. I'm certain of it. Atomic bombs versus atomic bombs, hydrogen bombs versus hydrogen bombs, and on top of all that, we'll have a new, terrifying weapon . . . As a scientist—no, as a human being—I can't allow us to add it to the mix . . . Don't you see?"

As Shinkichi quietly listened, he felt Serizawa's distress weigh upon him too. Yes, he understood the older scientist's anguish, but even so, he had to take a chance and place his trust in him.

"But what are we to do about the misery and death right in front of us? Should we just give up? Say there's nothing we can do? The only one who can save us right now is you, Dr. Serizawa. Suppose you were to use it. As long as you remain firm in your conviction not to share your research publicly, there shouldn't be any danger of it being used as a destructive weapon, should there?"

"You've got to understand, Shinkichi, that human beings are weak. Even if I burn all the documents, the knowledge will stay with me. As long as I'm alive, who can guarantee that someone or something won't force me to use it again? . . . Human beings are weak . . . Darn it . . . I wish I'd never made the damn thing . . ." He let out a groan.

Poor Serizawa. Doubts upon doubts. Worries upon worries. His heart was full of grief.

Right then, they heard the faint strains of a girl's chorus. It rose like a wave, and in the voices was something like a prayer. The three of them felt their eyes drawn to the television.

The screen was showing scenes of different parts of Tokyo. The great metropolis had been completely transformed into a disaster zone in the course of a single night.

Smoke rising from smoldering fires. Crushed buildings. Wreckage of burned-out cars.

Big trucks were carrying the seriously injured to the makeshift hospital rooms of the Anti-Godzilla Task Force. The television broadcast the groans of the wounded.

And then, the television showed the prayers of some newly

orphaned elementary-school children who had been entrusted to a temple . . . The screen showed a shot of some child's lost and abandoned gym shoe. Big drops of rain were falling on it.

The song continued. At some school, a children's choir was singing a prayer for peace.

Oh, peace and comfort! Oh, light of the sun!
Hasten your return, take pity on us
Feel our sorrow as we pray
And pour our very lives into this song

Serizawa was deeply moved and sat stone still, as if transfixed to the spot. Shinkichi and Emiko also felt their hearts swell with emotion . . . The voices of the girls' chorus rose to a climax.

Suddenly, as if he couldn't stand it any longer, Serizawa flipped the TV switch. Then, reaching into a case, he pulled out several secret documents and threw them into his kerosene-burning stove in a firm act of resolution.

As they watched, Shinkichi and Emiko could sense his determination. They were overwhelmed. For years, he had poured his tears and sweat into those schematics and equations, and now, they were crackling and burning as they went up in flames . . .

Emiko couldn't watch. She leaned forward and buried her face in her hands.

Shinkichi stood up, still in obvious pain. He started to say, "Dr. Serizawa . . ." but the words trailed off.

Their eyes met. They were full of tears, already overflowing.

Serizawa took Shinkichi's hand firmly in his own, and a moment or two later, he cast his eyes down to the stove. The papers were completely engulfed in flames.

Emiko couldn't stand it and started weeping. "I'm sorry . . . Forgive me . . ."

Serizawa forced a smile. "That's fine, don't worry, Emiko . . . These are the blueprints for the device. I've got to make absolutely sure that no devil ever gets his hands on them . . ."

Whoosh! The burning documents collapsed in pile of ash.

Prayer for Peace

The headline in the paper the next day read, "Who is the Tokyo Godzilla Society? An enemy of Japan?"

According to the article, the day before, when the Japan Ground Self-Defense Force was working its way through some of the burned-out ruins, it came across the body of a twenty-three- or twenty-four-year-old male. His pockets were stuffed with printed half sheets of paper that spoke about "Our Lord Godzilla."

Although he seemed to think of the kaiju as some kind of leader, Godzilla had trampled him to death, brutally crushing his midsection underfoot. It seemed clear he didn't really have any connection with Godzilla. He'd just used the monster terrorizing society as a way of scaring people.

Judging from his clothing, it seemed clear he was the same fellow who'd pasted the flyer to the wall in front of Ogata and Shinkichi before trying to get away.

When the authorities ran his fingerprints, it turned out he had four prior criminal convictions, all of which involved threatening people for money or valuables. It seemed likely that this time, too, there was no real, prior connection with anything called the "Tokyo Godzilla Society." He seemed to be acting on his own. At least, that's what the article suggested.

Rumors had been flying that Professor Yamane must be the head of the Godzilla Society, so Ogata, Shinkichi, Emiko, and the others were relieved at the news, especially when they thought about how the professor must feel.

A few days later, the survey ship *Seagull* once again set sail. Dr. Serizawa was on board, carrying his invention, the Oxygen Destroyer.

After Godzilla's wild rampage through Tokyo, citizens were furious at the monster. For that reason, people were holding out lots of hope for the Oxygen Destroyer.

As if praying for the *Seagull*'s success, the Maritime Safety Agency had sent out a group of patrol boats to form a row around the port. The quick, excited voice of a live-broadcast announcer resounded across the bow.

"At long last, the great moment of truth is nearly upon us. Will Godzilla—the monster of the century, and one of the greatest threats to the world as we know it—sink to his grave at the bottom of the sea? Just now, Dr. Serizawa has quietly stood up on the deck of the *Seagull* . . ."

Meanwhile, the authorities were proceeding with their survey aboard the *Seagull*. Suddenly, their Geiger counters started making an unsettling string of clicks.

Everyone looked at one another. Ogata immediately raised his hand and shouted, "Stop! . . . Go astern! . . . Stop the engines!"

The ship floated quietly on the surface of the sea.

"He's here! Right below us!"

Hearing this, Serizawa's face became unusually tense. As he called out Ogata's name, his voice trembled slightly. As Ogata turned to look, Serizawa shouted in a brooding voice, "Get me into a diving suit!"

"What're you saying?"

Ogata spat out the words, "You're not an experienced diver. What're you going to do once you get that suit on?"

Professor Yamane chimed in from the side, "Serizawa, I'm with Ogata . . . Don't be unreasonable."

Serizawa stiffened. "Professor! This is the only Oxygen Destroyer we've got. It's the only one in existence. I've got to go underwater to ensure it works properly. There's no choice." He spoke decisively, but there was great sadness in his voice.

The professor sensed his resolve and said nothing more.

Shinkichi, who was standing behind the professor, shouted, "Alright! Then let me go too!"

"No, I'm going alone!"

"That's crazy! You're not an experienced diver. You're going to jump into the ocean all alone?"

Ogata tensed up, then looked at Shinkichi's expression. "That makes sense. I'll feel better if Shinkichi goes too. I'm trusting you, Shinkichi."

As Ogata helped get Serizawa into the diving suit, he confirmed, "Now listen . . . You're going to follow all Shinkichi's instructions, OK?" Serizawa nodded meekly.

Ogata made a sign to the bridge. "Stand by . . . Now, very slow . . ."

The boat gently began to move. Someone switched on the pump for the underwater air feed.

Silence. Everyone held their breath.

Holding the Oxygen Destroyer in his hands, Serizawa turned to Yamane. "Professor, I never even dreamed this would be the way I'd show my invention to the world." He tried to crack a forced smile.

The professor was moved by Serizawa's readiness to do the right thing. He approached him and gave him a big bear hug.

Emiko stepped forward too. "I'm praying for your success."

Serizawa gave a slight smile and nodded.

Right under the spot where the *Seagull* had stopped, Godzilla was squatting down silently between some boulders. With a slow motion, he raised his head.

Shinkichi and Serizawa slipped quietly into the sea.

Leaning over the edge of the boat, the professor said, "Shinkichi, I'm counting on you. Take good care! Got it?"

The two nodded at one another. With a *glug-glug*, Shinkichi and Serizawa sank into the water, leaving a trail of big bubbles above them. Emiko held their lifeline tightly, praying as she watched them disappear under the surface . . .

The lifeline kept unraveling and unraveling the deeper they went.

Sometimes a stripe of brightness would waver on the gloomy sea floor, casting an uncanny light. Forests of gigantic kelp were growing there just like the forests on land, and below them, Godzilla was huddling in the shade of some rocks.

As they reached the bottom of the sea, the two looked around.

As if sensing some slight change, Godzilla lifted his head a bit.

There was a quick flash in the water.

Godzilla rose up slightly and looked in that direction.

Shinkichi tapped Serizawa's shoulder and pointed to the shade of the rocks, near where the kelp was waving eerily in the water.

There, barely visible in the hazy water, was the outline of Godzilla! As if startled, Serizawa looked at Shinkichi. Shinkichi began waving the underwater flashlight in his hand in big motions.

Godzilla began to move, propelling himself rhythmically through the water as if pulled by a string.

As he stepped farther and farther back, Shinkichi shook his flashlight for all he was worth, trying to protect Serizawa.

On the surface of the water, the *Seagull* moved at minimal speed. Emiko grasped the lifeline tightly in her hands as Ogata stood by her side. The lifeline continued to spool out into the water. Behind them stood Professor Yamane, who was practically holding his breath.

Slowly but surely, on the seabed, Godzilla was closing in on them! The two divers retreated as best as they could.

By this point, Serizawa was quietly getting the Destroyer in position.

On the *Seagull*, the sailor with the communications headset was dripping with sweat from all the tension. In a shrill voice, he called out, "Stop!" The sound of the quietly turning propellers died down to nothing.

The entire crew felt as if their hearts were standing still.

Step by step, Godzilla approached.

Serizawa raised his right hand.

Shinkichi pulled ferociously on the lifeline. With a *whoosh*, he floated upward.

Serizawa, however, stayed in position with the Destroyer.

Godzilla got even closer.

As he rose to the surface, Shinkichi screamed inside his helmet. "Dr. Serizawa! Dr. Serizawa!"

But Serizawa was determined. With a swift movement— *WHOOSH!!*—Godzilla closed in.

It was now or never! *Click!* Serizawa released the Oxygen Destroyer's safety catch!

Water began to rush into the device. The round, cannonball-sized capsule slowly began to open, and bubbles started rising from the Destroyer.

Thrusting it toward Godzilla, Serizawa pulled himself back into the shade of the rocks.

Glub-glub-glub-glub . . . Godzilla moved forward into the cloud of rapidly churning bubbles.

No sooner had his entire body entered the cloud of bubbles than *whoosh!!*—Godzilla did a somersault and turned around.

Serizawa watched while hiding against a boulder. Quietly he pulled out a jackknife from where he had it hidden near his hip . . .

Back on board, Shinkichi had removed his helmet as he watched the bubbles rising to the surface grow more intense. He grabbed the radio transceiver and shouted over and over, "Dr. Serizawa!! Dr. Serizawa!! . . ."

Emiko and her father watched with sad faces.

On the seabed, Godzilla was clawing furiously at the underwater rock outcroppings. He was writhing in agony. Driven to painful desperation, he struggled to make it to the surface of the water.

As he watched, Serizawa whispered to himself, "Shinkichi . . . I wish you a happy life. Take good care of Emiko. Sayonara, sayonara . . ." And with that, *whoosh!!*—he cut the breathing tubes and the lifeline with his knife.

In the maelstrom of bubbles rising from the Destroyer, Godzilla writhed in distress. Each time he started to topple over, he managed somehow to get up again.

The fiercely bubbling water formed a swell like a small mountain, pushing the surface of the water upward, and the *Seagull* with it.

Suddenly, the professor, who had been hauling in the lifeline that Ogata was guiding, pulled up the end of the cord. There was no longer any tension in it.

He began shouting at the top of his lungs. "Serizawa! Serizawa!! . . ." There was deep sadness in his voice.

The slack lifeline was dead. It felt strange and unsettling as they pulled it up. The end showed it had been cleanly severed with a sharp knife.

Still holding the radio transceiver, Shinkichi stood there in a daze.

"Dr. Serizawa! Dr. Serizawa! I should have helped . . . Dr. Serizawa . . ."

Emiko grabbed onto him. She was already in tears.

Then, right before everyone's eyes, *splash!!*—Godzilla's anguish-filled face appeared at the surface, spraying everyone.

Summoning up what remained of his last strength, he was trying to attack the *Seagull*.

"*Aaaagh!!*" Emiko let out a sharp shriek.

Shinkichi grabbed her and held her tight.

Everyone gasped and threw themselves down, face-first on deck.

Godzilla writhed around, making some big movements with the last of his strength, then *SPLASH!!*—he collapsed back into the sea, sending up a waterfall's worth of spray. His form started to sink.

Glug-glug-glug-glug . . . Godzilla's dead body sank quietly into the still-bubbling water . . . For some time, his form lay on its side between the seabed boulders, but then it dissolved before everyone's eyes.

Professor Yamane started hard at the surface of the water. There were tears running down his face.

The Japanese people had succeeded in wiping Godzilla, that hateful monster, from the face of the earth.

On the deck of the patrol boat, which had been observing from a distance, the press and other VIPs jumped with joy.

One announcer was speaking with such delirious excitement that he looked ready to swallow the mike whole. "What a moving moment! What joy! We've won! With our very own eyes, we watched as Godzilla's dead body sank deep in the ocean to its grave. No mistake about it! This victory was made possible by the young Dr. Serizawa—the scientist of the century!"

On the deck of the *Seagull*, Ogata was weeping. He had been Serizawa's classmate back in school. Shinkichi and Emiko were also crying.

Shinkichi didn't even try to wipe the tears from his face as he whispered, "Dr. Serizawa wasn't able to trust people in our day and age. Not even himself . . . Who could guarantee that the Oxygen Destroyer would never be used as a weapon of mass destruction? Not even the man who invented it."

Emiko nodded, and Shinkichi continued. "At the end, he told me to have a happy life . . ."

Hearing this, Emiko broke down shaking in an even greater bout of tears.

Trying to stifle his voice, Shinkichi also wept.

Professor Yamane wore a dark expression as he whispered quietly to himself. "But . . . I can't imagine that the Godzilla we saw was the last of his kind . . . What if . . . What if the hydrogen bomb tests were to continue? . . . Who knows? Maybe more of his kind might appear somewhere on earth."

The intense bubbling in the water eventually settled down. A quiet prayer for peace flowed over the surface of the water.

Oh, peace and comfort! Oh, light of the sun!
Hasten your return, take pity on us
Feel our sorrow as we pray
And pour our very lives into this song

Crossing the deep-sea swells that had returned to silence, the *Seagull* headed back into port. Flying from its mast was the flag of the Rising Sun.

Ka-boom! Ka-boom! The patrol boats sent a whole series of celebratory shots into the air. However, none of them had any way of knowing just how much sadness each of the passengers aboard the *Seagull* had in their hearts.

GODZILLA RAIDS AGAIN

Godzilla in Osaka

Flight over the Ocean

The light roar of the engines sounded like music as the dark shadow of the airplane cut across the undulating waves of the great expanse of endless ocean.

The silver wings glinted in the light as the small seaplane made a large circle over the water. Painted on the body of the plane was the company name Marine Fisheries, Ltd.

Two or three white clouds floated across the sky like frayed, white, flossy silk. The light, rhythmic sound of the plane reverberated off to their side as Shōichi Tsukioka chased after a school of fish below. He wore a firm, determined expression.

His eyes were masculine, shoulders broad, and arms sturdy. Lightly gripping the steering column, he stared down at the ocean's surface, and a smile rose to his face.

He slowed the engine slightly and pushed the steering column firmly forward, sending the plane into a steep decline. In view right before it was a big school of fish swimming in tight, jostling formation, sending up white foam. Their fins were visible here and there above the waves.

Five hundred meters altitude. Tsukioka pushed up so he was flying level with the water. He pressed the transmitter hanging around his neck. "Calling HQ, calling HQ. Tsukioka here, Tsukioka here. There's a large school of bonito near the surface at XX° N, XX° E. Report to the ship *National Dragon No. 3*. Over."

"HQ here, HQ here. Roger, roger. Keep us updated on the whereabouts of the school of fish. Over."

"Roger, roger. Over and out."

By this point, the plane had made a large circle in the sky. It continued to circle the school of bonito like a raptor circling its prey.

Marine Fisheries was located in a three-story building on the Osaka shoreline. Hidemi's face shone brightly as she answered the call in the radio room on the top floor. Outside the window, the tower of Osaka Castle rose into the sky, pretty as a picture.

With a rustle, Hidemi passed the memo on which she'd jotted down Tsukioka's message to Yasuko Inoue, seated immediately beside her. Yasuko immediately began tapping out the message on the telegraph radio.

The clicking seemed to fall into a rhythm of sorts. The two seemed to be having a good time.

"*National Dragon No. 3, National Dragon No. 3* . . . HQ here . . . Big school of bonito at XX° N, XX° E. Head there at full speed . . ."

As soon as Yasuko finished tapping out the message, she received a response on the telegraph radio receiver in front of her. "*National Dragon No. 3* here . . . Roger."

The *National Dragon No. 3* quickly shifted its direction and sped toward the spot, sending up a wake of white waves behind it.

On deck, there was a long row of fishing poles. The captain, who was holding a pipe in his mouth, was staring off at a point in the sky.

The sea was quiet, with no wind at all. The sound of the diesel engine combined with the waves slapping the side of the boat formed a song that could have lulled even a baby to sleep.

"Captain, there he is. There he is." The navigation officer pointed into the sky at a small, black dot coming closer and closer.

With its broad wings, Tsukioka's plane circled twice, three times over the *National Dragon No. 3*. "Tsukioka here, Tsukioka here . . . Will guide the *National Dragon No. 3* now . . . Over."

Immediately, Hidemi responded, "Roger, roger . . ." Then she lowered her voice. "Aren't you exhausted?"

"No way . . . We're going to have a good catch today! How about the two of us go celebrate tonight?"

"Sounds good. I'll be here, just get back soon." Her voice was lively and happy. "There's something else . . ."

"What?"

"Well, nothing really. It's just that I told my father I'd borrow the car."

Yasuko, who was eavesdropping, gave a little chuckle and teased Hidemi, as if to give her a little nudge. "No fair, Hidemi! The two of you whispering like that. Outrageous! Even if you are the daughter of the company president!"

"Oh no! Sorry, sorry! I'll make it up to you by treating you to some zenzai."

"OK, I take it back. Continue your conversation then. Did you hear that, Tsukioka? Over."

Hidemi smiled. "My goodness, always thinking of your own interests. I'm done talking."

They could hear Tsukioka give an energetic laugh at the other end of the line.

"Yasuko, do you mind taking over for a sec? I'm going to step out and see my dad."

But then, right as Hidemi was standing up from her seat, they suddenly heard a high-pitched, excited voice over the wireless.

"Kobayashi here, Kobayashi here . . ." It was from Kobayashi, another of the company's pilots, also out at sea. "Trouble in the right engine, trouble in the right engine . . ."

Startled, the two girls looked at one another.

"Kobayashi! Kobayashi! . . . HQ here . . . Report your current location, report your current location."

"Approaching the southern shore of Iwato Island . . . Oh, no! The right engine gave out . . ."

Kobayashi's plane wobbled and shook, letting out a disturbing vibrating sound. The plane began to gradually lose elevation. Gritting his teeth, Kobayashi desperately tried to guide his plane toward the island, relying only on the left-engine propeller, which was still turning groggily, but then the left engine also began to emit an odd noise. Then suddenly—*poof*—it stopped entirely, as if a gear had broken somewhere.

"Oh no! Engine failure! Can't fly . . . Request emergency assistance!"

"Kobayashi! Kobayashi! . . . Please respond . . . Kobayashi! Kobayashi!" Yasuko frantically called into her receiver, but there was no further response.

Hidemi immediately turned to her own radio transmitter and flipped the switch. "Calling Tsukioka, calling Tsukioka! . . . Kobayashi is making an emergency landing near Iwato Island. Request immediate assistance!"

"What?!! Kobayashi? . . . Yes, roger, roger! Heading there immediately."

Tsukioka revved up his engine, and tracing a large, steep circle in the sky, he changed course and headed straight for Iwato Island.

Hidemi rushed from the radio room and flung open the door to the office of the president of the company. "Father!" She was paler than usual. Her father, Mr. Yamaji, was talking to one of the section chiefs and lifted his head in surprise.

"What? Something urgent?"

"It's Kobayashi's plane . . ."

"What!? . . . What did you say?" The color promptly drained from his face too.

Two Kaiju

As Tsukioka circled once over Iwato Island, then once again, he turned his eyes to the edge of the water in a continuous search. The island was nothing but a rocky outcropping that soared right out of the vast Pacific Ocean. The waves were high, making it impossible to approach by boat. For more than a dozen kilometers around it, there were some small rocky islands, which sliced upward from the water like blades. The islands were covered with nothing but bare, dark-gray rock. Just looking at them gave him an uncomfortable feeling.

He swiftly dropped his altitude. As he flew, his glittering eyes scanned the bare rock.

"Oh, there he is!"

Near the middle of the island was a small cove where all kinds of rocks, both big and small, were jutting out into the sea. By them was a sandy, fairly flat beach, so small that it barely deserved that name, but right by it, the horrifying wreckage of Kobayashi's plane was floating on the waves, shining in the sunlight.

As Tsukioka continued to lower his plane, his face grew visibly brighter. Hearing the approaching roar of Tsukioka's plane, Kobayashi had climbed on top of a small boulder and was waving his handkerchief so frantically it was a wonder it didn't rip to shreds.

"Tsukioka here, Tsukioka here . . . Found Kobayashi and his crashed plane. Headed there now for the rescue . . . Over."

"Roger, roger . . . We're praying for your success. You're in our thoughts!" Hidemi's voice was full of excitement.

Yamaji, the company president, also chimed in. "Tsukioka, we're counting on you." His voice was trembling with anxiety as it reached Tsukioka's ears.

"All right now," Tsukioka thought to himself, tightening the muscles of his stomach. He pressed his steering column firmly forward and got into position for a sea landing.

As he landed, the seaplane sent up a huge, white splash. He navigated the plane to the water's edge and quickly jumped out.

"Hey, thanks, Tsukioka!" Kobayashi came running up. His shirt was wrapped around his right arm.

"You OK? Are you hurt?"

"I'm fine. I think I just sprained it . . . But you saved my life! You got here so fast!"

"You should save your thanks for the ladies in the radio room."

"What? You mean I owe my life to those two? They're always on my case . . ."

Tsukioka laughed. "You'll be so indebted to them that you can't afford to look them in the eye."

The two gave a good, hearty laugh.

Suddenly, they heard an indescribable, terrifying howl, and a bunch of rocks tumbled down one of the nearby rock faces. Shocked, the two of them looked up.

Overhead, a gigantic kaiju had stuck his head out from the shadow of the rock wall. He looked down at the two of them with bright, glaring eyes.

He lifted his head and let out a *GRAAAWWR!!* The sound was terrifying. It was so overwhelming you would have thought a hundred bolts of thunder were sounding all at once.

"Oh, my god!!" The two of them instinctively ducked down.

"Kobayashi! Run!!"

The two dashed into a crevice in the rocks and held their

breath. They stared intently out of the crack in the rocks, then turned to look at one another.

"What the hell was that?! Do you know, Tsukioka?"

"Godzilla! It's gotta be."

"Godzilla?!"

"It must be! It's got to be the same monster that attacked Tokyo."

The kaiju did something that caused a rattling and tremendous crash outside. The two men looked up at the monster, and a shiver ran down their spines. They ducked down and huddled, wrapping their arms around one another in fright.

Through a high crack in the rocks, the monster peered down at the two of them. His eyes were shining, and he wore an angry expression on his face.

In their spot far below between the rocks, Tsukioka and Kobayashi must have looked like little dolls to Godzilla. Was he going to grab the two of them and pull them out of their hiding spot in the crevasse? His gigantic hand, which looked like that of a wild beast, tried to work its way into the fissure, but fortunately the space between the rocks was too small. Godzilla struggled in vain, unable to reach them.

That seemed to just enrage the monster all the more, and he let out another *GRAAAWWR!* But right then, he pulled back and stretched to his full height. The rocks rattled and began to fall.

Each time he moved his gigantic hand, a shower of sand, stones, and large boulders fell from above the two men.

"My god!! . . . What're we gonna do?"

They shuddered in fear. With each shower of debris, the two men pressed against one another. They frantically tried to escape the avalanche of rocks, but that only made Godzilla's eyes glitter with an even more berserk look. The rocks began to rattle and break. The gap between the rocks was growing bigger, and they could see more of the monster's full form. His gigantic hand was getting close. He let out one more loud roar and plunged his hand into the widened gap, nearly reaching them.

The two men let out a shriek and curled up. As Godzilla stuck his hand in and unfurled his gigantic claws, he could almost reach them. He was less than two meters away.

The boulders Godzilla dislodged had sealed up the only escape route. Now, his hand was right over them. He continued to wriggle his hand closer and closer. Anxious sweat dripped from the brows of the two terrified men. Godzilla was practically on top of them.

"Damn it!" The sweat was pouring off Kobayashi by this point. Every time Godzilla moved his hand, Kobayashi tried to evade it. He had turned white as a sheet, and he was shaking in terror.

"Kobayashi . . ." Tsukioka's voice was unexpectedly calm, as if he had already resigned himself to fate. A smile rose to his lips, which held an unlit cigarette. "This'll be our last smoke, I suppose." His tone was incredibly calm as he handed a cigarette to his companion.

Godzilla was still trying to reach them. Tsukioka bit his lips and quietly closed his eyes.

Right then, something happened.

WROOOWR! There was a terrifying roar behind them. Another kaiju had stuck his head out from the surface of the water. On his back was something like a gigantic turtle shell covered with terrible, sharp, bladelike projections. The kaiju's body was covered with hard scales and probably measured something like forty or fifty meters in height.

The new monster let out another terrifying roar— WROOOWR!!—and crawled up onto Iwato Island, sending a tremendous rumbling through the earth.

Godzilla's fingers, which had been reaching toward Tsukioka and Kobayashi, suddenly stopped, and Godzilla's face, which had been visible through a high opening in the rocks, vanished so quickly that one might have thought he'd disappeared entirely. This was followed by a deafening roar and terrible rumbling of the earth that shook the air. It was like getting caught in the middle of an earthquake.

"Ahhh!!" The cigarettes fell from the mouths of the two astonished men. Fearfully, they looked up to see what was happening overhead.

The two furiously roaring kaiju were rolling and tumbling over the opening in the rocks above them. They were wrestling and angrily trying to bite one another.

The second kaiju came at Godzilla with unimaginable speed. As their two colossal bodies crashed into one another, they let out a terrifying roar, and the ground shook ferociously. Each time that happened, the rocks crumbled. The monsters were fighting with all their might.

The two men held their breath as they looked up.

The second kaiju quickly moved away from Godzilla and circled around with remarkable agility. Sensing the right moment, he swiftly closed in for an attack.

Godzilla readied himself by pulling himself up to his full height. As the two kaiju glared at one another, they let out a series of continuous, menacing roars.

From their space between the rocks, Tsukioka and Kobayashi held their breath and watched this unimaginable standoff. They were witnessing the fight of the century!

For a few moments, the second kaiju continued to stare Godzilla down. Then for reasons that were unclear—perhaps he didn't sense any opening in Godzilla's defenses—he gave a look of scornful disdain and plunged into the sea, producing a huge splash.

That seemed to only make Godzilla all the angrier, and he too promptly leaped into the water. The splash from the two kaiju plunging into the sea fell onto the beach like rain and sent higher-than-usual waves crashing onto shore.

The two promptly returned to their senses. "Kobayashi, now's our chance. Let's run . . ."

"OK. Quick."

They dashed to the edge of the water where Tsukioka's plane was floating.

"Quick! We don't know when they'll return." Tsukioka quickly pushed Kobayashi, whose arm was still hurting, into the plane, then jumped in himself. He immediately pressed the button to start the engine.

Brrum, brrum. The engine made a light noise, and the front of the plane right away began kicking up waves as the plane headed toward deeper water.

The plane floated lightly into the air and made one, then two circles over Iwato Island. From the air, Tsukioka and Kobayashi looked down at the sea. It had swallowed the two enormous kaiju completely. A tremendous whirlpool was turning in the water, and there were strange waves on the surface, as if somewhere on the bottom of the ocean, the two were still battling it out.

Professor Yamane

Osaka, the second largest metropolis in Japan.[1] Osaka Castle, still retaining its appearance from the distant past, towered over the city, soaring over its surroundings. The Osaka Metropolitan Police Station formed a stark contrast to it, looking entirely modern. In one of the conference rooms, more than twenty people had gathered. Among them were the superintendent general of police, officers from the Japan Ground Self-Defense Force, and admirals from the maritime branch of the Self-Defense Forces. Professor Yamane had just hurried in from Tokyo via airplane, along with his fellow zoologist Dr. Tadokoro. Tsukioka, Kobayashi, and President Yamaji of Marine Fisheries were also there. On the table was a tall pile of photographs of primitive creatures, divided and individually classified.

Tsukioka and Kobayashi were studying each one of the pictures so intently that they could have bored holes in them with their eyes. The light had drained from their eyes.

Among the nearly two hundred photographs of primitive creatures, they had not found a single photo of the kaiju they had seen battling Godzilla so fiercely on Iwato Island.

A policeman picked up the final picture and said, "That's it. No more." With that, he placed the photo quietly on the table.

---

1. Since this novella was published in 1955, Yckohama has overtaken Osaka as the second largest city in Japan, pushing Osaka to number three.

As soon as Tsukioka and Kobayashi saw it, they shouted in unison, "That's it!!"

"Really? Are you sure?"

Their answer came quickly. "Yes, completely sure . . . No doubt."

"I see . . ." Dr. Tadokoro looked over at the officers from the police force, officers from the Self-Defense Forces, President Yamaji of Marine Fisheries, and Professor Yamane with a dark look in his eyes.

"Professor Yamane, that means we guessed right . . . Our worst guess turns out to be right . . ."

The professor nodded slightly.

For a moment, no one spoke, but after a few seconds, the superintendent general of police spoke. He had gone pale. "What does this mean? There's another monster besides Godzilla?"

"That's right. Hydrogen bomb testing awakened not just Godzilla but also this other monster too—Ankylosaurus."

"Ankylosaurus?"

"That's right. Ankylosaurus." Slowly and quietly, Dr. Tadokoro picked up the picture and handed it to the police superintendent.

Everyone's gaze turned to the photo in the superintendent's hands as if magnetically drawn to it.

"This is Ankylosaurus, also known by the common name Anguirus. This dinosaur roamed the earth between 150 million and 70 million years ago. Godzilla also existed around the same time . . . Right here, I've got a report written by the leading Polish paleontologist, Dr. Peteri Hordon. Let me read a little for you."

He picked up a book from the table and, after casting a glance across everyone in the room, began to read. "'Anguirus was between 150 feet (45 meters) and 200 feet (60 meters) tall and was a carnivorous dinosaur known for its aggressive behavior. Its movements were remarkably nimble, given its enormous body size. Moreover, the thing that is most remarkable about Anguirus is that unlike other animals, it had multiple brains in its body—namely in its chest, abdomen, and elsewhere—to maximize its speed and agility. Anguirus bore a fundamental hatred for other creatures. It was a gigantic, violent creature given to savage behavior.'"

He quietly closed the book, placed it on the table, then kept his eyes shut a moment before continuing. "In fact, our two witnesses to the struggle have confirmed that Anguirus was violent—he did attack Godzilla from behind. I'm afraid that's all that I have today to report on this new kaiju." The professor quietly sat down in his chair.

A heavy silence followed, undisturbed even by a single whisper. The high-ranking officers from the Ground Self-Defense Force hung their heads as if stunned, but one of their underlings broke the quiet. "Professor Yamane, you were kind enough to make the trip by airplane all the way from Tokyo. We'd like to hear from you about what we can do to combat Godzilla."

The professor gave a quick nod of acknowledgment and stood up again. "Just now, you asked about what we can do to combat Godzilla. Unfortunately, there isn't a single thing we can do. We can't prevent Godzilla from coming again."

"What?!" A small commotion washed across the conference room as the startled audience stirred in their seats.

"That's right. We're completely powerless, without any defenses against Godzilla. I've got no plan. That's the situation."

A hush fell over the room.

"I brought a film with me to show you the destruction that Godzilla wrought in the capital. After that, I'll take some more questions, but I would also like to brainstorm with all of you about what we could do to combat Godzilla. Let me show you . . ."

Professor Yamane made a sign with his hand, and the light illuminating the conference room switched off. Projected on the screen was a gigantic image of Godzilla.

Godzilla had come ashore in Shinagawa, but even though the

Ground Self-Defense Force had organized lines of artillery and tanks to stop him, none of their firing seemed to bother him in the least. Within the blink of an eye, his gigantic form appeared. The defenders had stretched high-voltage electrical lines around Shinagawa to protect it, but not even tens of thousands of volts of electricity stopped the monster. Godzilla broke through the electrical lines in seconds. Then he began spewing a white-hot beam from his mouth, melting the tall, sturdy towers supporting the high-tension electrical wires. They sagged, withered, and melted to the ground. Godzilla proceeded from Shinagawa to Shiba, then into the heart of Tokyo, growing more destructive the whole time. He smashed buildings underfoot, ripped apart a train in his teeth, and smashed the National Diet Building before retreating into the sea and disappearing underwater. The artillery and aerial bombardment didn't seem to have any effect whatsoever. The film the professor had brought made that perfectly clear.

When the film finally ended, the lights clicked on once again. Indescribable, helpless sighs could be heard throughout the room.

"As you can see, Godzilla's a violent, terrifying creature with radioactive genes. No matter how many weapons we gather, no matter how much knowledge we collect, we can't stop him. He just does whatever he pleases despite us."

A representative from the Self-Defense Forces stood up. "But, Professor, didn't we manage to exterminate Godzilla?"

"That's right, using the Oxygen Destroyer . . . It sent Godzilla, along with its inventor, Dr. Serizawa, to a watery grave at the bottom of Tokyo Bay. However, it's now clear that not even the Oxygen Destroyer can completely exterminate monsters like Godzilla."

"Professor! Are you telling us that there was more than one Godzilla?"

Dr. Yamane nodded, deep in thought. "That was the thing that we feared the most . . . But now, here we are threatened by a second Godzilla plus Anguirus, a new kaiju . . . The threat we're facing is comparable to that of a hydrogen bomb."

Biting his lip, Tsukioka listened to the professor with closed eyes.

The superintendent general of police had a worried look on his face. "But, Professor, there must be some way to minimize the damage."

"That's right. Thinking about how to minimize damage is all we can really do now. For that purpose, we need to confirm the current location of the kaiju and alert everyone. At the same time, we should order an evacuation of citizens in nearby coastal regions and order all lights shut off . . . When Godzilla came on land in Tokyo, we learned he was extremely sensitive to light. In fact, if anything, bright lights make him burn with intense rage . . . I imagine that's the result of having been burned by hydrogen bomb tests in the past. No doubt he remembers. I imagine he's learned to react to lights in strange ways, so perhaps we can use his reactions to our advantage. We could drop flares to lure him farther out to sea . . . This is a rather passive way to deal with the situation, but it's all I can come up with for the moment . . . The most important thing, in my opinion, is to implement a strict blackout policy . . . I hope you in the police and Self-Defense Forces can do that for us."

All throughout Professor Yamane's speech, Tsukioka stood motionless and listened.

Godzilla Approaches

Two figures were climbing up a sloping path to a high spot overlooking the city of Osaka. The two seemed to grow taller as they climbed.

The landscape was beautiful. The buildings seemed to fold in on top of one another, and beyond that, Osaka Bay sparkled clearly under the night sky. Tsukioka and Hidemi were silent as they walked shoulder to shoulder, climbing the steps along the path.

Hidemi turned to look at Tsukioka and said, "What's on your mind?"

"Nothing really . . ."

"No way! Something's on your mind for sure."

Tsukioka gazed with a friendly expression at Hidemi.

As if to deflect his attention, Hidemi burst out, "You know, Kobayashi was saying something just a little while ago . . . He admires your courage. He really takes his hat off to you."

"What do you mean, 'takes his hat off to me'?"

"That day, when you were being attacked by Godzilla, you gave him a cigarette."

"Oh, that." He nodded slightly as he remembered.

"He thought you were being courageous."

"Courageous!? Not really."

"What then?"

"Well . . . I'm not exactly sure how to put it into words."

Hidemi pressed closer to him. With his hand in hers, she wore a bright expression on her face. "In any case, I'm glad you were OK . . ."

"I thought my time had come . . . And right then, your face flashed before my eyes."

"Really?"

Hidemi flushed bright red. A grin crept over Tsukioka's face too.

"That makes me happy," she said.

The two seemed content as they climbed the steps, humming a little tune. They locked gazes, clearly enjoying themselves.

Right then, there was a loud *whoosh*. Something that sounded like an explosion filled the air around them, then flew away, headed toward the dark ocean waters. It was the roar of a jet setting out to search for Godzilla. Without thinking, Tsukioka stepped ahead of Hidemi for a moment as if being tugged away from her.

"So, the search has started . . ." Tsukioka affixed his eyes at the black water of the bay extending into the distance. His gaze shone with a spark of determination.

Hidemi stared at Tsukioka's back. She felt as if a cold wind had just blown over her.

When Tsukioka eventually returned to his senses and turned to look at her again, she was smiling forlornly.

"It's not going to work out for us, is it? . . . At least, as long as Godzilla is around . . ."

Tsukioka felt as if he should answer somehow, but right then, there was another loud roar overhead as more jets flew by.

An uneasy feeling settled over the two as they quietly turned and walked back toward the city streets.

At the headquarters of the Anti-Godzilla Task Force, everyone spent the night full of apprehension. In that regard, they were just like all the other citizens of Osaka. At the same time, however, the police and defense forces were pouring all their energy into the search for Godzilla that had started the night before.

The superintendent general's eyes were bloodshot as he radioed orders to his underlings. "Roger, roger. HQ here with orders for all involved in the search for Godzilla. We've been searching since last night, but there's still no sign of him. All of you, do your utmost. If you catch sight, give us at HQ a thorough report of his movements. Over and out."

When the superintendent general was done with the orders, he moved away from the mike and shuffled over to where Dr. Tadokoro was seated. "Where on earth could Godzilla have gone? Did he sink into the water?"

Dr. Tadokoro reflected for a moment. "Long ago, in past geological ages, the seabed experienced tectonic movement, so there are countless caves and crevasses out there. If Godzilla dived into one those, well, we might never find him at all."

"That bastard's causing us all sorts of trouble!" The superintendent general sounded exasperated.

Right then, a buzzer sounded. All at once, a look of nervousness appeared on all the faces in the room.

"Roger, roger. This is Yamashita. At 15:24, my radar picked up something in the water that might be Godzilla. Location: XX° N, XX° E. In pursuit. Over and out." There was a large map spread out on a table. Someone immediately placed a small model of a plane at the coordinates the pilot had just mentioned.

Then, another message came over the radio. "Roger, roger. This is Frigate T-10. At 15:32, we glimpsed something that appears to be Godzilla. Location: XX° N, XX° E. In hot pursuit. Over and out." Someone put a miniature frigate down at the spot on the map.

All the people involved with the search had been full of nervous anticipation, but suddenly they sprang into life.

"Roger, roger. This is HQ. All search party members should proceed as quickly as possible to XX° N, XX° E. Repeat. This is HQ. All search party members should proceed to . . ." The radio broadcast the orders repeatedly to all the airplanes and frigates out at sea.

All the reconnaissance planes made quick, sharp turns and headed to the designated spot. Far below, on the surface of the ocean, frigates headed to the same destination at full speed, leaving long, white wakes behind them.

On the map were a handful of small models showing where Godzilla had been sighted. Their movement across the water seemed to indicate a certain direction. The superintendent general and Dr. Tadokoro looked at the models long and hard.

"Professor, extrapolating from these movements, it seems Godzilla might be going . . ." His words trailed off.

Dr. Tadokoro nodded slightly. "Yes, it looks like he might be headed toward the southern coast of the Kii Peninsula, or perhaps the coast of Shikoku . . ."

"If so, what does that mean for us here in the Osaka and Kobe region?"

"Well, the greatest probability is that Godzilla will come ashore somewhere there . . ." The professor slid his finger straight on the map from the spots where the sightings had occurred toward Marugame on Shikoku.

The news of the Godzilla sightings was immediately dispatched to radio stations, newspapers, and all other media outlets. All the newspapers printed large headlines on the front pages asking, "Will Godzilla land on southern Shikoku?"

The radio stations also started making emergency broadcasts to share the news.

"As of 3:00 p.m., the Anti-Godzilla Task Force headquarters has ordered an emergency evacuation of southern Shikoku. Aerial reconnaissance has shown Godzilla appears to be headed in from the Pacific Ocean along a slightly northeastern trajectory. It appears inevitable that either today or tomorrow, he'll reach the southern shores of Shikoku and come on land. Seafaring vessels in the area and people living along the shores should clear the area immediately. Repeat . . ."

Yamaji, Tsukioka, Hidemi, Yasuko Inoue, and the managers at Marine Fisheries were all listening to the radio. Their faces were dark and sunken.

Suddenly, Tsukioka shouted, "Mr. Yamaji!" startling the company president, who was taken completely off guard. "If Godzilla appears in the sea over there, that means . . ." His words trailed off.

"It means we'll lose some of our most important fishing waters, I suppose."

One of the managers, who was standing at his side, pursed his lips. "If so, this will have a huge impact on our industrial production, among all sorts of other things . . ."

Once again, someone chimed in from the sidelines—Yasuko this time. In a shrill voice, she cried, "Why don't they hurry up and use some flares to guide him somewhere else?"

"If they did, I certainly wouldn't complain." Kobayashi seemed more composed than usual.

Yasuko added, "But I suppose that even if they did, no one would want to eat the fish from there anyway." At this comment, everyone let out a small, uncomfortable burst of laughter.

In the evening papers that day, the large headlines read, "Did Godzilla miss? Osaka and Kobe breathe a sigh of relief."

The tension had finally eased in Osaka, and in stark contrast to the day before, the city had returned to normal. The neon lights were glowing, and the reflections of countless signs in just about every color twinkled on the surface of the river. The sounds of raucous bands spilled from the dance halls, along with the sweet voices of singers and the noise of people dancing.

Tsukioka and Hidemi were finishing up some shopping. Earlier that evening, they'd been having fun walking through the streets with so many other people.

Right then, they heard the uncanny squeal of a siren, and all at once people started running in every direction through the city streets outside.

The excited voice of a female announcer flowed from a speaker. "This announcement just in. An emergency is in effect for everyone in the Osaka region. At 19:30, the Anti-Godzilla Task Force HQ made this announcement. Previously, it had been believed that Godzilla would reach the southern shore of Shikoku; however, there are signs that he is in the process of making his way into Osaka Bay. In just a few moments, flares will be dropped into the water to lead Godzilla back out of the bay. To that end, a blackout will be put into effect right away. Everyone, we humbly ask that you please remain calm and quiet as you evacuate the area. This announcement will repeat . . ."

The announcement hadn't even ended before everyone lost their cool and started shoving one another noisily. The store was thrown into confusion as everyone rushed for the nearest exit, including Tsukioka and Hidemi, who had finished making their purchases.

In the middle of this hellish crucible, Tsukioka tried to protect Hidemi from the jostling crowd as they moved toward a door. With a *snap*, the light shut off, and the room filled with angry, scared screams even shriller than before.

One by one, the power to each of the Osaka neighborhoods was shut off, and in just a matter of moments, the entire metropolis was plunged into the darkness of night. Bright and eerie, the moon shone in the nighttime sky. A series of jets rushed by at top speed, leaving an uncanny roar to echo in the ears of everyone below.

Crowds of Evacuees

Godzilla had raised his head above the surface of the water. As soon as he saw the beam of the lighthouse by the entrance to Osaka Bay, he made a huge splash and started rushing toward it.

GRAAAAWRRRR, Graaaawrrrr, Graawrr . . . Godzilla let out a tremendous roar, which echoed into the distance.

In the blink of an eye, Godzilla snapped the lighthouse off at the base like a piece of chalk, and the top sank into the bay. Godzilla's eyes glistened wildly as he pressed forward. Step-by-step, he approached the concrete breakwater.

Right then—*flash, flash!!*—streaks of fire fell from the sky. The airplanes flying over Godzilla's head had dropped a series of flares to blind the monster. The strong lights floated down through the air, tracing gently sloping lines like the ropes of a swing.

Godzilla seemed taken aback. He was still staring at the lights when the jets made another pass over his head, roaring through the air. Again, they dropped more flares, creating arcing lines that fell from above, illuminating the nighttime sky with sparkling light.

Godzilla grew tremendously enraged. Perhaps the lights recalled the loathsome hydrogen bomb tests he'd been through. He suddenly dove into the water, then rushed toward the lights, using all his terrifying strength.

The falling flares illuminated the area outside Osaka Bay as brightly as midday. In the light, the silhouette of the gigantic monster stood out in clear relief. Everyone watching from a distance shivered with fear.

At the Anti-Godzilla Task Force Headquarters, the telephone had been ringing nonstop. Each call was a report for the superintendent general.

One announced that such and such district was almost completely evacuated.

Another call told him that another district was also nearly emptied.

The superintendent general nodded quietly. "Good work, men." Using a brush with red ink, he marked off one by one the different regions of the Osaka map spread out on the table before him. At the same time, he issued a series of orders to all police stations. "This is an order from the Anti-Godzilla Task Force headquarters. Repeat, this is an order from the Anti-Godzilla Task Force headquarters . . . All stations should quickly relocate all remaining citizens in their jurisdiction to safety . . . Repeat, this is an order from the Anti-Godzilla Task Force headquarters . . ." These words went out repeatedly over the airwaves.

All throughout the city, police stations prepared to relocate the criminals locked up in their care.

Every street outside central Osaka was swamped with refugees, who only had time to grab a tiny number of their most important personal belongings before fleeing for higher terrain on the city's outskirts. The long line of people stretched on and on like a line of ants.

The crowds also carried Tsukioka and Hidemi along. Finally, the long, snaking line brought them to Hidemi's home in the hills. They had only just arrived. Hidemi's heart was pounding fiercely. She was out of breath, and her face was visibly paler than usual.

Kobayashi suddenly popped out of the gate, where he had been hunkered down with a steel helmet on his head. "Oh, Tsukioka!

It's you!" No sooner did he see Tsukioka's face than he burst out, "I understand the company president has gone to the factory."

"What? To the factory!?"

"Yeah, I'm about to head there too." He opened the door of the car waiting by the gate and jumped in energetically.

"OK! I'll go too." Tsukioka gave a small nod, then turned to look at Hidemi. She had taken a sharp breath and was standing transfixed to the spot. "OK, Hidemi," he said. "Take care of yourself."

"What? You too?"

"I'm going to see what's happening . . . I think it's safe here, but on the off chance something does happen, head for the hills over there . . ." He pointed at the dark mountains behind her.

"OK, you take care too."

The three paused and looked one another in the face as the long, continuous flow of refugees continued to spill forward, passing them by.

"Alright then! We're off."

"Tsukioka, take care of my dad, OK?"

He nodded energetically and promptly jumped into the waiting car. Kobayashi let out the clutch, ejecting a small amount of gasoline-scented smoke into the air, and the car quietly began to move.

Hidemi gazed at the car uneasily as it pulled away. Right then, she heard the oppressive sound of a buzzer coming from a radio to signal breaking news. "This just in. The clever strategy of using flares to gradually lure Godzilla out into the deep sea beyond Osaka Bay appears to be working. To protect our lives and assets, as well as to protect the city of Osaka itself, we urgently request that you continue to observe a complete blackout. This is of grave importance . . ."

Some more jets flew across the sky, screeching off into the distance.

Hidemi had pricked up her ears and was listening to the radio broadcast with an uneasy expression on her face. She was gazing out at the flares, which she could see far out, illuminating the waters beyond Osaka Bay. *Flash, flash* . . . Seen together, the round bursts of light looked like a bunch of fireworks raining down quietly through the pitch-black sky.

Had the airplanes' daring plan to lure the monster away been successful? The lights appeared to be gradually retreating from the city. Everyone on land quietly gazed at the waters of Osaka Bay, feeling as if they were at least somewhat safe now.

A group of people was standing on the roof of the Marine Fisheries office along the seashore. Among them were Yamaji, the company president who had just clad himself in military gear, and several other employees who had come to protect the company premises. They were all looking far out to sea.

One of them shouted through a megaphone, "Mr. Yamaji, it looks like they've lured that damn monster out to the deep ocean, approximately two kilometers beyond the breakwater of the bay."

The company president smiled. "That settles it. Osaka has used its ingenuity to evade Godzilla's attack."

"Right. All we need to do is be patient a little longer." The employees were nodding as a new round of jets flew overhead.

Everyone looked up and raised their voices. "You go, guys! We're counting on you!"

The Escaped Prisoners

Because the citizens had fled, the streets of central Osaka were empty. It was as quiet as a city of the dead, with scarcely a single soul to be seen. In the occasional distant light cast by the falling flares, two vehicles seemed to rise out of the darkness. They were two paddy wagons, and they had set out from a prison shortly before.

In the flickering light, some evil-looking prisoners were huddled in the corners of the wagons, looking at one another as if signaling something with their eyes. Right then, one of the men began to howl, "Uuuuhhhh, uuuuhhhh!" as if he was in pain. He dropped from his seat to the floor.

"What's going on?" One of the guards riding with them rushed to the prisoner's side and leaned over, seemingly ready to throw his arms around the man to lift him up.

"Get him!" The other prisoners, who had been quiet until that moment, suddenly stuck out their hands to grab the guards. In the blink of an eye, they had grabbed the guards' pistols and— whack!—used the butt of their guns to knock them alongside the head.

The prisoners quickly kicked open the back doors and dashed outside, fleeing in all directions like a bunch of baby spiders. Alarmed by the ruckus, the policeman in the driver's cab hurriedly looked over his shoulder and slammed on the brakes. The brakes squealed loudly as the paddy wagon ground to a sudden halt.

The policeman threw open the door and jumped to the ground. "Stop right there! I'll shoot!!"

The outlines of the escaped prisoners could be seen clearly in the light from the flares.

Pap-pap! The policeman let out some warning shots. One of the prisoners crouched down and grabbed his knees, but the others rushed right and left, trying to escape into the small side streets.

Right then, they heard a siren approaching from the direction that the paddy wagon had been headed. A police car was speeding toward them.

Some of the startled prisoners raised their hands into the air. Meanwhile, the police car illuminated three of the others who were trying to escape into the side streets. The prisoners were clearly visible in the headlights.

The guards broke into two groups and chased the fleeing prisoners.

Breathing hard as they ran, the three escaped prisoners jumped into a gasoline tanker parked in front of a gas station. There were yellow flags and signs on it warning about hazardous materials inside. Ignoring them, the prisoners quickly hit the ignition and slammed on the accelerator, fleeing at top speed.

"Darn it!" The guards stomped their feet in anger, but there was nothing they could do but stare at the tanker as it pulled away.

Just then, a passenger car turned toward them, approaching from a side street. Kobayashi was at the steering wheel, gripping it hard. The guards threw their hands in the air, forcing the car with Kobayashi and Tsukioka to a sudden stop.

One guard threw the door open and dived into the back seat. "Please! Don't let that car out of your sight!!" He pointed at the tanker speeding away.

Kobayashi and Tsukioka quickly understood what was happening. "Here we go! Think you're gonna get away, huh?!"

The clutch made a dull thump as Kobayashi put the car in gear and began the chase. As if realizing what was happening, the prisoners' tanker dashed with ever more ferocious speed through the city streets, but Kobayashi also sped up. Every time Kobayashi sped around a curve, the car seemed to nearly lift into the air. The chase was on, and the speed was terrifying.

The prisoners were driving frantically, as if their lives were at stake. They sped down one side street after the next, going as fast as they could, trying to lose their pursuers.

Then suddenly, a police car appeared out of a side street before them. The alarmed prisoner at the wheel immediately gave the steering wheel a hard turn to the right, rushing into a narrow side street.

"Damn it! A dead end!!" Right before them was a wooden fence. It was coming at them fast. The prisoners shut their eyes and grabbed onto their seats as tightly as they could.

There was a CRASH accompanied with the sound of the bumper crumpling and the wooden fence splintering. As fate would have it, the gas tanker had barged into a petroleum storage facility. The front of the tanker rose into the air, and for a moment, it was clearly visible against the night sky. The prisoners continued driving frantically through the large grounds of the storage facility, desperately trying to get away from Kobayashi and the police car, which remained in hot pursuit. With terrifying speed, they turned right and left, raging through the large grounds of the facility full of gasoline storage tanks. Kobayashi and the patrol car followed closely behind, trying to find a way to somehow obstruct their path.

At that moment, a patrol car cut right in front of the gas tanker. The prisoner at the wheel made a sharp turn to avoid hitting it, creating an odd *screeeech* as the tires slipped. In a flash, the tanker flipped onto its side—*crash!*—almost before the men inside even knew what was happening. The metal sliding across the concrete let forth a volley of sparks that set the gasoline spilling from the crashed tanker on fire.

It only took a fraction of a second. The tanker was enveloped in a ball of fire, and with the speed of a bullet—*ka-blam!*—it flew high into the air and crashed down on a filling station.

KA-BOOM!! The enormous explosion of the tanker sent flames soaring high into the sky. The pillar of fire seemed to extend all the way into the heavens.

Flames spread across the spilled gasoline, which carried the fire to the storage tanks one after the next. All at once, the place was enveloped in a gigantic flower of red flames. The conflagration rose high into the air, scorching the night sky.

The metropolis of Osaka was still completely dark, but in a single instant, the scarlet flames of the massive fire burning all the way to the heavens exposed the city to Godzilla.

Fire trucks dashed through the streets toward the fire, their sirens piercing the ears of everyone in the vicinity.

Until that moment, Godzilla had been preoccupied with the flares dropped over the sea, but now, he seemed to perk up. He turned and glared in the direction of the city. *GRAAWRR!!* He let out a loud bellow, and gazing at the city with wildly glistening, bloodshot eyes, he turned his huge body toward Osaka and started toward it, kicking up gigantic splashes of water along the way.

The aerial squadron was now desperate. They dropped a series of flares right in front of him, trying to distract him, but the monster didn't pay them any heed at all. He approached the city with great speed.

At that moment, Kobayashi and Tsukioka energetically dashed up the stairs at the Marine Fisheries office, their feet pounding against each step.

"Damn it! He's seen us . . ." They looked at the company president. "What on earth's gonna happen now!?"

Everyone's eyes were fixed on the bay. They didn't dare look away for even a moment. The top half of Godzilla's gigantic body had risen above the surface of the sea, and the monster was proceeding with great energy toward them.

The aerial squadron had changed tactics and were now taking turns nose-diving toward him, trying to shoot at Godzilla's heart. They let out one volley of rockets after the next; however, Godzilla's body was covered with a thick layer of scales, and the rockets simply grazed off him without doing a thing.

With intent, bloodshot eyes, the pilots performed another round of sharp nosedives toward Godzilla. As they sped toward him, his gigantic form grew ever larger in front of their windshields. The rockets seemed to be drawn right into his body, but his enormous body just simply repelled the explosives one after the other. They didn't affect him in the slightest.

Once the jets stopped firing, they tried flying quickly through the enraged monster's path to distract him, but his frenzied eyes glistened with anger. A beam of white-hot light shot out of his mouth.

In an instant, the jets were enveloped in flame. They tumbled once, then twice through the sky and fell into the sea, sending up a big, white splash as they struck the surface.

"My god!!" As the crew on the roof of the Marine Fisheries office watched the disaster unfold, they stamped their feet in anger and disappointment. Still, they couldn't tear their eyes away from Godzilla.

"Say! What's that?" Yamaji pointed to the surface of the water. In Godzilla's wake, something was splashing about, sending up a great spray of water as it approached.

It was the other kaiju! With terrifying force, he pounced at Godzilla from behind.

"Oh no!" Tsukioka shouted, unable to contain himself. "It's Anguirus!"

Yamaji exclaimed, "What? Anguirus!? . . . That? . . ."

A look of surprise and terror appeared on the faces of everyone gathered there.

Anguirus wasn't a fair fighter. He leaped on Godzilla from behind, letting out an enormous howl. Using the sharp spikes on his head, he turned on Godzilla, furiously trying to hurt him.

Godzilla hadn't anticipated this attack, but he managed to stand up straight, growing even more angry in the process. A fierce scuffle ensued.

As they fought, Anguirus turned toward the shoreline at one point, perhaps because he sensed some danger to himself. There, he hunkered down, taking aim for any chink in Godzilla's defenses that he could find.

Godzilla let forth a loud *GRAAWWRRRRR!!* that reverberated high into the heavens. And with that, he dashed toward Anguirus and leaped onto him.

Like Godzilla, Anguirus also rose onto his hind legs to receive the attack. With even greater force than before, he rushed at Godzilla, lashing out at him.

As the two terrifying, ancient monsters grappled and wrestled, their gigantic bodies drew ever closer to the wharves of Osaka Bay.

Godzilla Makes Landfall

With each passing moment of this life-and-death struggle, the colossal bodies of Godzilla and Anguirus closed in on the wharves at the edge of the bay. A line of heavy artillery and tanks were in formation along the shore. All at once, they opened fire, but was it already too late?

Ka-bang! Ka-bang! The deafening volley was aimed at the two kaiju, which the military held in their searchlights, but the shelling didn't do a thing. Instead, the shells raining down around the two monsters only seemed to enflame their rage. Caught in the searchlights, Godzilla and Anguirus looked all the more terrifyingly angry and agitated.

The continuous volley of shells created arcs of red flame as they rained down on the grappling forms of the monsters. They exploded in pillars of flame and ocean spray, which enveloped the kaiju.

Still, they continued grappling in the water, biting one another, slapping one another with their tails, and spitting out beams of white-hot light. Meanwhile, they moved gradually toward the wharves until their humongous bodies reached the breakwater wall.

Terrified by the sight of the monsters, the soldiers and police stationed there trembled and scattered in all directions. Seeing this, Godzilla quickly pulled away from Anguirus and let out a ferocious roar. He smashed a tank underfoot and crushed a building with his hand. At the same time, he breathed a strong beam of white-hot light at the defensive troops, who were running around frantically, trying to get away.

GRAAWWWRRRR!!

The troops writhed about, screaming and shrieking in agony. Seeing this, Anguirus also used his supernatural abilities to spit out a beam of white, incandescent light, which was every bit as powerful as Godzilla's. It was clear Anguirus also didn't care who or what was in his path.

In the blink of an eye, the strip of buildings near the two monsters was enveloped in a sea of flame—factories, buildings, everything. Still, the two continued fighting, moving ever closer to central Osaka in the process. Their struggle was so intense that all the power of science seemed useless in the face of their tremendous strength.

Yamaji, Tsukioka, and the others on top of the building had been staring at all this with wide-open eyes. Sensing danger approach, they started dashing down the staircase.

Kobayashi was the first to start yelling, but the other worried employees quickly followed, screaming at the company president to come down the stairs off the roof. "Mr. Yamaji! Mr. Yamaji! You've got to come. It's dangerous! You've got to come down now!" Their faces were twitching, trembling with fear.

Tsukioka quietly approached him. "Sir, please. It's time to go."

The company president glanced quickly at Tsukioka but almost immediately turned back to look at Godzilla and Anguirus. "My god . . . What happened? They were using the light from the flares to lure Godzilla away, but instead, that same light ended up drawing in Anguirus . . ." He bit his lower lip in anxiety and frustration.

The employees below were still shouting, worried about his safety. One person shouted, "Mr. Yamaji! Please, you've got to come down . . . Now! No time to lose!" Another followed, "Mr. Yamaji! There's nothing you can do. Come down, and let's go. Hurry!"

By this point, Godzilla was less than a hundred meters away. Tsukioka forcefully grabbed Yamaji's arm and pulled him down the stairs, his feet pounding loudly against each step as he ran.

Godzilla and Anguirus were getting close. They smashed the factory that lay in their path. The tall chimneys and nearby cranes broke, clattering loudly to the ground, but there was nothing anyone could do to stop the destruction.

As Anguirus searched for an opening in Godzilla's defenses, he nimbly leaped at him from behind, but that only provoked Godzilla's anger, and he delivered a strong, irritated blow with his powerful, colossal tail. He repeatedly swung his tail back and forth as if putting all the force of his body into it.

Still clinging tightly to Godzilla's back, Anguirus persistently tried to get at his opponent's neck. He showed no sign of letting up the attack.

As Godzilla twisted and writhed, trying to throw Anguirus from his back, his tail slammed into the Marine Fisheries canning factory, smashing it to bits with a single blow. Then, in the blink of an eye, the strange, white-hot light shooting from the mouths of the two kaiju set the ruined factory on fire, and it went up in flames.

"Oh no, the factory . . ."

The company president started to run toward it. Tsukioka and Kobayashi each grabbed one of his arms and held him back. "Please! If we don't get out of here right now, the fire'll get us."

Yamaji was staring with a blank look on his face at the factory, which was engulfed in flames. Pulling him by the hand, Tsukioka and Kobayashi tried to lead him to safety, but suddenly, they were thrown face-first to the ground. They heard the ear-shattering crunch of the building crumbling overhead, and flames and black smoke belched forth.

"Mr. Yamaji!! Mr. Yamajiiiiiiiii!!"

"Are you alright? Mr. Yamaji?!"

Tsukioka and Kobayashi could just barely be heard over all the noise as they called out worriedly.

On higher land, up in the hills, Hidemi was watching the fierce, bright flames spreading across the shoreline. "Please, God . . ." She clasped her hands together at her chest in fervent prayer.

Fire engines sped at top speed through the burning city blocks. Since there were hardly any people left in the city, they drove through the streets faster than ever.

Two people came running toward the fire engines, fleeing frantically from the very direction the firemen were headed. "Hey!!" the two men shouted, then stopped. Their forms seemed to rise out of the darkness in the brightness of the fire engine's headlights.

Since the engines blocked their path, they turned and dashed into a subway entrance, which was standing wide-open nearby. They ran down the staircase into the station, which was completely empty of people. They hurried along, trying to escape along the subway tracks.

Overhead, the two kaiju continued their struggle to the death. On the other side of the river, they trampled the Central Telegraph and Telephone Bureau building as if it was nothing at all, then shot more blinding beams of hot, incandescent light at one another.

Anguirus continued his unrelenting attack, still looking for a hole in Godzilla's defenses. In the middle of the great flower of red flames, Godzilla stood up straight on his back legs and grappled with his enemy using slow, heavy movements.

Anguirus quickly shifted to the side. Having dodged Godzilla's blow, he recovered and lunged at Godzilla again.

The hair-raising battle between the two monsters was gradually approaching the spot over the subway where the two prisoners had fled. Belowground, the footing was treacherous, but the two escapees continued to run along the subway tracks, stumbling and falling along the way. They were breathing extremely heavily, just about out of breath. They were incredibly pale, unable to say a thing in their exhaustion.

The life-and-death battle between the two terrifying monsters raged overhead. The kaiju rammed into one another, and locked in one another's embrace, they fell down, smack in the middle of the Dōjima River.

Crushed by the weight of the monsters overhead, the ceiling of the subway cracked apart, and all at once, the river water poured into the subway tunnels below. *Whooosh!*—the sound it made was deafening. The water rushed like a massive flood into the tunnels where the prisoners were cowering. The chairs, barriers, and everything else were immediately swept away.

"Aaaaaagh!!" The escapees let out a shriek, but the water swallowed them in a flash. Not even an additional moment went by before the violently surging water had completely submerged the entire subway, filling the tunnels.

Anguirus

Brrrring, brrrring. The telephone was ringing at the Anti-Godzilla Task Force headquarters.

The commander quickly grabbed the receiver. "Um, hello?" Almost immediately, the color drained from his face. "Huh?! What? Godzilla's done what? . . ." He began screaming, "Everyone evacuate! Evacuate everyone from here immediately!!"

Hearing the commander's order, people began running out of the Metropolitan Police Station in every direction. However, it was already too late for most. There was a loud rumbling, and the ground beneath the station building shook violently. Godzilla's foot had already smashed part of the station.

He was facing off with Anguirus, who was standing tall in the inner moat of Osaka Castle, which rose dramatically into the sky behind him. Godzilla boldly stood his ground, taking a posture that showed he was about to attack. For a moment, the two monsters glared at one another with the central keep of the castle in the background, then Godzilla lunged bravely at Anguirus, coming straight at him as if he had found some chink in his opponent's defenses.

Anguirus summoned up all his force, and with a loud thud, the two gigantic kaiju slammed into one another. They trampled the nearby buildings underfoot and spit their strange beams of white-hot light at one another. They had both summoned up all their strength for an all-out battle to the death.

Even the defensive troops who had been running around madly, trying to escape just a moment before, were so awestruck by the tremendous sight that they forgot to run. Instead, they just stood there staring with blank looks on their faces.

The monsters wrestled, then separated, wrestled, then separated again, then kept repeating this over and over. Their howling was tremendous. But were there limits to a kaiju's strength? Perhaps so. There was a moment when it looked like Anguirus was beginning to lose his strength, and Godzilla suddenly pulled away. With his tremendous, powerful tail—*whack!*—Godzilla delivered a single hard blow to his opponent's neck. Anguirus bent forward, collapsing halfway to the ground. Godzilla seized this opportunity to attack with his tail again, delivering one blow, then another.

It looked like the end might have come for Anguirus. He seemed to have lost the will to fight, and he let out a forlorn howl. Seeing this, Godzilla lifted his gigantic body into the air, and putting all the force of his massive body into his hind legs, he delivered a powerful kick to Anguirus's chest—*Bam!*

At precisely that moment, the two massive kaiju fell over, collapsing onto the main keep of Osaka Castle. There was a terrible rumbling in the earth as they fell. *Crash! Kaboom!*—The castle broke to pieces beneath their weight, making another awful sound. In the blink of an eye, a monster born of the hydrogen bomb had destroyed one of the most famous castles in the world.

Anguirus rolled over once, then once more, and collapsed into the castle moat. After that, there was no more movement.

GRAAAAAAWR!! Godzilla let out a loud roar and shot a beam of white-hot light from his mouth. In a flash, the corpse of Anguirus, the remains of Osaka Castle, and all the surrounding buildings were completely enveloped in a sea of wildly burning flames.

Godzilla had won, but he continued to rain his destructive white, incandescent light down on his surroundings. As a result, practically everything in the vicinity was caught up in a sea of fire.

Osaka was burning. Flames, flames, flames were leaping up everywhere. From the higher ground behind the city, the citizens of Osaka looked down, hardly knowing what to say or do. Everyone had gone completely pale.

Bombs, cannons, and airplanes—all the weapons proudly produced by the most advanced, modern science—had proved completely ineffective against the gigantic monster. All anyone could do was wring their hands and watch.

It seemed as if there was no will to do anything left among the citizens of the city. In the distance, a group of people sat down despondently on the ground, and closer by, seven or eight people followed suit. With empty eyes, they turned their gazes toward the brightly burning city. All they could do was watch.

From somewhere came the faint sound of a radio broadcast. "The most terrifying battle of the century has come to a close. But at what cost? Our world-famous Osaka Castle has collapsed into rubble, and Japan's second largest metropolis has been thoroughly trampled underfoot by Godzilla, offspring of the hydrogen bomb . . . Has Godzilla's anger subsided? . . . Godzilla appears to be retreating solemnly and silently . . ."

Even after the radio broadcast ended, the citizens didn't move. Instead, they silently watched the burning city streets and the retreating outline of Godzilla as he disappeared into the distant waters of Osaka Bay.

The Hokkaido Branch

The city streets of Osaka were still smoldering from the fierce
flames of the night before. In every direction, the place looked
like a blackened, burnt field. Perhaps because of that, even the
light of the rising sun seemed duller than usual. The people who
had been burned out of their homes were simply standing around
as if they had lost all energy to clean up the ruins. Hardly anyone
said a word.

Yamaji, the president of Marine Fisheries, and Shibaki, the
head of the Hokkaido branch, were standing on what was left of
the roof of the Marine Fisheries offices. They were quietly gazing
out over the heartbreaking spectacle of the ruined city.

Yamaji said to his younger companion, "Over there, where the
smoke is still rising . . . That's what's left of our cannery." He lifted
his hand slowly to indicate the area.

"My god, the destruction is much worse than I'd imagined."
Shibaki turned to look at Yamaji with a pained expression in his
eyes.

Yamaji seemed to read something in his gaze. "Cut it out. No
need to look at me with pity."

"Yes, sir."

Then in a firmer, more formal voice, the president added, "I,
Kōhei Yamaji, promise we'll get back on our feet again . . . Rest
assured."

"Just hearing that lifts my spirits . . ."

Yamaji chuckled. "I hope I made your long trip all the way from Hokkaido worth it." He grinned, and Shibaki smiled and nodded back.

The employees were already hard at work cleaning up the mess in the blackened, blistered buildings. They were working efficiently, and their efforts were already paying off. Hidemi and Yasuko, both devoted workers, had tied neckerchiefs over their hair and towels over their mouths and noses. They gathered the employees with free hands and indicated they should straighten up the radio communications room. "We've got to get to work here straight away . . ."

Yamaji and Shibaki happened to be passing by, so they stopped to give the room a good look. The damage was greater than Shibaki had expected, and he was knitting his brow worriedly. As he scanned the room, Hidemi caught his gaze.

She quickly pulled down the towel covering her face. "Oh my! When did you get here?" She gave him a little smile.

"Oh, look . . . It's you . . . I flew in first thing this morning. I had to rush to the airport to make it."

"Thanks for coming all this way . . . Yasuko, do you mind taking over for me?"

The three of them walked to the office next door. All the rooms were in a frightful state of disarray. There was hardly a thing left of the window frames, and everything had collapsed. So many of the desks had burned that there really wasn't even one left to use comfortably. The place was such a mess that Shibaki became despondent and couldn't utter a word.

"Father, why don't I put on some tea for all of you?" Without hesitating, Hidemi started over to the door and put her hand on the knob.

Right then, the faces of Tsukioka and Kobayashi suddenly appeared in the window of the door. The glass had all broken away, leaving an empty hole where the window should have been. They pulled the door toward them, opening it into the hallway, and plodded with loud footsteps into the room.

"Goodness," Hidemi welcomed them with a smile. "Glad to see you back!"

Tsukioka didn't answer. He had a severe, strained look on his face. "Sir, we can't figure out for the life of us where Godzilla went . . . Apparently, the Maritime Safety Agency hasn't been able to locate him either."

"I see . . . Thanks for trying."

"We put everything we had into the search but to no avail." Kobayashi's tone was full of regret.

Tsukioka unzipped his aviator uniform. He pulled a cigarette case out of his pocket and stuck a cigarette in his mouth. Standing at his side, Kobayashi also helped himself to a cigarette, which he stuck between his lips. With a *click*, he flicked his lighter, took a deep puff of smoke, and held it for a moment before exhaling. A pleased look came over his face.

Yamaji seemed to be mulling something over. As he looked up, he asked, "Say, Kobayashi, would you do me a favor? Would you go up north to the branch office in Hokkaido?"

"Hokkaido?" The president's sudden request surprised not just Kobayashi but everyone else too.

"I was discussing it with Shibaki, the branch manager. After the disasters here at the main office, we can't afford to lose time and money by letting our ships sit by idly. We were thinking that for the time being, we could use the branch office in Hokkaido as the main center for our operations. We'd fish the waters up there, then use the canneries up in the north . . ."

"Sure. As long as I get to fly, I'll gladly work wherever you want."

"Thanks," Shibaki said. "We're counting on you to give it your all." He clapped his hand down on Kobayashi's shoulder.

"I'm happy to, sir."

Hidemi chimed in. "So does this mean that Tsukioka and I get to go too, Dad?"

"No, we've got tons of work here for you, rebuilding the main office."

"Oh, I see . . ." Hidemi was discernably disappointed. She glanced over at Tsukioka and caught his gaze.

Yamaji added, "We can head up to Hokkaido once we get things in shape here."

"Alright. Got it."

Kobayashi chimed in flirtatiously, "Hidemi, I feel for you, having to stay all alone in Osaka for the time being without me. This place is a mess . . ."

Hidemi gave a little chuckle. "Kobayashi, you're nuts." She pointed her finger at her ear and made a little twirling motion.

"Me, nuts?"

"That's right. When you look forward to something, you dream about it, and that makes it all the better when you finally get it—that is, *if* you ever get it." She was clearly teasing him. "The longer you wait, the better."

Kobayashi laughed. "You just won't give in, will ya?"

All five people in the room laughed out loud.

Kobayashi continued, "But when you finally make it up to Hokkaido, there might be some surprise competition waiting there for you."

"You do say! Now who's refusing to give in?"

"Whatcha talking about? There might be someone up there in Hokkaido waiting for me right now . . . She's not shameless like a certain somebody right in front of me who was born and raised in Osaka. She's a lot more naive and innocent . . ." Kobayashi smiled flirtatiously.

"Oh, come on!" she teased. "No way, I don't believe there's anyone waiting for you in Hokkaido . . ."

"Now that you've said so, I'm going to have to find her and prove you wrong."

"See, there we go! Look how easily your fibs come crumbling apart."

"Fibs?"

"That's right! The fib that there's someone up there waiting for you . . ."

"Alright! You got me!" Kobayashi scratched his head in feigned embarrassment.

Tsukioka, who was standing next to him, chimed in. "Don't worry, Kobayashi—your specialty is hunting down things in your plane. You'll track her down in no time."

Hidemi jumped in again. "Just remember, Kobayashi, tracking down girls and tracking down fish aren't the same thing."

"Well then, I'll have to find me a wingman . . ." He clenched his hand lightly and pretended to spar with another guy.

Shibaki said, "Want me to step in the ring and be your go-between when the time comes? . . ."

"Please! I need all the help I can get." Kobayashi bowed his head slightly.

Immediately, Tsukioka added, "Yeah, he bungles everything."

"Don't listen to this jerk," Kobayashi joked. Everyone in the room—not just the five in the conversation—burst out laughing.

Later that day, Shibaki, the manager of the Hokkaido branch office, climbed into Kobayashi's plane. With the whirr of the propellers echoing behind them, he and Kobayashi set off for the northern island.

The Far North

Snow, snow, and more snow. Hokkaido, located in the far north of the country, was covered with a blanket of white. Not a speck of color was visible on the snow-covered mountains. Just the sight of them was enough to make a person feel cold. The houses and roads were covered with a thick accumulation of snow, and icy wind howled in from the sea, making the seashore where Marine Fisheries was located so frigid that all one had to do was step outside to feel the cold cut to the bone.

Inside, a bright-red flame was burning in a kerosene stove. In fact, it was so toasty inside that just walking around the room would make a person break into a light sweat. Kobayashi was wearing his thick aviator uniform as he strolled up to Shibaki. There was a light, energetic quality to his footsteps.

"Sir, I'm going to go out looking for my future bride again . . ."

Shibaki chuckled. "Great, thanks." Since the conversation with Hidemi back in Osaka, "searching for a bride" had become Kobayashi's lighthearted way of referring to his aerial searches for schools of fish.

"So, where do you think I'm going to find the matchmaker today?"

Shibaki quietly stood from his chair and indicated a spot on the map pinned to the wall behind him. "The matchmaker's probably eagerly waiting for you somewhere out here . . ."

Kobayashi took down the coordinates in a small notebook. "Well then, it's about time for the groom to make an appearance."

Shibaki gave a little laugh and said, "I'll prepare the celebratory sake then. It'll be waiting when you get back."

"Roger, roger!" Kobayashi cheerfully raised one hand, gave a quick salute, and walked quickly out of the manager's office.

As he was leaving, one of the workers in the main office teased him, "Take care of yourself, Mr. Groom-to-be!"

"OK," Kobayashi quipped. "I've thought through it and have everything under control . . . But it's through strength and technique that I'll get the job done. These arms will do the job!"

He walked toward the small seaplane that was waiting for him, right on the edge of the ocean. The engine was already purring, and the propeller was spinning with a pleasant hum.

He sat in the pilot's seat and ran his eyes over the instruments. As he pressed the throttle, the engine purred more loudly, and the plane began to glide across the waves. Before long, the nose of the plane began to lift lightly into the air.

As he picked up altitude, he began to bank the plane, curving back in the direction of the office. The engine made a pleasant purr as the plane flew.

Shibaki watched the plane through the window as Kobayashi flew off. There was a bright, cheerful expression on his face.

The surface of the northern sea sparkled with light, and the dark currents dancing underneath created large but innocent waves. The currents carried along large chunks of ice that shone like white sails above the water. Out on the open sea, the *Northern Seas,* one of the ships owned by Marine Fisheries, had to shift its course a little to the right, then a little to the left, to avoid the icebergs in its path.

The captain of the ship had been tanned a reddish-brown color from all his exposure to the sun. He was holding a pair of binoculars to his eyes with one hand as he gazed hard at the horizon and shouted orders to his crew.

Behind him, one sailor ran out of the ship's radio room. "Captain! Cod, cod! We've spotted a gigantic school of codfish! It's at XX° N, XX° E . . ."

A grin spread across the captain's face. He snatched the memo with the coordinates from the radio operator and ran his eyes over its contents. Then in one corner of the sky, he heard the pleasant sound of an engine traveling toward them. "Oh! There he is. There . . ." The plane was just a black speck in the sky, no larger than a poppy seed. "Look, it's Kobayashi . . . Hey, everyone, Kobayashi's come to visit today!"

Hearing the captain's announcement, the crew rushed out to the deck and looked up. Kobayashi's plane approached rapidly. It circled twice, no, three times around the *Northern Seas,* then started leading them toward the gigantic school of cod.

Once Kobayashi reached his destination, he began to descend rapidly to indicate where the fish were. Then, he descended a little more so that he was right above the deck of the ship. Once there, he dropped a tube containing a message.

One sailor picked up the cylinder, and the others gathered around. They quickly opened it and read the note contained inside. "Praying for a huge catch," it said.

The sailors gave a loud cheer and waved at Kobayashi above. As if in response, Kobayashi made a big curve around the ship, then headed back to the hangar. The pleasant whirring of his engine reverberated across the sky as he flew away.

"Here we go, men. Now that Kobayashi's shown us where the catch is, let's make 'im proud!"

With magnificently skilled movements, the sailors of the *Northern Seas* began pulling up their nets, one after the next. They all were filled with gigantic cod. *Thud, thud.* The fish landed on deck. They flapped around, *whap-whap,* as more netfuls full of cod landed on them, one after the next. Before long, the sailors had a small mountain of fish.

The ship sent a volley of radio messages back to the office. Cheers went up at the office to celebrate the successful catch.

"We got your bride, Kobayashi!!"

"An unbelievable catch!!"

Even Shibaki, the branch manager, was beaming. He called over the nearby employees. "Hey, you guys, call that restaurant we like so much . . . Yeah. That's the one—the Yayoi. Tell them to prepare some extra-special celebratory sake for us tonight. We're gonna celebrate."

"Right on it, sir . . ."

All of the employees were smiling. Everyone seemed to be in high spirits.

Now that he'd finished the task at hand, Kobayashi started crooning "Sōran-bushi," a folk song from Hokkaido, as he flew back toward shore, lightly gripping the steering column. He was in a merry mood.

A woman's voice came over the radio. "Calling Kobayashi, calling Kobayashi . . . This is the branch office. Please respond. Over."

"Roger, this is Kobayashi, this is Kobayashi."

"Kobayashi, you need to come back right away. Return immediately. Return immediately." He heard some chuckling at the other end of the radio.

"Huh?" For a moment, he screwed up his face in confusion. "Wait . . . Hidemi? Is that you?"

Her voice softened. "Right! You got it. I arrived just now."

"Really? Did Tsukioka come too?"

"Yup, I flew up here with Dad in Tsukioka's plane."

"Really? I've been waiting!"

Tsukioka, who was still wearing his aviator uniform, was standing beside her. He put his mouth up to the radio transmitter. "Hey! Kobayashi!"

"What? You're there too, eh?"

Tsukioka laughed over the radio airwaves. "Yeah, we managed to get settled in Osaka, at least for the time being. I flew up here as soon as I could."

"You don't say . . ." Kobayashi's tone of voice shifted, as he'd just thought of something. "That reminds me. There's someone who wants to meet you, Tsukioka."

"Huh? Me? . . . Who?"

"Someone special."

"Someone special, you say?"

Hidemi jumped in. "Kobayashi, who're you talking about?"

Kobayashi laughed. "You'll see."

"Come on, tell me . . ."

"It's a secret. S-E-C-R-E-T . . ."

"What a tease! Then I'm not going to give you the gift I brought."

Kobayashi feigned being upset. "Awwww, you've got me," then he laughed.

With that, the transmission abruptly ended. Tsukioka and Hidemi looked at one another.

"Who do you think he meant?"

"No idea . . . Who'd be all the way up here in Hokkaido?" A puzzled look came over Tsukioka's face, and he tilted his head in confusion.

Celebrating the Big Catch

A powdery snow was blowing in, striking the hanging lantern that faintly illuminated the eaves outside the restaurant. Tsukioka and Hidemi followed Kobayashi inside.

"Say, tell me. Who were you talking about earlier?"

"I told you, you'll see . . ." Kobayashi proceeded to the back of the restaurant and called out to the lady manager, "Hey, missus! You've got a customer . . . Man, what bad service!"

Hearing Kobayashi's loud voice, the manager came rushing out to greet him. "Well, if it isn't the groom himself! Everybody's waiting for you."

"Are they now?" Hardly paying attention to his two guests, Kobayashi was about to kick off his shoes when he heard some heavy footsteps approach.[2]

"Say, Tsukioka! It's us, it's us!"

The energetic voices belonged to Tajima and Ikeda, two friends from way back. They were dressed in uniforms of the Self-Defense Forces.

A look of joy spread across Tsukioka's face. "My goodness! You guys! Still alive . . ."

---

2. In a traditional Japanese restaurant like the one here, it is customary to take off one's shoes before stepping up and into the hallway or the room where the food and drink will be served. Once inside, everyone sits on the floor and uses low tables close to the ground. This allows people to move around and interact more freely without the hassle of shifting chairs around.

The two men threw their arms around Tsukioka in a warm embrace. The three hugged like enthusiastic children. Even though Tsukioka hadn't yet taken off his shoes, they pulled him up into the raised corridor outside the room where they'd be eating. They were as jubilant as kindergartners.

Tsukioka laughed. "Fancy meeting you here of all places—way up here in the far north!"

"Yeah, well, the north's been good to us."

"I'm so glad! I'm so happy you guys are here!" With that, Tsukioka playfully made a fist and gave his friends each a small but audible knock on the chin. The two men laughed and took turns playfully knocking him on the chin back. A painless little knock like that could only be a sign of the close friendship between the men.

Meanwhile, Hidemi was looking on wide-eyed. Kobayashi explained, "These guys were pilots with Tsukioka back during the war. They managed to make it out alive—they're heroes." Hidemi found men who expressed themselves in a rough-and-tumble fashion like that really attractive.

Another sturdily built man emerged from the back room where everyone was seated. He was wearing an unsophisticated suit and had a mustache. "Tsukioka!!"

"What?! It's you, Captain!!" Tsukioka immediately raised his hand in a salute. Back during the war, Captain Terazawa had overseen the torpedo bombers.

The captain gave a big grin. "Tsukioka, I got word from the groom here that you flew all the way up here." He and Kobayashi smiled and nodded.

Hidemi was standing beside them, looking perplexed.

"Captain, it's so good to see you looking strong and healthy."

"Come on, let's skip the formalities. We need a toast for old time's sake. It's been ages!"

"Right on!"

Terazawa started leading the new arrivals into the room where everyone was seated. Tajima said to Hidemi, who was standing next to Tsukioka, "Missus, please. After you . . ."

"My, what manners . . ."

Hidemi blushed, and that made Tsukioka lose his composure slightly. "Tajima, you're quick to the draw as always . . ."

Ikeda responded in his place, "No need to worry, Tsukioka."

The two men took Tsukioka and Hidemi's hands and led them into a smaller room across from the one where the main party was gathered. "It's been ages since we've seen you, Tsukioka. We're gonna celebrate tonight by drinking like fish!" Tajima and Ikeda were already fairly tipsy as they pressed Tsukioka to drink.

"I don't know . . . I've already . . ."

"Come on! What's not to celebrate? You've got a beautiful wife right next to you."

"You've got it wrong. She's not my wife."

"So, who is she then?"

"The daughter of the company president."

Tajima leaped in, "But I bet you're going to get married someday."

Ikeda added, "You must've guessed right. Hit the nail on the head. Look, the happy couple is blushing . . ."

"My goodness." Hidemi had turned bright red and shifted her gaze downward uncomfortably.

Terazawa was already red from the alcohol. "You guys are incorrigible."

Tajima picked up a flask of sake with a shaky hand. "Come on, let's have another toast."

"Alright!" Tsukioka held out his sake cup.

Across the corridor was the room where most of the party was. The guests raised their voices in the song "Sōran-bushi." Kobayashi probably started it, and the rest of his coworkers must have joined in.

Hearing the song from the other room, Ikeda stood up unsteadily. "Alright, I'm going to sing too! I can't let them do a better job than me!"

> In the capital, under the lavender clouds of spring,
> The scent of flowers wafts across the straw mats
> Where we gather together to celebrate
> Dreams of inexhaustibly luxurious dark scarlet
> And all the other shifting hues of the late spring
> Burn for a moment in our hearts—dense, rich, and green
> We admire the pure hearts of the people of the world
> And yearn for the north where the starlight burns so bright

Tajima, Tsukioka, and Terazawa all joined Ikeda in song. Singing together made them feel like they were back in the good old days. Hidemi sat back and enjoyed the music.

Across the corridor in the other room, the employees of Marine Fisheries were celebrating the day's tremendous catch. The captain of the *Northern Seas,* several of the workers from the ship's boiler room, and five or six of the office employees were present. There was also a geisha performing there too, plucking her samisen. Meanwhile, Kobayashi tapped out the rhythm on a drum as the group raised their voices wholeheartedly in song.

> *Sōran, sōran*
> *Sōran, sōran*
> When we ask the seagulls in the sky
> About the timing of the tides:
>> I, a bird in flight, answer,
>> Ah, you should ask the waves!
>> *Enya-sa, dokkoisho*

Seated in the front of the room were Yamaji and Shibaki, who were drinking as they watched the singers. Kobayashi was beating the drum with vigorous hand movements as he sang—"*Sōran, sōran.*" He overheard a refrain from the song in the other room and pricked up his ears. He turned to Yamaji and gave a slight nod.

Yamaji noticed and said, "I see they're trying to keep up with us over there . . ."

Kobayashi chuckled and said, "Mind if I go visit them for a bit?"

"No, of course. Take your time." He smiled.

Kobayashi was a little unsteady on his feet as he stumbled into the corridor. A waitress happened to be carrying by a tray with several small flasks of sake. He helped himself and grabbed two. "Thanks."

"My goodness, Mr. Groom!"

He pretended to pour the sake in the flasks into his mouth, then said, "Shhhh . . . Keep my secret!"

The waitress appeared to be used to his antics and just laughed. "No problem . . ."

When Kobayashi joined the others, Tajima was the first to acknowledge him. "Hey, it's the groom-to-be! Have a drink!"

"OK, sure." He held out a cup, and once it was filled to the brim, he downed it in a single go.

"Oh my . . ." From her expression, Hidemi seemed to be fed up. She lowered her voice and said, "You've been acting weird all night, Kobayashi. What's going on? Everyone's been calling you a 'groom' all day . . ."

"Yeah, a weird nickname, I know." He laughed.

Hidemi was drawn in, despite herself. "So it's just a nickname?"

"Well, for the present time at least . . ."

"You don't seem serious. You still haven't found one?—A bride, I mean."

As she said this, Kobayashi felt his heart suddenly breaking, but he struck his chest firmly with his fist. "I'm keeping one candidate for a bride right in here."

"Oh really? You'll have to show me!"

"Nope, not yet."

"You're such a tease." She turned away from him with a pouty expression, and Kobayashi laughed.

Right then, Tajima shouted, "Now, it's the groom's turn to sing!"

"OK . . ."

And with that, the men started singing the same song all over again.

Godzilla Appears in the Northern Seas

Toward the end of their song, the shōji door slid open, and Shibaki peeked in. He was paler than usual. Tsukioka and Kobayashi beckoned him in with a welcoming gesture.

"Listen, you guys. I need to talk for a second!"

Surprised by the unusual nature of this interruption, the group stopped singing, and Tsukioka and Kobayashi stood up. In a low voice, Shibaki said, "I need you to come with me immediately! It seems that our ship the *National Dragon No. 2* has sunk . . ."

"What!? Sunk, you say?" Tsukioka and Kobayashi looked at one another in astonishment.

"They're saying Godzilla was responsible!"

"Godzilla? . . ."

The color drained from everyone's faces.

In the other room, everyone had promptly sobered up. Yamaji was giving them orders. He turned to one employee and said, "You, I need you to go to the Maritime Safety Agency . . ."

"Sure," the man responded, jumping up.

Tsukioka came dashing into the room with loud footsteps. "Mr. Yamaji!"

Captain Terazawa, who was standing there among the employees, stepped forward, bowed to Yamaji, and said, "Excuse me, sir. Remember, I'm in the Self-Defense Forces . . . What's all this about Godzilla?"

"Just now, I learned something from this man . . ." He pointed to an employee, who was still out of breath. The man had obviously just run into the room. "Just a few minutes ago, we had a radio message from the *National Dragon No. 2*. They said they'd spotted something at sea that appeared to be Godzilla. They were at XX° N, XX° E. Then they radioed in an SOS, but that was the last we heard from them. Just radio silence after that."

"Hmm," Terazawa muttered. The color drained from his face as he mulled it over. "Ikeda! Prepare for emergency deployment immediately!!"

"Yes, sir! Right on it, sir."

"Tajima! First thing in the morning, you're going out to sea on a search."

"Yes, sir!"

After receiving their orders, the two men dashed out of the restaurant. Terazawa appeared so stern that one might have mistaken him for an entirely different person than a moment ago.

Tsukioka took a step forward. "Captain, I've got a request, sir." Terazawa nodded.

Kobayashi and the others had hurriedly left the room after receiving Yamaji's orders. All Hidemi could do was look on uneasily. In a fraction of a second, the atmosphere had changed completely. The room felt far bleaker and more desolate.

The rest of the night passed with everyone feeling anxious.

▶

In the morning, the clouds hung low in the sky. Tsukioka's plane flew under them as he searched for Godzilla. He stared down at the water's surface so intently that his gaze could have bored a hole in it. He had already been looking for many hours, and the strain was clearly visible on his face.

Hidemi's crisp voice came over the airwaves into his ears. "This is the branch office. This is the branch office . . . Calling Tsukioka . . . Please respond . . ."

"This is Tsukioka . . . No sign of Godzilla yet . . . Over."

"The weather is rapidly degrading. We are temporarily halting the search. Return immediately . . . Over."

In a sullen voice, Tsukioka responded, "But I've been hard at work searching. My current location is XX° N, XX° E . . ."

Hidemi suddenly changed her tone. "No! You must return. Please, I'm begging you. Come back immediately . . ."

"Roger, roger . . . No need to worry . . ."

"Calling Tsukioka, Calling Tsukioka . . . Please respond . . . Calling Tsukioka . . . Calling Tsukioka . . ." Hidemi continued calling out to him.

"Tsukioka here, Tsukioka here . . . With all due respect, I'm not going to abandon the search . . ."

"Tsukioka . . . You need to return immediately, Tsukioka . . ."

He made no more attempts to respond.

In a worried voice, Hidemi said, "You're so stubborn!"

Tsukioka gave a little chuckle, despite himself, as he flew the plane in a large curve through the air.

Hidemi kept calling, but Tsukioka didn't answer. Consumed with anxiety, she continued to sit, irritated, in front of the radio system.

Not realizing what was going on with Tsukioka, Kobayashi pulled on his aviator uniform and went over to Hidemi, still behaving like his usual jovial self. However, Hidemi wasn't feeling sociable and pretended not to notice him.

Not quite sure what to do, he joked, "Well then, I suppose it's about time for me to go look for my bride-to-be . . ." He spoke in a low voice as if he were speaking to himself, but Hidemi didn't even turn to look. Feeling awkward, he zipped up his aviator uniform and said, "Look, Hidemi, there's something I'd like to ask you."

She simply turned but didn't say anything.

Kobayashi tilted his head quizzically and commented, "You're acting strange today."

"I'm acting the same as every day," she retorted, not sounding especially friendly.

"Really? Something's different . . ."

She softened her voice somewhat and replied, "What? Tell me."

He hesitated for a moment, then asked, "Say . . . Um, what kinds of things, um, do girls like?" It was clear that he was rather embarrassed.

She was somewhat taken aback but immediately realized what was going on. She looked hard at Kobayashi, who looked shy and perhaps even slightly upset.

"Um, if today's not good, you don't have to tell me right now . . ."

"No, fine . . . I'll tell you." She softened her voice and put her finger against her cheek, pretending like she was thinking hard.

Kobayashi hurriedly pulled out a small notebook from his pocket, then flustered, said, "No, wait. You're the daughter of a rich man. Your answers might be . . ." His voice trailed off.

"Fine, I won't tell you then." She quietly turned toward Kobayashi. Her expression had softened somewhat.

"Well, maybe I ought to ask you after all."

"Girls like all sorts of things."

"Sure. For instance?"

"Purses."

"Purses. Got it." Kobayashi scribbled in his notebook.

"And watches."

"Getting more expensive . . ."

"Socks too. Nylons."

"Nylons . . . What else?"

"It's hard to say. There are all sorts of things girls like . . ."

"No doubt."

"Well then, why don't you let me think for a while."

"Good idea. Please do."

"So tell me . . . About how old is this girl?"

"Ummmm . . ." He was on the verge of making a careless mistake. "Goodness! I'm afraid I can't say. I'm in dangerous waters here . . ."

"It doesn't matter. You can tell me . . ."

Kobayashi flushed, and he tried to change the subject. "Man, Tsukioka's taking forever to get back . . ."

Right around that same moment, something startled Tsukioka, who was still flying over the ocean. He opened his eyes wide and looked down.

Godzilla was below. The monster was moving through the water, leaving a white wake in his trail.

"Oh!" Tsukioka shouted his excitement. Tsukioka rapidly lowered his airplane and started approaching Godzilla, who kept on appearing and disappearing between the waves. The fuel gauge on his plane was already approaching zero.

He clicked his tongue and reached for the radio headset around his neck. "Tsukioka here, Tsukioka here . . . I just found Godzilla. Am in hot pursuit . . . Over."

Tsukioka's voice immediately bounded over the airwaves to Hidemi and Kobayashi. They were astonished by the news.

"Roger, roger . . . Please! I'm begging you. Don't follow him any farther out to sea . . ." Hidemi was pleading with him.

Kobayashi also jumped in. "Tsukioka! You OK on fuel!?"

"Just enough to make it back . . ."

"You idiot!! I'm going to go get you. What's your current location?"

"XX° N, XX° E. I'm in the air over Kamiko Island. It looks like Godzilla's headed ashore."

"Alright, got it. I'm coming to get you immediately!" Hurriedly readjusting the straps of his uniform, Kobayashi made for the door.

"Kobayashi!"

"What?"

"Be careful. Please."

"Roger that!" Kobayashi chuckled, but before he left, he said, "Say, Hidemi. In return for me being careful, I want you to think about what kind of present you think would be best."

"Sure, let me think. I'll have come up with something by the time you get back, Mr. Groom-to-be."

"Promise?" Still clowning around, Kobayashi dashed out of the room with a smile on his face.

As she headed back to her seat, Hidemi noticed the small notebook he had left behind. She picked it up and opened it. There was a photograph of Kobayashi inside. He was seated in a pilot's seat with a slight smile on his face. Hidemi went to put it back on the desk when something else fell out and onto the floor.

It was another small photograph. Without thinking anything about it, she picked it up. Much to her surprise, the photo showed a young woman wearing her hair in two ponytails on either side of her head. Her eyes were bright and showed a sweetness as she smiled.

A realization struck her. "Oh my, this must be the girl he was talking about . . ."

Overhead, she could hear the roar of Kobayashi's engine as he flew away.

Kobayashi's Plane Meets Its End

Ga-chunk! Captain Terazawa slammed down the radio receiver. "Tajima!"

"Yes, sir?" He came running.

"Load all the planes with bombs. Prepare to attack!"

"Yes, sir!" Tajima quickly dashed out of the room.

The news about the Godzilla sighting had immediately been reported to the Self-Defense Forces.

Tsukioka was still keeping an eye on Godzilla from his plane, and he was sending minute-by-minute updates about the monster, who had already crawled ashore on Kamiko Island. The entire island was covered in a thick layer of ice. On three sides, there were tall icy cliffs that jutted up from the water, but on the other, front side of the island, there was a narrow strip of low land facing the sea. The water there formed something like a small bay, and the strip of low land along it led inland to the center of the island, which was shaped like a crucible. Godzilla had climbed ashore by the bay and was plodding toward the center of the island step by step.

Tsukioka watched this as he flew over the island. As he banked the plane, forming a large arc in the air, he caught sight of Kobayashi's plane flying straight toward him. He banked the nose of the plane so that he was headed toward Kobayashi, who waved at him in response. The planes zipped right past one another, and Kobayashi began rapidly decreasing his altitude, dropping from the sky toward the island below.

The mountains of ice grew bigger and filled his vision. At the bottom of the crucible created by the mountain walls sat Godzilla. All alone there on the island, he looked especially huge as he stared up at the plane with sparkling eyes. Kobayashi made two or three more quick dives, trying to lure him farther back toward the center of the island. Each time, Godzilla made big motions in the air, trying to grab at the plane and knock it to the ground, but with each swing, he made a step or two backward toward the island's interior.

Tsukioka had already flown back to home base. As soon as he arrived, he rushed by car to the headquarters of the Self-Defense Forces.

Tsukioka pointed to Kamiko Island on a large map affixed to a blackboard. "If Godzilla's able to escape through this open area back to the sea, it'll be too late. We've gotta think of some way to stop him and keep him penned in . . ."

Terazawa pondered Tsukioka's suggestion for a moment. "All right. Let's block his exit with a wall of flame. That should buy us some time. Ikeda?!"

"Yes, sir?"

"Fill an amphibious assault ship with drums of gasoline. I want you to set out right away!"

"Yes, sir!" Ikeda bowed crisply, then turned and left, his shoes echoing loudly through the hallway.

"Tajima, I want you to take command of the aerial squadron."

"Yes, sir." Tajima dashed out energetically toward the airfield. Tsukioka accompanied him.

The jet engines were already roaring, and the bombs had been loaded underneath the wings, ready to drop. The planes were ready to take off as soon as the command arrived. Tajima hopped into the pilot's seat, and Tsukioka jumped into the passenger seat behind him. Tajima waved his hand in a broad gesture back and forth, and the ground assistant removed the blocks beneath the plane's landing gear.

The jets roared even louder. One took off, then another. They created an impressive formation in the sky as they flew low over the Marine Fisheries Hokkaido branch office. The pilots turned the noses of their planes toward Kamiko Island.

Through the window of the radio room, Hidemi watched the departing squadron and waved.

The drums of gasoline had been loaded onto amphibious landers, which had started coasting over the ocean, leaving a wake of white waves behind them. Ikeda and others were on board, headed at full speed toward Kamiko. The rough waves of the northern seas lapped loudly at the sides of the landers.

Above Kamiko Island, Kobayashi was still circling over Godzilla's head, doing his best to lure the monster farther back into the center of the island. Godzilla kept persistently swinging, making dramatic movements as he tried to knock the plane out of the air. At some point in the process, however, he spun around, taking one step, then another toward the bay from which he could exit the island.

"Darn it!!" Kobayashi pursed his lips in frustration. What would happen if he let the monster escape? He took a sharp dive, nearly grazing the head of the kaiju.

GRAAAWR! Godzilla swung at the air and let out a loud cry. Then he stood still, glaring with glittering eyes at Kobayashi's plane.

Kobayashi made circles just above Godzilla's head as he waited for the jets with the bombs to arrive. "Kobayashi here . . . Godzilla's moving toward the sea. Get the Self-Defense Forces here as quickly as you can. Over."

Hidemi listened through the radio receiver and responded in a soft voice, which traveled back to him across the airwaves. "The airplanes from the Self-Defense Forces left here at fifteen-hundred hours, twelve minutes . . ."

"Roger, roger." Kobayashi immediately looked over at Godzilla.

The monster had once again started walking toward the bay where he could exit the island.

"Shoot! I'm not going to let him get away." He made another sharp nosedive in front of Godzilla, just barely making it out over the ocean. He glanced up into the air. The Self-Defense Force jets were rapidly approaching, and their roar reverberated over the island. Their trajectories began to curve in the air.

The roar of the engines only seemed to intensify Godzilla's anger. *GRAAAAAAAWR!!*—he growled and took a couple more steps toward the bay.

In one of the jets, Tajima gave a quick glance over his shoulder at Tsukioka. He turned the plane toward Godzilla in preparation for a bombing run. He picked up the radio transmitter around his neck and shouted, "Prepare the attack!!" His voice was crisp and loud so the squadron mates flying alongside him could hear over the noise of their engines. "Drop!!"

The bombs began falling one after the next from the wings of the jet squadron. *Whoosh*—the bombs cut through the air. They fell around Godzilla, engulfing him on all sides. They began to explode into columns of fire at his feet—*KA-POW! KA-POW!* However, the explosions didn't shake him in the least.

"Tajima, the attack isn't working . . ."

Tajima nodded regretfully. Once again, Godzilla let out a tremendous howl and took a few more steps toward the bay.

Kobayashi watched as the attack squadron made a large curve in the air, trying to stop Godzilla's movement.

"Darn it!!" Kobayashi's plane suddenly began to lose altitude. The wing began to vibrate with a loud *brrrrrrrrrrr*, and the plane began to fall toward Godzilla.

Tsukioka saw this and shouted, "My god! He's in danger!!"

Kobayashi's plane was rapidly descending toward the monster. He was practically right in front of Godzilla as he tried to give his plane more altitude.

Right then, there was a sudden *FLASH!* A beam of white-hot light flooded from Godzilla's mouth. Kobayashi's plane wobbled and shook from the blast. In the blink of an eye, it was engulfed in flames.

"My god!" Kobayashi gritted his teeth. The glittering mountainsides, all covered in ice, were coming right at him. His plane slammed into the mountain.

Tsukioka shouted at the top of his lungs. "No! Kobayashiiiiii!!"

But right then, there was a tremendously loud *ROOOOOOOAR* like thunder as the glittering slopes of the mountains collapsed. There was a huge avalanche of snow and ice, which slid down the mountainsides, forming a thick wall of ice in front of Godzilla.

The kaiju was half-buried under the avalanche. He tried to struggle free, but the limitations on his movement just enraged him even more.

Kobayashi's plane crash was over in a fraction of a second, but it left Tsukioka stunned. He stared without any expression on his face for a moment before returning to his senses. "Tajima, look! Look at that!" From his seat behind Tajima, Tsukioka lifted himself up and pointed to the avalanche Kobayashi's plane had unleashed.

"Wow!" Tajima nodded vigorously. "Calling all planes. Commence bombing raid from above."

The jets headed toward the mountain slopes, picking up altitude along the way. One bomb . . . Two bombs . . . Five bombs . . . Ten bombs.

As the bombs rained down around Godzilla, only a little more snow and ice came tumbling down from the soaring mountain peaks. The bombing raid was ineffective.

Tsukioka gritted his teeth and shouted regretfully, "It's not working!"

"Then let's fire some rockets directly into the mountainside." Tajima held his radio transmitter up to his mouth and said, "First,

Squadron Number One needs to return to home base to arm itself with rockets. All remaining planes should stay here and keep Godzilla occupied!"

Accompanied by two jets, Tajima flew off toward the base on the mainland.

Godzilla was gradually starting to work his way out of the avalanche caused by Kobayashi's plane. Before long, the monster's entire body would be showing.

Nature's Victory Song

"Dad!" Hidemi was pale as she bounded out of the radio room and ran to where Yamaji and Shibaki were gazing uneasily out the window at the deep sea in the distance.

Yamaji wore an apprehensive look as he asked, "What's the matter, Hidemi?"

"It's Kobayashi . . ." That was all she could say before her words trailed off.

"Kobayashi?!"

"Yeah . . . He won't be coming back . . ."

"What?! . . . Are you serious? . . . Our Kobayashi? . . ." Yamaji looked at Shibaki astonished, then turned his eyes downward as he understood what must have happened.

A tear rolled down Hidemi's cheek, followed by another.

"But Kobayashi gave us something . . . He discovered how to defeat Godzilla . . ." Unable to withstand her grief any longer, Hidemi broke into sobs.

"My goodness . . . Kobayashi's really dead?" Yamaji closed his eyes tightly and was silent for a moment.

But then, as if he had suddenly shaken off all his emotion, he barked, "Hidemi! Get back to your station!!" She was still in tears, but he was resolute as he scolded her.

She returned to the radio room with shoulders sagging. She took out the two photographs that had fallen from the little notebook Kobayashi had forgotten earlier that day. She quietly lined them up on the table by the radio, and she turned her upset, pained gaze toward the pictures of Kobayashi and the cute, young woman with the ponytails. "Kobayashi, you two will never see each other again . . . The thought breaks my heart . . ." Her eyes clouded with tears as she gazed at the photos. As if unable to stand it any longer, she put her head down on her hands on the table and wept.

Right about then, back at base, Tajima and the other pilots who had returned were drawing a cutaway map of Kamiko Island on the blackboard. Three of Tajima's subordinates stood in front of him as he explained his plan of action. Standing beside them were Captain Terazawa and Tsukioka, also listening.

"Understand?" Tajima pointed to a spot halfway down the ice-covered mountains on the cutaway map. "To create a big avalanche, you'll have to aim here. It's the only way . . . However, it will be really hard to land your shots in the right place. See what I mean?"

"Yes, sir!"

Tajima looked silently at the faces of the other pilots and said, "You're going to have to fly to right here, release your bombs, then lift the nose of your plane in a steep rise parallel to the mountain slope . . . The greatest danger will be Godzilla's white-hot ray. The second thing you'll need to watch for will be after you fire the rockets and are pulling upward. You'll have to be super careful you don't hit the top of the peak . . . It'll take superhuman agility to clear both hurdles. But this is our only choice. We need a win here! . . . Got it?"

"Yes, sir."

Tajima stared at the other pilots again.

Right then, another member of the squadron ran in and bowed to Terazawa. "Sir, the rockets have been loaded onto the jets."

"Good. Well then, men, you're off!" Terazawa gave his order, and the entire crew dashed outside.

Tajima turned to Terazawa, saying, "I'll be back, sir!"

Just as Tajima was readying to go, Tsukioka rushed up and pleaded, "Tajima, please, take me with you! I hate to ask you again, but please, let me help you! Please!"

Seeing the determination in Tsukioka's eyes, Tajima was at a loss for a moment, but then he turned to beseech Captain Terazawa. "Godzilla killed Kobayashi . . . But not just that. He's taken so many precious lives and destroyed so much valuable property. That hateful monster! Please, sir, let us get him! . . . Captain, we beg you."

For a moment, Terazawa didn't seem to know what to say, but then he spoke. "Tsukioka, you'll be putting your life in danger!"

"I'm aware, sir!"

"Fine. Then you can go too, Tsukioka." Terazawa grabbed Tsukioka's hand and gave it a firm squeeze.

By that point, back on Kamiko Island, Godzilla had managed to claw more than halfway out of the avalanche. His top half was sticking out of the ice and snow, and he let out a continuous series of howls.

Ikeda and the other members of the Self-Defense Forces had made landfall with the amphibious landers, and one after another, they were busily carrying out the drums of gasoline. They hurriedly stacked them one by one in a row. The plan was to try to block Godzilla's path to the sea with a wall of fire.

Godzilla continued to try to knock down the wall of ice holding him in. By this point, much of his body was visible. With each passing moment, things were becoming more dangerous for the workers stacking the gasoline drums.

"Hey, hurry up! Who knows how long it'll be before Godzilla gets free and pounces on us!"

All the men were working frantically. Ikeda looked up into the air and whispered, "Man, I wish the squadron would get here fast . . ."

Right then, there was a tremendous noise of something falling.

Godzilla had broken free of the wall of ice, and it came tumbling down below him. He lifted his colossal body high into the air.

"Watch out! All men aboard!!" No sooner did the men hear the order than they all rushed toward the amphibious landers.

It took only a fraction of a second for Godzilla to step over what was left of the wall created by the avalanche, and he squashed one of the soldiers underfoot. As if proud of himself, Godzilla made a loud *GRAAAAAWR!*

Ikeda shouted, "Take the landers out!!" The amphibious landers started kicking up a trail of white waves as they sped away from the island.

Now that Godzilla had crossed the wall of the avalanche, he headed toward the bay. Right then, a plane that had been circling overhead and observing him made a turn and started a nosedive that took him right in front of the monster. For a split second, Godzilla flinched!

"Ready! Fire!!" As Ikeda shouted the orders, the machine guns on the amphibious landers opened fire. *Rat-tat-tat-tat-tat-tat* . . .

The gunfire rained down on the drums of gasoline. *KA-BAM! KA-POW!* The drums exploded one after the next. The gasoline poured out, covering everything. The flames spread instantly, leaving the entire place engulfed in terrifying, ferocious flames.

Seeing the conflagration, Godzilla grew increasingly violent and started stepping into them; however, he didn't get far before turning back in the direction from which he had come. He seemed unable to break through the wall of flames that burned between him and his destination.

The gasoline burned even higher. The heat caused small avalanches to come tumbling down from the surrounding ice-covered cliffs, blocking Godzilla's path.

"What are those darn planes doing? Hope they get here soon! The fire's only going to last another three minutes or so." Ikeda looked up at the sky through his binoculars. "Wait, there they are!"

"Is that them?" A wave of joy washed over the men in the landers.

In one corner of the sky was Tajima's jet followed by four other planes.

No sooner did the planes start banking above the island than Tajima's plane's wings tilted a little to the left, then to the right. The planes were moving into single file. Ikeda and the others down in the landers stared up at them, unable to tear their eyes away. The planes were entering an attack formation.

As Tajima entered into a sharp nosedive, Godzilla's angry face grew bigger and bigger in Tajima's windshield.

Suddenly, the monster began shooting out his ray of white-hot light! Managing to skillfully fly around Godzilla's beam, Tajima fired his rockets toward a spot halfway down the mountain.

In an instant, the icy mountainside came rushing toward the plane. Tajima quickly rolled the plane onto its side, just barely missing the mountain peak. The plane nearly grazed it while dancing upward into the vast heavens.

Making a large arc in the air, Tajima glanced back. With a thunderous sound, followed by a loud echo, an enormous avalanche poured down the mountainside, headed right for Godzilla. "There we go! That's it!"

"Plane No. 2, ready the attack!"

The soldiers on the landers raised a shout of joy. Following orders, the pilot of the second plane flew in for the attack.

Godzilla had wriggled halfway free. In his anger, he once again spat out another beam of white-hot light. The second jet burst into a ball of flame, and with a loud bang, it exploded in midair.

But what should happen next? The plane had managed to fire off its rockets during its last moments. They flew straight into the mountainside, creating another avalanche even bigger than the last. An incredible score!

Snow and ice poured down on Godzilla. Once again, he struggled to break free. Roaring, he spat out more white-hot light. Each time he did, some of the snow and ice fell away from his body, tumbling downward.

"Darn it!!" Ikeda and the others on the landers gritted their teeth. The third jet was closing in for its run. "Come on now! Be careful!"

Godzilla swung his huge hand at the third plane. Meanwhile, the plane used the opening to shoot its rockets into the mountainside behind him. As the plane started its rapid ascent, it slammed into the mountain peak. *KA-BOOM!* The third jet exploded into a shower of debris.

The soldiers in the landers looked up in astonishment, as the fourth jet readied its attack position.

"Careful, careful!" The soldiers' shouts weren't just encouragement; they also contained a prayer.

"Darn it! Here we go!!" In the pilot's seat was Tsukioka, tightly gripping the jet's steering column. He flew straight at Godzilla, who was struggling to raise his head from the ice. The monster was roaring again ferociously.

Godzilla's face expanded to fill Tsukioka's vision as he approached. The monster frantically spat out a beam of white-hot light. It was like a scene right out of hell.

Tsukioka managed to skillfully dodge the deadly ray. He firmly pressed the button to launch his weapons. *Whooosh!*—the rockets shot out of the wings on both sides of his plane, leaving white trails of smoke in their wake. The glittering, icy mountainsides rushed ominously toward the windshield.

Tsukioka pulled on the steering column with all his might. The plane shot quickly upward, letting forth a disconcerting rattle as the plane just barely missed the peak.

"Wow!" The troops below let out a cheer. At the same moment, there was an avalanche so great that it seemed to shake the earth's very axis. Tsukioka's rockets had unleashed it.

The avalanche set off a series of other avalanches on the surrounding mountains. The primitive monster let forth a continuous, terrifying roar as Mother Nature buried his colossal form underneath a massive flow of ice.

The despicable monster Godzilla, who had claimed so many lives and destroyed so much valuable property, had finally disappeared at the bottom of a mountain of ice in the farthest reaches of the northern sea.

"Kobayashi . . . We finally got him. We got Godzilla!" Tsukioka's eyes began to glisten and well up.

The massive avalanche that swallowed Godzilla continued to roar, showing no signs of abating.

"Kobayashi, Tsukioka and your friends did it. They got him for you."

Back at the Hokkaido branch office, the two photos were still sitting next to one another on the radio desk. Kobayashi was chuckling in one, while in the other, the young woman with ponytails smiled innocently.

Hidemi, Yamaji, and Shibaki gazed at the photographs. They solemnly put their palms together in a gesture of prayer and, motionless, took a moment of silence.

The snow and ice continued to tumble down the slopes of Kamiko Island. In the sky above, Tsukioka's plane flew in a big curve. Was Tsukioka having a difficult time leaving the island that had claimed the life of his dear friend?

Oh, peace and comfort! Oh, light of the sun!
Hasten your return, take pity on us
Feel our sorrow as we pray
And pour our very lives into this song

The avalanche continued as if it might never end. It seemed as if perhaps nature herself were singing a song of victory.

Afterword

Translating an Icon

Jeffrey Angles

Here, as elsewhere in this book, all names appear in the English order (with surname, or "last name," last) instead of the traditional Japanese order, which puts the surnames first.

Because the monster Godzilla is one of Japan's most famous cultural exports, loved by countless fans and extensively analyzed by Japanese historians, film critics, students, and viewers all over the world, it is practically unbelievable that no one has produced an English translation of the two Godzilla novellas published in conjunction with the release of the first two films. The novella *Godzilla,* as well as the sequel *Godzilla Raids Again* (which more literally might be translated as *Godzilla Counterattacks*), were both written by Shigeru Kayama (1904–1975), the same science fiction novelist who developed the scenario for the first two Tōhō Studios films that introduced the famous monster to the world.

Because Kayama was the main architect who laid the foundations of the Godzilla story, the two novellas translated here reveal a great deal about his personal intentions and vision for the story, even though they were published around the time of the release of the second film. Indeed, these novelizations clarify some of the ideas that went into the films. Interestingly, the plot in these novellas sometimes differs slightly from what one finds in the movies, giving a sense of some of the issues Kayama personally hoped to explore with his now iconic monster.

Kayama, Man of Monsters

Before delving into the content of the novellas, a few words are in order about Kayama and his involvement with the famous films. Shigeru Kayama is the pen name of Kōji Yamada, born in 1904 in Tokyo. As a boy, he had a great love for animals, including insects, but he was particularly fascinated with lizards and reptiles. Soon before college, he read the book *Zensekaishi* (A prehistory of the world) by the Japanese paleontologist Matajirō Yokoyama, which inspired a love of dinosaurs and a fascination with their size and power. Even as he pursued a different path, studying economics at Hōsei University, he continued to read on his own about paleontology, geology, and ancient animals. In 1927, he dropped out of university without graduating, but that same year, he took a job with the Ministry of Finance, where he continued to work through the difficult years of World War II.

In his thirties, Kayama experimented with writing tanka poetry; in fact, among his earliest publications were some poems published in the journal *Sōsei* (The public) in 1940. However, it was in 1947, two years after the end of the war, that he submitted what would become his first published short story, a three-part story called "Oran pendeku no fukushū" (The revenge of Orang Pendek), to the journal *Hōseki* (Jewels), which was having a contest with a cash prize for new writers. This journal would rapidly become one of the most important and influential mystery magazines in postwar Japan, incubating the careers of numerous important writers, including Kayama, whose story was one of seven selected out of approximately two hundred entries for publication. Interestingly, this first story reflected the author's interest in the natural world and drew upon a myth about a mysterious, mythological creature who, like Kayama's later creation Godzilla, lived most of its life hidden from humankind.

This success kickstarted Kayama's career, and in 1948, he won the inaugural Detective Mystery Club's New Writer's Award for his second story, "Kaimansō kidan" (The strange tale of Sea Eel Estate). In 1949, soon on the heels of these two successes, he left his position in government to become a full-time author. Literary historian Kawatarō Nakajima has commented that Kayama quickly became a sensation, publishing stories with astounding speed. In 1948 alone, Kayama published a jaw-dropping total of forty-four pieces of writing, and in 1949, he published another thirty-seven.[1] Over the next few decades, he would write hundreds more short stories and novels, many of which used elements gleaned from biology, paleontology, and other branches of the natural sciences to enrich Kayama's plots full of mystery, detection, and adventure. The collection of his complete works published between 1993 and 1997 by the publisher San'ichi Shobō stretches to fifteen thick volumes, and many of his most famous short stories are widely available in various print and digital editions.[2] Many of these, including the Godzilla novellas translated here, were written primarily with young audiences in mind, although his work still has an adult following today, especially among science fiction and mystery fans.

While mystery, science fiction, and adventure might seem to modern American audiences like profoundly dissimilar genres involving different expectations and ideas, this was not necessarily the case in midcentury Japan. For instance, if one looks at the wildly popular stories written by the seminal mystery novelist Ranpo Edogawa (1894–1965), one finds a blurring of genres—science, adventure, ratiocination, and even the supernatural collide in just about every story. (Incidentally, Ranpo, whose full pen name is "Edogawa Ranpo" in the Japanese order, modeled his pen name after the American writer Edgar Allan Poe and served as a key figure in the history of Japanese mystery fiction. He even served as a founding force behind the magazine *Hōseki,* where Kayama published his first stories.)

It was in 1954 when Kayama was at the height of his fame that Tōhō Studios called upon him to work with them on a movie. In midcentury Japan, screenplays were almost never the product of a single individual. Instead, multiple people would work together with a studio, collaborating, brainstorming, and repeatedly revising until ideas took concrete form as a screenplay. It is, therefore, an exaggeration to describe the Godzilla story as solely Kayama's invention; however, he did develop a vague idea from a forty-four-year-old Tōhō movie producer into a concrete story, which others then produced as the famous film. Even though most discussions of the monster's history, especially in English-language scholarship, credit director Ishirō Honda (1911–1993) and his special effects director Eiji Tsuburaya (1901–1970) as Godzilla's primary creators, the story of Godzilla's birth is woefully incomplete unless one considers Kayama's critically important contribution.

Godzilla, Child of Nuclear Anxiety

The inspiration for the film came in early 1954. Tōhō producer Tomoyuki Tanaka (1910–1997) was in Indonesia, planning a big-budget film about a Japanese soldier who fell in love with a half-Indonesian girl and fought in the Indonesian War of Independence.[3] Unfortunately for him but luckily for future Godzilla fans, Indonesian officials suddenly withdrew permission, apparently due to rising political tensions at the national level, leaving Tanaka with the need to come up with a new, attention-grabbing project as quickly as possible.

As he fretted on the flight back to Japan in April 1954, he came across an article in a Japanese movie magazine about *The Beast from 20,000 Fathoms*, an American smash-hit film from 1953 based on a 1951 Ray Bradbury story called "The Fog Horn." This film was, in turn, inspired by the film *King Kong*, which was finished in 1933 but rereleased in 1952 by RKO. This rerelease, which cost the company little, grossed more money than all of the previous releases of *King Kong* combined, making it clear to movie producers that films about big monsters could be extremely profitable.[4] In *The Beast from 20,000 Fathoms*, an atomic bomb test in the Arctic Circle awakens a hibernating dinosaur trapped below the ice. Now awake and angry, the beast makes his way down the east coast of North America, destroying buildings, killing, and terrorizing along the way. The monster's goal is the ancient breeding grounds of the Hudson River by New York City, where fossils of his species had also been found. He comes aground in the city, causing panic and destruction both by his brute force and the ancient contagion released from his blood. Finally, in a climactic scene at Coney Island, the monster is killed by more atomic science—this time, a radioactive isotope fired into his neck from the top of a roller coaster.

Intrigued by this story, Tanaka realized that if he were to create a film about an ancient monster awakened by a nuclear blast, he might capitalize on the tremendous fears and concerns surrounding nuclear weapons and radioactivity in Japan—the same country that had suffered the atomic bombings of Hiroshima and Nagasaki less than a decade before. Interestingly, until that point, the mainstream Japanese population had not had much opportunity to stop and reflect upon the horrors of what had happened in those cities in 1945. During the Allied occupation of Japan, which lasted from 1945 until 1952, the Civil Censorship Detachment of the Supreme Commander for the Allied Powers (SCAP) hired a large number of Japanese citizens to create a censorship system that would examine everything published in Japan, which as scholar Jay Rubin has noted, included "newspapers, books, magazines, radio and theatrical scripts, movie scenarios, even pamphlets of clubs and professional societies," plus sometimes even mail and telecommunications.[5] The goal was to sideline discourse that might derail or complicate Allied attempts to build a new, postwar order in Japan. The Press Code issued by SCAP in September 1945 states, "There shall be no destructive criticism of the Allied Forces of the Occupation and nothing which might invite mistrust or resentment of those troops."[6]

One subject that the SCAP authorities feared might incite the most hostility toward the occupiers was open discussion of the atomic bombings of Hiroshima and Nagasaki, especially the lingering aftereffects of radiation sickness, which were only coming to light following the war. Of course, it wasn't possible to hide the fact that the American authorities had vaporized two major cities with only two bombs—even the emperor of Japan himself mentioned this seemingly unbelievable fact in his radio broadcast of August 15, 1945, in which he announced the plan to surrender unconditionally and bring the war to the end. There, the emperor noted, "the enemy has begun to employ a new and most cruel bomb, the power of which to do damage is, indeed, incalculable, taking the toll of many innocent lives." He mentioned that unless Japan surrendered, it might lead to "an ultimate collapse and obliteration of the Japanese nation" and perhaps also "the total extinction of human civilization."[7]

Certainly, it wasn't possible to keep the atomic bombs a secret, so the Civil Censorship Detachment concentrated on trying to keep discussion of the bomb at the level of objective and scientific facts, while limiting editorial opinions and literary works about the subject.[8] In fact, they did not even allow publication of photographs of Hiroshima and Nagasaki victims until the early 1950s. One of Japan's most famous postwar poets, Rin Ishigaki (1920–2004), recalls that in August 1952, the newspaper where she worked asked her to write a poem to accompany a photograph showing a victim of the bomb blast. It was the first time she had ever seen a photograph of an A-bomb victim, and she recalled that "both the union official who ordered me to write the poem and I myself were profoundly shaken. My response arose like the scream of one who cries out while being beaten."[9]

As a result of censorship, during the first years of the postwar period, there were fewer books, films, and articles about radioactivity, nuclear weapons, and their use against Japanese cities than there would have been under a freer system. As one commentator points out, until *Godzilla* came along, there were only "documentaries and sentimental movies" made about Hiroshima and Nagasaki.[10] In fact, a melodrama called *Genbaku no ko* (Children of Hiroshima) from 1952—the film Japan entered into the Cannes Film Festival as its 1953 entry—actually received criticism for not being anti-American enough. Complicating this was the fact that many directors didn't want to be associated with politics, and Japanese distributors at the time tended to shy away from films with explicit protest messages. When such films were shown, they were typically in off-the-beaten-path theaters with small promotion budgets.[11]

One should remember that during this time, many Japanese citizens were preoccupied simply with picking themselves up from the burned-out ruins of the major cities and moving forward, making new lives, trying to struggle free from the rampant hunger and black markets of the immediate postwar years. Going to see entertainment that would make them relive some of the worst moments of the war wasn't necessarily terribly appealing, and movie studios were cautious about such sensitive material. If a film were to explore concerns regarding radioactivity, it made sense for it to be at least somewhat indirect—perhaps not touching upon Hiroshima or Nagasaki directly but using some other monstrous form to represent the horrors and danger of nuclear weapons. In short, in early 1954, when Tanaka first conceived of making a film about a monster born of nuclear bombing, there had been nothing like it in Japanese film—certainly, not a big-budget, action-packed thriller on the order of *Godzilla*, which puts concerns about nuclear weapons and lingering radioactivity at the center of the plot.

Concern about radioactivity had reached new heights among the Japanese population earlier that same year, right around the time that Tanaka was cooking up the idea for a monster film. On March 1, 1954, a group of Japanese fishermen on a boat named the *Dai-go Fukuryū-maru* (*Lucky Dragon No. 5*) were accidentally caught in the path of the Castle Bravo hydrogen bomb tests in the Bikini Atoll (now part of the Marshall Islands). Although they were ninety miles to the east of ground zero, all twenty-two members fell severely ill with radiation poisoning, and one, Aikichi Kuboyama (1914–1954), died within months. This disaster, which critics described as America's third time using an atom bomb against Japan, became front-page news in Japan and severely complicated Japan's relationship with America.[12]

In the ensuing investigation, scientists discovered that tuna irradiated by this and other American hydrogen bomb tests in the Pacific were making their way to Japanese markets and into stomachs. Not only did this shocking discovery lead to a tuna boycott and give new strength to the antinuclear movement, it also drove home the continued danger of nuclear weapons. The accident showed the Japanese population that even in peacetime, even when decisions about nuclear policy were being made far from Japanese shores, Japan still suffered radioactivity's negative effects. No one was safe, no matter where they lived, and so it is not surprising that Tanaka would capitalize on this anxiety to create a film that gave Japan's nuclear anxiety concrete physical form.

Kayama's Scenario

In mid-May 1954, a little more than two months after the *Lucky Dragon* incident, Tanaka pitched to Tōhō Studios his idea for a monster movie, which he tentatively called *Kaitei ni-man mairu kara kita dai kaijū* (The giant monster from 20,000 miles under the sea)—a title that clearly reveals how much inspiration he derived from the American film *The Beast from 20,000 Fathoms.* After getting the green light, he rushed to Kayama's home in Tokyo. Tanaka was a fan of Kayama's work and excitedly urged him to develop the idea into a movie scenario.

Kayama eagerly accepted, and within the short time frame of one week, he delivered the scenario on May 25, 1954. This scenario, called the "G-sakuhin kentō-yō daihon," became the basis for the film. (Literally, this means "script for the purposes of consideration for the work G," but English sources usually describe the scenario simply as the "G-Project.")[13] Kayama's scenario has been described as creating "the entire foundation for the film; in broad terms, the plot, characters, themes, and structure of his writing would remain intact in the final cut."[14] In the scenario, Kayama drew upon ideas in *The Beast from 20,000 Fathoms* as well as a story he had written earlier about a giant lizard that walked on its hind legs.[15]

In an interview published in October 1954, around the time of the release of the film, Kayama stated that in writing the scenario, "I wanted to try to throw myself to the best of my ability into my own form of resistance against nuclear weapons."[16] To that end, Kayama came up with the idea to put a key scene right at the beginning of the film to remind viewers of the bombing of the *Lucky Dragon No. 5.* In the G-Project scenario, the references to the real history of the event are far more heavy-handed than what eventually went into the film or the novella translated in this volume. The G-Project scenario starts with an off-screen voice making the following announcement:

November XX, 1952—on this day, our planet Earth was terrorized by a fearful experiment that until that point, no one could have possibly imagined and that left the world unable to do anything but tremble in fear. The first hydrogen bomb test! It didn't involve destruction as much as outright murder. In the blink of an eye, the test site in Nirugeraabu [sic] Atoll was returned to "nothingness," and a radioactive cloud tore thirty-two miles wildly up into the stratosphere, rising like the hair of the Devil himself.

Then on March XX 1954, a new hydrogen bomb, proudly and newly completed, was tested on Enewetak Atoll.

We have not been informed about the details of that test. However, judging from the fact that the scientists in charge of the experiment described it as involving "destructive abilities beyond our wildest imagination," one cannot help but feeling one's skin crawl at the thought of its fearful power.

Can we say that fortunately, this power's range only extended to the area of the tests themselves?

No! The answer is a resounding no![17]

Perhaps the reason Kayama didn't include the exact dates was because of American government secrecy surrounding the tests, but he was correct that the first test of a hydrogen bomb, nicknamed "Ivy Mike" as part of "Operation Ivy," took place on Elugelab Island in the Enewetak Atoll in the Marshall Islands on November 1, 1952. (Kayama misspelled the name of Elugelab Island, which is just one part of the larger Enewetak Atoll.) He was incorrect in that in March 1954, the Castle Bravo test took place not on Enewetak Atoll but in an artificially enhanced part of the Bikini Atoll, located not far to the east of Enewetak. As chance would have it, the unlucky Lucky Dragon No. 5 was approximately ninety miles east of there, and around two hours after the blast, a shower of radioactive particles rained down upon them. The important point for our purposes here, however, is that Kayama originally hoped to make the Godzilla story even more direct in its condemnation of American nuclear weapons than the final film turned out to be. One sees this especially clearly in the fact that right after the off-camera speech quoted above, Kayama's scenario lists several ideas for shots for a montage that would have tied the film strongly to real historical events and fears:

- *Lucky Dragon No. 5* pulling into port, burned
- The disposal of radioactive tuna
- The unsettling faces of the harmed fishermen
- The heavily wounded patients being taken to the hospital
- Placards on May Day stating "No to Hydrogen Bombs"
- Children looking sadly at the empty nests of sparrows which did not come with their usual migration
- Paranoid men who are walking and pointing up at bats in a clear sky, fearing that they are radioactive ashes falling[18]

Tanaka took this script with all of its heavy-handed references to the *Lucky Dragon* incident and turned it over to the director Ishirō Honda and his assistant director, Takeo Murata, a talented and experienced screenwriter. Murata drafted a revised screenplay, then the two men sequestered themselves in a hotel to map out the details of individual scenes. Murata recalls, "For three weeks, we racked our brains and collaborated to turn Kayama's story into a workable screenplay."[19]

The opening scene provides an informative example of how Honda and Murata modified Kayama's scenario to fit the screen. Film historians Steve Ryfle and Ed Godziszewski have noted that Honda rewrote the scene because he "saw his monster not as an indictment of America but a symbol of a global threat."[20] Honda was worried that Kayama's G-Project scenario was too overtly political, and he and Murata toned down Kayama's criticism. Honda once stated, "Putting a real-life accident into a fictional story with a monster would not be appropriate. . . . Instead, it became a matter of . . . the feeling that I was trying to create as a director. Namely, an invisible fear."[21] As a result, Honda and Murata removed Kayama's long off-screen announcement and the proposed shots directly related to historical events—things that would put the film squarely within the territory of protest film. In the film, viewers simply see an underwater explosion destroy a boat filled with fishermen. However, this was enough for contemporary Japanese audiences in theaters in late 1954. Even if audiences didn't notice the fact the ship was labeled "No. 5," the mere sight of fishermen dying at sea from a mysterious blast immediately recalled the sensational incident that had rocked the nation earlier that year.

In public, Kayama didn't seem especially upset at the fact that Honda and Murata watered down his message. In the same October 1954 interview quoted earlier in which Kayama remarks that he wanted the G-Project scenario to serve as his own form of antinuclear activism, he states that he was writing just a "plot outline" for the film. Even though some of the most overtly antinuclear scenes were removed, he said, "I believe that my core intention was fulfilled by the character of the scientist Daisuke Serizawa"—the figure who warns viewers about the dangers that scientific developments, when unrestrained by ethics, can inflict upon humanity.[22] In a separate roundtable interview published in November 1954 when the film had been completed, Kayama comments, "As the one responsible for the creation of the story, I was really worried about what kind of film it would become; however, the film exceeded all my expectations."[23]

While Honda and Murata were developing Kayama's scenario and working with special effects director Eiji Tsuburaya, who took charge of the monster's action scenes, Tanaka visited them frequently, urging all involved to consider budgetary restraint. Some at Tōhō Studios were worried that with this science fiction monster film, they were entering new, unfamiliar territory, and no one knew if it would be a success. In fact, *Godzilla* did become the most expensive Japanese film ever produced until that point, and studio executives were on pins and needles until the release, worrying about whether it would be a financial success or sinkhole. The production budget was around 60 million yen, three times the budget of an average Japanese feature film, and advertising and prints brought the total figure to around 100 million yen.[24] Honda's wife, Kimi, recalls that after filming started, she detected constant worry in her husband's expression. "I wondered, 'Is this going to end his career as a director?' . . . And he, too, must have thought, 'God forbid if this fails.' This was considered such a bizarre idea back then."[25]

Godzilla on Screen, Take I

On June 10, 1954, Honda and Murata brought the development stage of Kayama's scenario to a close, and filming started a little more than a month later. As numerous fans and film scholars have noted, a constellation of talented individuals all contributed to the success of the film.[26] These include Eiji Tsuburaya, who directed the action scenes with the monster; Teizō Toshimitsu (1909–1982), who helped design the Godzilla costume; Akira Ifukube (1914–2006), the genius composer who wrote the unforgettable soundtrack and even came up with the sound effect for Godzilla's distinctive roar; and Masao Tamai (1908–1997), who while serving as cinematographer had the idea of using monochrome and nitrate film to give the film its distinctive noir look. One also cannot forget the prominent actor Takashi Shimura (1905–1982), who starred as Professor Yamane; the dashingly handsome newcomer Akira Takarada (1934–2022), who stole the show with his performance of Ogata; the beautiful actress

Momoko Kōchi (1932–1998), whose tears as the character Emiko created a strong sense of urgency; the handsome Akihiko Hirata (1927–1984), who starred as the sullen scientist Serizawa; and actor Haruo Nakajima (1929–2017), who developed a method to make the monster's movements look relatively believable from inside the exhaustingly hot, heavy, clumsy Godzilla suit.

When Kayama first saw the completed film on October 25, 1954, during a private celebration and screening of the film at Tōhō Studios, he was deeply moved.[27] After the Oxygen Destroyer kills Godzilla at the end of the film, Kayama was said to have remained in his seat, silently weeping. Soon afterward, an event was held at the Takarazuka Theater in Asakusa, Tokyo, to share the film with the media, and again, Kayama wept. Special effects director Tsuburaya said that Kayama was so pleased with the quality of the film after this showing that he invited the whole staff to come to the seaside resort of Atami for an overnight celebration. The film was released in Nagoya in October 27, 1954, and nationwide (including Tokyo) on November 3. Only about half a year had elapsed since Tanaka had found the initial inspiration for the film on his flight home from Indonesia—an astonishingly quick turnaround for what turned out to be such an ambitious, innovative, and influential project.

Despite the studio's concerns about the cost of the film, it was a tremendous financial success. When the film opened in Tokyo, it sold out the Nichigeki Theater in the Ginza (a building that Godzilla conspicuously destroys in the film), and long lines of moviegoers waited for hours to get tickets. It set a record for a Tōhō film, with around thirty-three thousand tickets sold around the capital on opening day alone. According to the film magazine *Kinema junpō*, it earned 183 million yen in theaters, becoming the eighth-highest grossing Japanese film of 1954.[28] Soon afterward, Tōhō Studios sold the rights to producers in Hollywood, who chopped up Honda's original and spliced in new scenes with actor

Raymond Burr playing an American journalist in Tokyo. Incidentally, Tōhō sold the film rights for somewhere between $20,000 and $25,000, but the American theater run brought in $2 million, netting a handsome profit for the American producers.[29]

Although reception of the original Japanese version was mixed among Japanese film and newspaper critics, the film spoke both to children, who were thrilled by the monster scenes, as well as adult audiences, who witnessed Godzilla's destructive rampage and recalled, sometimes with emotional distress, their own experiences surviving World War II. Godzilla's destruction of Tokyo couldn't help but remind viewers that not just Hiroshima and Nagasaki but nearly all of Japan's major cities had been destroyed in Allied air raids. In fact, the firebombing of Tokyo on March 9–10, 1945, was the most destructive single bombing raid in human history, killing perhaps as many as one hundred thousand people in a single night—more than the total number of people who died in Hiroshima both from the immediate bombing and subsequent radiation poisoning. One viewer, the mystery novelist Jō Masayuki, remarked in a roundtable interview with Kayama, "The parts where Godzilla destroys Tokyo are really vivid. . . . They recall the war devastation, and make you feel like old wounds are being exposed again."[30] As historian Yoshikuni Igarashi has pointed out, in the film, "the United States returns as an enemy—albeit an unnamed one—through the figure of Godzilla, invoking memories of the war."[31] One scene in which the director Honda and his assistant director Murata poignantly evoke these memories comes when a doctor with a Geiger counter discovers a young child contaminated by Godzilla's radiation. Although the words *Hiroshima* or *Nagasaki* are never mentioned, no audience in 1954 could see this scene without thinking of the horrifying, lingering aftereffects of the American atomic bombings, which left victims, including innocent civilians and children, suffering for years.

Soon after, when Ogata and Emiko go to Serizawa to plead for his help, they happen to see a national television broadcast, which shows a girls' choir singing a prayer for peace. (The lyrics for this now-famous song come from Kayama's original scenario and are set to music written by soundtrack composer Akira Ifukube.) As critic Mark Anderson points out, this scene uses the medium of television, which was still fairly new in Japan at the time, to unite the nation.[32] It brings together a series of shots that transcend the kind of limited perception that would have resulted if the camera had only followed an individual character. By showing televised images in the frame of a television set, the director puts the movie-going audience in the same position as the characters in the film watching the broadcast, and for a moment, all share the same perspective. Through this clever visual alignment between the film's characters, the national audience watching the TV broadcast, and the audience watching in movie theaters in 1954, the directors establish a mood of grief shared both inside and outside the world of the film. Within the film, it moves the characters Emiko and Serizawa to the point of tears; it serves as a turning point, convincing Serizawa that he has no choice but to use his weapon for the good of the nation. Outside the film, this scene also profoundly moved moviegoers and became one of the most frequently remembered moments in the plot.

In short, *Godzilla* was not only an exciting and dramatic film, it was also purposefully constructed in a way that allowed the Japanese to reflect on their recent past and traumas. It gave the Japanese population an opportunity to grieve and experience emotional catharsis—something that might not have been possible just a few years earlier when so many people were struggling just to pick their lives back up and get by. Scholar William Tsutsui has mentioned that for adult Japanese viewers at the time, watching the film "was a gut-wrenching experience. And yet it was also cathartic in many ways. It captured in a very accessible, visceral way something that no graphs or charts or statistics could ever show."[33]

Godzilla on Screen, Take 2

Given the commercial success of the first film, Tanaka at Tōhō Studios wanted to strike again while the iron was hot. He quickly approached Kayama about writing a sequel that could capitalize on *Godzilla*'s success. The result was the rapidly produced sequel *Gojira no gyakushū*, known in English as *Godzilla Raids Again*, although a more accurate translation might be "Godzilla Counterattacks," since most of the work is about a second "Godzilla" reacting to attacks from another prehistoric monster. The director was not Honda but Motoyoshi Oda, a director who has been described as bringing a "more action-oriented approach" to the sequel.[34]

Once again, Tanaka turned to Kayama for a scenario, and Tōhō Studios paid for him to sequester at a seaside, hot-spring resort in Atami for one week to work on it intensively. In an essay published in March 1955, a little more than a month before the opening of the film sequel, Kayama comments, "If you stop to think about it, this was a tremendously difficult task. Even if you *don't* stop to think about it, you'll realize it was just about impossible."[35] The reason was that at the end of the first installment of the Godzilla film series, the Oxygen Destroyer definitively kills the monster, so how could the monster be resurrected? Kayama was worried that unless he buckled down and came up with something good, the film would end up a miserable failure.[36]

As he jumped into the hot-spring bath on the first day of his stay at the resort, an idea came to him: he would build upon Professor Yamane's comments at the end of the first film. There, he said that if nuclear tests continued, another Godzilla might come along. That is precisely what happens in the sequel; a second creature of the same species emerges and behaves just as destructively as the first. Also, he decided to write in a second monster, Anguirus. This addition not only complicated the story but also permitted a different kind of exciting action scene with two monsters pitted against one another. This time, Kayama shifted the backdrop to Osaka, Japan's second largest city at the time, thus giving the viewing audience a vicarious thrill in seeing another major metropolis destroyed on screen.

In his 1955 essay, Kayama admits he had difficulty thinking of an end to the sequel. It didn't make sense to come up with another "exceedingly convenient solution" like the Oxygen Destroyer. The answer didn't come to him until two days after the scenario was due. He states that he had tied a towel around his head and spent all night awake thinking. Tokyo was celebrating the Christmas holiday, and as he imagined his friends drinking champagne and partying, his anger at Godzilla mounted. As a chilly dawn was breaking, he hit upon the idea of killing this frustrating, second Godzilla by burying him in an avalanche.[37]

The sequel appeared in theaters in April 1955, around half a year after the release of the original 1954 film—a quick turnaround nearly unthinkable by contemporary standards. The sequel didn't provide quite the same fresh shock to viewers as the original film, which was so unprecedented. Moreover, since the solution did not involve defeating Godzilla through advanced technology, the sequel did not raise the same questions implicit in the first film about the ethical responsibilities of scientists—in fact, one clear message of the first film was that scientists need to ensure that technological developments are never perverted toward destructive ends. Moreover, military defense helps solve the problem of the second Godzilla, whereas in the first film, the military was completely ineffective. Clearly, the second film had moved away from Kayama's initial eagerness to raise questions about the ethics of science, the use of weapons of mass destruction, and the military's ability to protect the nation from nuclear contaminants.

In an essay published in December 1955, a half year after the film came out in theaters, Kayama published an essay called "*Gojira* zange" (Godzilla confessions), in which he expresses doubts about the direction the Godzilla franchise was taking. He recalls something that happened one day when he was in a dentist's office. A child near him happened across an image of an ancient creature in a *Life* magazine and began excitedly shouting, "It's Godzilla! Godzilla!"[38] Kayama realized that in the eyes of children, any creature from the geological past that looked like a reptile had become a "Godzilla" or "Anguirus." He notes that what had started as a symbol representing his fear of atomic weapons had morphed into a character with a "manga-like appeal" that the viewing audience loved.[39] He comments that in theaters, many people would smile or even laugh when Godzilla would come on the screen, and viewers sympathized with Godzilla at the end of the second film as he dies.

Clearly, Kayama's story about a monster who embodies the nation's nuclear anxiety had morphed into something else. He therefore states, "*Godzilla Raids Again* will be the last for me. No matter how much the movie companies might request it, I have firmly decided I will not write another sequel, no matter what."[40] In his eyes, allowing the monster to live represented a tacit approval of the hydrogen bomb. Plus, he admits, even he had started to feel affectionate toward Godzilla.

Godzilla in Written Form

As this essay from late 1955 shows, Kayama thought the franchise was moving away from his original intentions, especially with the second film. It is unclear exactly when these doubts began to emerge, but it is likely he was already feeling them in 1954 when he helped to create a radio drama based on the film, and in July 1955 when he published the novelized versions of the story translated in this volume.

Although nowadays people think of *Godzilla* foremost as a cinematic phenomenon, even before the release of the first film, the

Japanese public had the opportunity to encounter Godzilla in another form. From July 17 to September 25, 1954, the broadcasting service Nippon Hōsō aired an eleven-installment radio version of the Godzilla story, and in early October 1954, even before Kayama saw his first private screening of the film, the publisher Iwaya Shoten published the radio drama as a stand-alone book titled *Kaijū Gojira* (Godzilla, the kaiju). Although Kayama's name appears as the sole author on the cover, the main author was actually Shirō Horie (1913–2009), who at the time was the head of the Tōhō Literary Arts Division and served as a writer, producing radio dramas and other literary works for Tōhō Studios under the pen name Bin Tatsuno. Horie wrote the radio drama version, while enlisting the help of mystery novelist Sango Nagase (1902–1990) in arranging the text, and then when that was complete, they showed the drama to Kayama, who put on the finishing touches and gave final approval.[41] Through this radio enactment, Tōhō was clearly attempting to generate interest in the Godzilla story in advance of the national release of the film in late October, and judging from the tremendous sales of the film on opening day, the strategy seems to have worked.

It is interesting to note that unlike the film version, the radio drama does not tone down Kayama's heavy-handed remarks that appear at the opening of the G-Project scenario, leaving the story tied more closely to actual historical events than the final film would be. In fact, Horie included verbatim the long introductory passage from the G-Project scenario quoted earlier, changing only the incorrect spelling of the place-name "Elugelab." As a result, radio listeners were reminded that the nuclear terror depicted in the story did spring from actual historical events. As mentioned earlier, Kayama had included in the G-Project scenario a list of shots of real events to be included as part of a montage that would remind viewers of Japan's all-too-real nuclear anxieties. The radio drama, however, skips right to the action of the story after the introductory speech. Listeners hear Emiko (who is working at Tokyo Bay Salvage in this version) pick up a telephone call for Ogata (who is the president of the company), and in the ensuing conversation, listeners learn about the destruction of the fishing boat *Eikō-maru*.[42]

Although there are numerous small differences between the radio drama and the Tōhō film, one of the more significant ones has to do with the ending. After Godzilla has been killed in the familiar film version, Ogata weeps with Emiko about Serizawa's death, and Professor Yamane closes the film with a somber warning that if nuclear testing continues, then another Godzilla may one day appear somewhere in the world. In the radio drama, however, Yamane is far less involved in the plan to use the Oxygen Destroyer. In fact, as Ogata and Serizawa are about ready to board the boat to deploy the weapon, Yamane appears out of nowhere, telling them that even though he doesn't know what new scientific force Serizawa is releasing with his invention, he doubts that it will kill Godzilla. When Emiko tries to argue on Ogata's behalf, Yamane hushes her with a rather misogynistic dismissal, but she refuses to be silenced, throwing her support behind Ogata and Serizawa's plan. When Yamane objects that the monster will be liquified, thus denying science a chance to study it, Ogata urges Yamane to abandon his strong curiosity as a paleontologist and instead prioritize the survival of humanity. With Yamane still objecting, Ogata and Emiko drive away, leaving Yamane running after them. As a result, Yamane is not in the final scenes at all.

Instead of having Yamane deliver a warning at the end, the radio drama leaves listeners with a message about the ethical imperatives of science. In the final scenes, as the sailors discover that Serizawa has cut his breathing tube and killed himself underwater with Godzilla, Ogawa recognizes that Serizawa had come to the conclusion that he could not trust humanity with his potentially dangerous weapon and decided to sacrifice his life. Addressing the absent Serizawa directly, Ogata remarks, "Through your actions, you brought us peace . . . Putting your life on the line, you fought for peace . . . Thank you, Serizawa . . . But will the crisis that humanity has brought about end with this? I don't know. Who knows, maybe a second Godzilla might appear one day . . . With your life sacrificed for us, we will likely have to fight again . . . Thank you, Serizawa . . ."[43] After these words, listeners hear the words of the chorus once again, and the radio drama draws to a close.

This version of the story ends with the world of science not coming to any consensus regarding its ethical responsibilities. Yamane objects to the destruction of a life-form that could provide possibilities for research, even if keeping Godzilla alive might lead to the loss of more life along the way. In this way, Yamane prioritizes short-term gains while ignoring larger collateral costs, not unlike Robert Oppenheimer and the others who prioritized the production of atomic weaponry while leaving aside questions about the potential long-term human and environmental costs. Serizawa, however, comes to the more humanistic conclusion that it is better to sacrifice possibilities for scientific learning if they could cause harm.

In 1955, Kayama published the two novellas translated in this volume in a single book as the first volume in a series for young adult readers titled "Shōnen Bunko" (Youth library) released by Shimamura Shuppan, Ltd. Since then, these novellas have been republished numerous times by different publishers, and currently, they are most widely available in an inexpensive paperback edition from publisher Chikuma Shobō. It is easy to assume that Kayama was simply trying to make money by developing his scenarios and the radio drama into novellas that were sure to sell, given the popularity of the first film, which had already been out for several months. However, by retelling the story in his own way, Kayama was taking the opportunity to present the public with his own, personal vision of the story, independent of the other forces at

Tōhō Studios that had shaped other versions. If one compares the films and the novellas carefully, it is clear Kayama used the films as a reference point when writing his novellas. In fact, numerous passages describe the scenes as if one is looking through a movie camera. For instance, in the battle between Godzilla and Anguirus in the second novella, Kayama carefully describes the two kaiju in the foreground as the keep of Osaka Castle rises dramatically behind them. In fact, the novellas generally follow the films more closely than the original G-Project scenario submitted to Tanaka in mid-1954, no doubt because readers who had seen the movie would have been upset if Kayama had diverged too radically from the film plot.

On the other hand, however, it is clear Kayama wanted to use the novellas to reassert his antinuclear message. In place of the introductory message that Honda and Murata had removed from the G-Project scenario but that had resurfaced in the radio drama, Kayama starts the novella with an author's introduction that categorically states that nuclear weapons "have taken on the form of Godzilla in this story." By proclaiming that he wrote the book as a concerned participant of the antinuclear movement, he shows young readers that his intention wasn't to create a cute and lovable monster; he was using the monster as a stand-in to depict his fear and distrust of nuclear weapons and radioactivity. In other words, we see hints that Kayama was already doubting whether his monster had effectively conveyed his nuclear anxiety and ethical concerns.

Given these doubts, it is interesting that in the novella, perhaps even slightly more than in the film, Kayama emphasizes the double-sidedness of the monster. Godzilla is not just a perpetrator of nuclear violence with white-hot, radioactive breath. Godzilla is also a victim of the bomb, awakened from underwater solitude by a hydrogen bomb that destroys the monster's natural habitat. Professor Yamane categorically states to the Diet investigatory committee, "Recent hydrogen bomb tests must have destroyed Godzilla's habitat. Let me be clear. Damage from the H-bomb tests seems to be what drove him from the home where he had been living in relative peace up until now . . ." Godzilla's destructive rampage against the homes of others is revenge for the destruction against the monster's own home. To put it in extreme terms, one might see Godzilla as an angry environmentalist who engages in guerilla-style warfare against human society, which through its inertia sits back and passively allows destruction of the natural world. In this sense, the story of Godzilla has a renewed significance in the Anthropocene, when human activity is rapidly changing the earth's environment, causing rapid climate change and mass extinctions of all types of wildlife. Godzilla reminds us that nature will fight back in ways humanity cannot possibly predict from the onset.

While Godzilla is also a victim in the film, it is easy for viewers to lose track of this idea in the dramatic, extended, carefully filmed scenes of Godzilla's violent rampage through Tokyo, where the monster acts primarily as victimizer. In the novella, Kayama repeatedly reminds readers of Godzilla's victimhood, especially in the heated discussion between Shinkichi and Yamane in the chapter "Koroshite wa naranai" (We mustn't kill). It is also significant that in that chapter, Kayama has Yamane refer to Japan's aggression during World War II when he states, "We Japanese have caused a great deal of trouble to people throughout the world. Carrying out this research [on Godzilla's amazing vitality] is our one and only chance to make reparations for all that." As a writer with leftist tendencies who regretted Japan's wartime actions, Kayama is underlining his main message, namely that scientific research must be guided by humanistic and ethical principles, and this represents the main way Japan can give back to the world and restore its image after its ethical wrongdoing during World War II.

At multiple places in the novellas, Kayama emphasizes that

trauma was the reason for Godzilla's rampage, especially in the second novella when we read that the flares dropped to lure the second Godzilla away from Osaka evoked the monster's memories of the hydrogen blasts. Certainly, these passages underline Godzilla's victimhood once again, but at the same time, the text also implicitly reflects the dangerous, new logic of warfare that quickly took hold at the beginning of the Cold War. As the United States and the USSR developed bigger and more terrifying weapons, the two settled on the logic of deterrence through mutually assured destruction. Each country felt that the only way of deterring the other was to develop ever bigger, more terrifying nuclear bombs that would make the threat of annihilation so great that the other side would never dare to use their weapons. However, in having a traumatic blast awaken an even greater threat to humanity in the story, Kayama's narrative points out the absurdity of this Cold War system—nuclear weapons can only beget more terror and destruction.

Interestingly, there are several places, especially in the first novella, where Kayama has reshaped the story significantly. One of the most obvious changes is that in the first novella, Kayama has demoted Ogata, the main protagonist of the film and the radio drama, to the relatively insignificant position of a side character. In the film, he appears to be around the same age as his love interest, Emiko, and is significantly older than Shinkichi, who serves as his adolescent sidekick and guide to Ōdo Island. (Kayama's original 1954 G-Project scenario suggests Ogata should be thirty years old, and Emiko, twenty-two—ages that a 1950s public in Japan would have found particularly suitable for a young, heterosexual couple.) In the 1955 novella, however, the action is refocused on Shinkichi, who appears to be in his late teenage years or perhaps around twenty. He has already left his home on Ōdo Island, is working full-time in Tokyo, and is of an appropriate age to become Emiko's primary love interest. The novella even invents a backstory, telling us that they became fast friends when they were evacuated together to the mountains of central Japan during the final years of World War II.

The most obvious explanation why Kayama made Shinkichi the protagonist is that young adult readers of the "Youth Library" would more likely identify with a protagonist closer to their age; however, there appears also to be something deeper at work. The film version involves a love triangle between the dashingly handsome Ogata, the beautiful Emiko, and the sullen, withdrawn scientist Dr. Serizawa, who has scars on his face and wears an eyepatch—a not-so-subtle suggestion he was likely wounded during the war. In fact, some have used this to speculate that as a researcher who was active during the war and clearly doesn't shy from "dangerous" science, Dr. Serizawa may have been working during the war on some nefarious project, such as the medical experiments carried out in Unit 731 in Manchuria or the development of weapons of mass destruction. (Nothing in the film or novella explicitly supports nor contradicts this.) Similarly, both the film and novella note that German scientists are the ones who seem to know most about Dr. Serizawa's current, potentially apocalyptic research—a small detail that seems to have no clear purpose other than to remind readers of the perverted use of German science for mass murder during the Holocaust.

By eliminating the film's love conflict between Ogata and Serizawa, two members of the wartime generation, and refocusing instead on the younger Shinkichi, Kayama shifts the story away from those men who were physically and psychologically wounded by the war and who waffle regarding their ethical responsibilities, and instead he turns his attention to a younger man with values forged during the peaceful, postwar rebuilding of Japan. In the novella, Shinkichi has greater ethical clarity than Serizawa, who clearly recognizes the danger of his research but refuses to abandon it entirely. (Of course, Serizawa does eventually redeem himself at the end, sacrificing himself so that he can take the mystery of the Oxygen Destroyer to the grave.) But before Shinkichi learns about the Oxygen Destroyer in the novella, he insists to Professor Yamane that responsible citizens must do what they can to help family and eliminate threats to the nation, even if it means forgoing certain potential scientific benefits. Shinkichi ultimately gains the upper hand by reminding Yamane, "If anything, Godzilla himself is the hydrogen bomb hanging over Japan right now!" Kayama appears to be implicitly suggesting here that humanitarian values, especially when coming from the postwar generation, will be what Japan needs to guide the country through its ethical dilemmas, which only grow more complicated when danger is in the air. Although Serizawa does eventually do the right thing, scientists, Kayama seems to suggest, cannot always be trusted since they are often too close to their work to have a clear moral compass. By contrast, Shinkichi appears as an ideal postwar citizen—hard-working, idealistic, and motivated by concern for his family, loved ones, and country. No doubt Kayama felt that this kind of moral clarity, especially when it came to weapons of mass destruction, was necessary as Japan found itself trapped between nuclear superpowers during the Cold War.

One striking addition to the first novella is the subplot about the Tokyo Godzilla Society—an addition that also revolves around moral responsibility. After Godzilla attacks, mysterious letters begin to arrive, followed by flyers posted around Tokyo, all praising the monster, treating it as a vengeful, angry god with massive destructive powers. One wonders if Kayama drew his inspiration for this part of the plot from King Kong—the early 1933 ancestor of kaiju films—in which an entire primitive society on Skull Island fears yet simultaneously worships the giant ape. In the novella, odd rumors circulate that Yamane, who has publicly resisted the idea of killing Godzilla, is perhaps in control of the monster, which might really be a gigantic mechanical robot. It quickly turns out, however, that the letters and posters were the work of an unscrupulous criminal with a prior record of threatening people for money and valuables.

Although the novella gives no clear explanation for the criminal's actions, it appears the so-called Tokyo Godzilla Society was the criminal's first step to manipulating and taking in the Japanese population somehow for his own personal profit. This small added subplot doesn't necessarily make a lot of sense unless one sees it as a warning from Kayama that there are always unprincipled people who will use disaster to advance their own agenda, however odd or reprehensible it might be on the surface. This was a fact that would have been obvious to anyone who lived through the immediate postwar period in Japan. By the end of the war, the systems of food production and distribution—indeed, the entire economy—had so thoroughly broken down that hunger and starvation were rampant everywhere. Black markets sprung up even in small towns, and people who had access to legitimate food products, clothing, and other necessities surreptitiously diverted them away from the official rationing system into the black markets to rake in enormous profits. The black markets were so pervasive that just about everyone who lived through the time remembers them as an unpleasant feature of immediate postwar life where greed and unscrupulous behavior were on full display.

Translating Kayama's Novellas

As the translator of these two novellas, I should conclude by saying a few words about a couple of small but significant issues that arose in translation. One thing readers will immediately notice is how often Kayama uses sounds in his writing. On nearly every page, Kayama describes at least one sound using an onomatopoeia—even relatively ordinary things such as the ringing of a phone (*brrrrrring-brrrrrring*) or the *click* of a light switch.

In fact, these onomatopoeias appear even more often in the Japanese original than in this translation because in Japanese there is a far greater set of vocabulary to represent sounds, and Japanese speakers frequently use onomatopoeias even to describe things English speakers would describe with words unrelated to sound. For instance, Kayama is particularly fond of the expression *hat-to suru*, which one might literally render "to make a '*ha*' [sound]," but I have rendered in various ways, such as "to be surprised," "to be taken aback," "to be startled," or even "to look up suddenly," depending on the context. Another common recurring word is *merimeri*, which in Japanese represents the sound of a building crumbling or a car fender crumpling. Obviously, putting the English letters *merimeri* into the text would seem odd—English readers probably would not understand at all—so in such cases, I used another sound or sometimes even an ordinary, non-sound-related word to replace it.

When Godzilla and Anguirus are rampaging, the numbers of onomatopoeias can reach levels that might seem comical to English-speaking readers. Multiple sounds—*crash, boom, rat-tat-tat, ka-pow*—come in rapid succession, spilling across the page. When I shared an early draft of this translation with a class of mine studying the Godzilla films, many students commented that the plethora of sounds reminded them of comic books and manga, which give visual representation of sound in stylized letters. While I recognize that all the onomatopoeias make this an unusually "noisy" translation, especially for English readers who might be unused to so much auditory description, the onomatopoeias helped Kayama appeal to the young readers who were his main audience, and by retaining them in this translation, I hope the book comes alive in all its clanging, crashing, booming, roaring excessiveness.

Although there were many onomatopoeias that were hard to capture in English, the most difficult had to do with the kaiju roars.

Through most of the two novellas, Godzilla's distinctive roar is represented in Japanese as グワーッ! (*Gwaaaa!*) or something similar. Since this doesn't especially look like a roar in English, I have opted for something a little more ferocious looking, such as *Gwwwaaaarrrr* or some variant thereof. I mention this because in the second novel, the newcomer Anguirus has a different roar, usually represented as ウオーッ! (*Wooooo!*) or something similar. Over the course of the long Godzilla franchise, the filmmakers at Tōhō Studios had fun coming up with different roars for their various kaiju, which became something like calling cards for the monsters—memorized, loved, and imitated by fans all over the world. Kayama clearly gave different sounds to the two kaiju, so even though my spellings of the roars might look odd to English readers, it didn't seem right to flatten them out into a single uniform *ROAR!* in English.

Another issue has to do with the transliteration of the name of the fictional island where Godzilla first appears to the world. In kanji, the name of the island is 大戸島. The subtitles of all the films, as well as all the English commentary that I have encountered, render this place-name "Ōdo Island" (or "Odo Island," without the macron that would indicate a long vowel).[44] When translating Kayama's text from the Chikuma Shobō edition published in 2004, I was surprised to find that Kayama gives the island the name Ōto, with a *T* sound instead of a *D* sound. When I checked another, earlier reprint, I again found that Kayama gave the pronunciation *Ōto*. Although the difference between the *D* and *T* sounds may not seem like a big deal, I debated long and hard about whether I should buck tradition in rendering the name of the island the conventional English way or Kayama's way. In the end, I gave way to tradition, for fear I might get stacks of angry letters from Godzilla fans assuming I got such an important detail wrong.

One final nod to English-language conventions in talking about Godzilla has to do with the gender of the monster. There is nothing anywhere in Kayama's original that indicates Godzilla's sex. Kayama's Japanese text leaves wide-open the possibility that Godzilla is female, hermaphroditic, or gender-non-conforming in some other way. (In Japanese, it is never necessary to use pronouns like *he* or *she*, so it is far easier in Japanese than English to avoid gendered language altogether.) My first draft of the translation tried to avoid this problem by calling Godzilla "it" instead of "he" or "she," but that evoked stunned and passionate reactions from my class of students, which included no small number of Godzilla fans. It became clear in our discussions that none of them had ever thought of Godzilla as anything but a rampaging, pissed-off male. I tried following contemporary trends and switching to the gender-neutral singular "they," but many students still rebelled. While I personally am fond of the idea of queering Godzilla and making him/her/it/them a little less gender nonconforming, I ultimately deferred to tradition and my most vociferous students, who wanted me to keep Godzilla an angry male. After all, if we accept Kayama's statement at the beginning of the novellas that Godzilla serves as a stand-in for nuclear weapons, and it was military men who were the main architects of America's military arsenal, perhaps it does make sense for Godzilla to be male, too.

Notes

1. Nakajima Kawatarō, "Kaisetsu," in *Kayama Shigeru, Shimada Kazuo, Yamada Fūtarō, Ōtsubo Sunao*, Gendai suiri shōsetsu taikei 7, ed. Matsumoto Seichō, Nakajima Kawatarō, and Sano Yō (Tokyo: Kōdansha, 1973), 416.
2. Kayama Shigeru, *Kayama Shigerū zenshū*, 15 vols. (Tokyo: San'ichi Shobō, 1993–97). The chronologies and notes included in this set provided a good deal of the biographical information about Kayama. Also helpful were the commentaries written by Hiroshi Takeuchi, a scholar of Kayama's work, for two different editions of the Godzilla novelizations: Takeuchi Hiroshi, "Kayama Shigeru to Tōhō tokusatsu eiga," in *Gojira*, by Kayama Shigeru (Tokyo: Chikuma Shobō, 2004), 443–47; Takeuchi Hiroshi, "Kaisetsu," in

Gojira, Tōkyō ni arawaru, by Kayama Shigeru, Four bunko (Tokyo: Iwasaki Shoten, 1997), 178–81.

3. Steve Ryfle and Ed Godziszewski, *Ishiro Honda: A Life in Film, from Godzilla to Kurosawa* (Middletown, Conn.: Wesleyan University Press, 2017), 85; J. I. Baker, ed., "The Birth of the Monster," *Life,* spec. issue, "Godzilla: The King of the Monsters," (reprint ed., 2021), 11–12.

4. Ryfle and Godziszewski, *Ishiro Honda,* 86.

5. Jay Rubin, "From Wholesomeness to Decadence: The Censorship of Literature under the Allied Occupation," *Journal of Japanese Studies* 11, no. 1 (Winter 1985): 84.

6. Rubin, 85.

7. "Text of Hirohito's Radio Rescript," *New York Times,* 15 Aug 1945, A3.

8. Rubin, "From Wholesomeness to Decadence," 88.

9. Quoted in Janine Beichman, "Ishigaki Rin, Poet of Today's Japan—and Yesterday's," Nippon.com: Your Doorway to Japan, 10 Dec 2021, https://www.nippon.com/en/japan-topics/b09012/ishigaki-rin-poet-of-today%E2%80%99s-japan%E2%80%94and-yesterday%E2%80%99s.html. For a translation of the poem Ishigaki wrote to accompany the photo, see Ishigaki Rin, "Greetings," in *This Overflowing Light,* trans. Janine Beichman (Tokyo: Isobar Press, 2022).

10. Baker, "The Birth of the Monster," 12. See also Mick Broderick, ed., *Hibakusha Cinema: Hiroshima, Nagasaki and the Nuclear Image in Japanese Film* (New York: Kegan Paul International, 1996).

11. Robert Feleppa, "Black Rain: Reflections on Hiroshima and Nuclear War in Japanese Film," *CrossCurrents* 54, no. 1 (Spring 2004): 106–7.

12. Rin Ishigaki, the same poet who wrote a poem after viewing a photo from Hiroshima, wrote an angry poem titled "Yawa" (An evening tale), decrying how quick Japanese newspapers were to celebrate America's consolation payment of 5.5 million yen to Kuboyama's family. She calls this "a pitiful spectacle." See Ishigaki Rin, "An Evening Tale," in *This Overflowing Light,* trans. Beichman.

13. Kayama's scenario is available as Kayama Shigeru, "G-sakuhin kentō yō daihon," in *Gojira,* 307–65.

14. Ryfle and Godziszewski, *Ishiro Honda,* 88.

15. Ryfle and Godziszewski, 88.

16. Kayama Shigeru, "*Gojira* kankō ni tsuite," *Gojira,* 255.

17. Kayama, *Gojira,* 308.

18. Kayama, *Gojira,* 308–9.

19. Ryfle and Godziszewski, *Ishiro Honda,* 89.

20. Ryfle and Godziszewski, 102.

21. Baker, "The Birth of the Monster," 14.

22. Kayama, "*Gojira* kankō ni tsuite," 255–56.

23. Jō Masayuki, Watanabe Keisuke, Takagi Akimitsu, and Kayama Shigeru, "Kagaku kūsō eiga *Gojira* o mite," in Kayama, *Gojira,* 257.

24. Ryfle and Godziszewski, *Ishiro Honda*, 84.
25. Ryfle and Godziszewski, 87.
26. For more on the film's history, especially a look at the roles that certain individuals played in it, see Baker, "The Birth of the Monster," 8–33; Ryfle and Godziszewski, *Ishiro Honda*, 83–107; and Higuchi Naofumi, *Guddo mōningu, Gojira* (Tokyo: Kokusho Kankōkai, 2011), 164–95.
27. Ryfle and Godziszewski, *Ishiro Honda*, 103.
28. Ryfle and Godziszewski, 104–5.
29. Ryfle and Godziszewski, 105–6.
30. Jō, Watanabe, Takagi, and Kayama, "Kagaku kūsō eiga *Gojira* o mite," 259.
31. Yoshikuni Igarashi, *Bodies of Memory: Narratives of War in Postwar Japanese Culture, 1945–1970* (Princeton, N.J.: Princeton University Press, 2000), 116.
32. Mark Anderson, "Mobilizing *Gojira*: Mourning Modernity as Monstrosity," in *In Godzilla's Footsteps: Japanese Pop Culture Icons on the Global Stage*, ed. William M. Tsutsui and Michiko Ito (New York: Palgrave MacMillan, 2006), 26.
33. Quoted in Baker, "The Birth of the Monster," 31.
34. Ryfle and Godziszewski, *Ishiro Honda*, 107.
35. Kayama Shigeru, "*Gojira* dai-ni-sei tanjō," *Gojira*, 262.
36. Shigeru, "*Gojira* dai-ni-sei tanjō," 263.
37. Shigeru, "*Gojira* dai-ni-sei tanjō," 265.
38. Kayama Shigeru, "*Gojira* zange," *Gojira*, 268.
39. Shigeru, "*Gojira* zange," 269.
40. Shigeru, "*Gojira* zange," 269.
41. Kayama Shigeru, *Kayama Shigeru zenshū*, vol. 7 (Tokyo: San'ichi Shobō, 1994), 526. Despite the fact that Kayama was not the sole author of the radio drama, it does appear in his complete works as Kayama Shigeru, "Kaijū Gojira" in *Kayama Shigeru zenshū*, vol. 7, 331–442.
42. Kayama, "Kaijū Gojira," 331.
43. Kayama, "Kaijū Gojira," 441–42.
44. The macron isn't especially important unless one speaks Japanese. I say this because Ōdo and Odo sound different to Japanese speakers and could mean two different things. Ōdo means "big door," whereas Odo can mean precisely the opposite: "small door."

Glossary of Names, Places, and Ideas

All names in this text appear in the traditional Japanese order, with family name first followed by the personal name. Words that commonly appear in English dictionaries, such as *Tokyo, Osaka, Hokkaido, Shinto,* and *kaiju,* are spelled in the English way, without the macrons over vowels to indicate the proper Japanese pronunciation. In a strict transliteration, those words would be spelled *Tōkyō, Ōsaka, Hokkaidō, Shintō,* and *kaijū.*

24° N, 141°2′ E: These coordinates are far out to sea in the Pacific, south of the farthest of the Izu Islands, namely, the tiny, uninhabited Sōfu-iwa (called "Lot's Wife" in English), which is located at 29°47′ N, 140°20′ E. Kayama likely chose these coordinates for the site of one of the accidents in the first novella since they were close to the very extreme of the postwar Japanese map.

After years, I return home and see . . . [song lyrics]: These lyrics were written by Kyūhei Indō (1884–1943) in 1907 and come from the popular song "Kokyō no haika" (Abandoned ruins of my hometown). The melody is borrowed from the 1871 American song "My Dear Old Sunny Home" composed by W. S. Hays; however, the Japanese adaptation became far more popular in Japan than the original English did in America.

Anguirus: See *Ankylosaurus*. Although Ankylosaurus were real, the word *Anguirus* was invented for the film, as was the passage from the fictional Polish paleontologist that Dr. Tadokoro reads.

Ankylosaurus: Real, armored dinosaurs of the genus *Ankylosaurus* dating from the Cretaceous period.

Buddhist altar: In Japan, it is not uncommon for people to have small Buddhist altars in their homes.

Central Meteorological Observatory: This governmental organization was created in 1887 when the Tokyo Meteorological Observatory (established in 1875) was transferred to the Home Ministry. In 1956, the observatory was reformed as the Japan Meteorological Agency, part of the Ministry of Transport.

clock tower on the top of a building [in the Ginza]: Although not named specifically here, Kayama is referring to the famous Wakō department store, founded in 1881. The version of the store that Godzilla destroys was a curved, Art Deco building completed in 1932 and topped off with a clock tower that played the Westminster Chimes hourly. With its striking look, this building, like the Matsuya Ginza, became known as a symbol of modernity, commerce, and cosmopolitanism. Although it was damaged, the store was one of few Ginza buildings to survive air raids of World War II. It also became a post exchange store for the Allied forces during the occupation of Japan. By destroying this building, Godzilla is trampling on postwar Japanese economic success as well as the postwar order created between Japan and the United States.

evacuation during wartime: Between 1943 and the end of World War II in 1945, when the Allied powers were firebombing the major Japanese cities, many families sent their children to the countryside to protect them. After half of Tokyo was burned in an air raid that killed around one hundred thousand people in a single night in March 1945, the overwhelming majority of young students who still remained in Tokyo were evacuated to the countryside.

Ginza: One of the major commercial and shopping centers of the city located in central Tokyo and filled with bright neon lights. For this reason, it was very much a symbol of Japanese modernity and capitalism.

Godzilla: In Japanese, the monster's name is *Gojira*. This word is written phonetically in the katakana syllabary (ゴジラ), suggesting that the word developed in spoken language among the people, not in formal writing. In fact, the name is a portmanteau that combines the names of two giant creatures: gorillas (*gorira* in Japanese) and whales (*kujira*). Also, the word has an archaic sound about it, as if it comes from the distant past. The clever decision to spell his name "Godzilla" in English, with the word *God* in it, was made when the film was exported to the United States. This manipulation of the English spelling sends a clear hint that there is something divine about the monster.

Haneda Airport: This was the main international airport for Tokyo until 1978, when a new international airport opened to the east of the city. Haneda is located on the western side of Tokyo Bay and is still in use.

Hokkaido (Hokkaidō): The northernmost of Japan's four main islands. It is well known for many things, including its stunning natural beauty, delicious food, and excellent fishing waters.

In the capital, under the lavender clouds of spring [**song lyrics**]: In Japan, it is common for schools and other institutions to have official songs. This is the first verse of the song "Miyako zo yayoi" (In the capital, spring), composed in 1912 as the song for one of the dormitories associated with the Northeastern Imperial University Agricultural School. (This school later became part of what is now Hokkaido University.) The lyrics were written by a student named Yoshisuke Yokoyama, and the music by a student and future religious leader named Kenji Akagi. Rarely do school or other official songs become known across the nation, but this song is an exception. It has been recorded many times, and choirs continue to perform it today, although less frequently than in the past.

Iwato Island: The fictional island in the Pacific from which the second of Godzilla's species emerges in the second novella. Its name literally means "rocky door island" (岩戸島 *Iwatojima*), but the name echoes a place-name that appears in the Japanese creation myth. After the creation of the world, the Sun Goddess Amaterasu felt vexed at her mean-spirited brother's treatment, and she hid herself away in a cave known as the Ama-no-iwato, or "rocky door of heaven," thus plunging the world into cold darkness. To save the world, one of the other gods danced in front of the cave to lure her out again. Considering this legend, it makes sense for Kayama to give this name to the island from which a new, second Godzilla emerged into the world.

Japan Ground Self-Defense Force: See *Japan Self-Defense Forces*.

Japan Self-Defense Forces: In 1950, during the Allied occupation of Japan that followed World War II, Japan created the National Police Reserve to help protect the nation as war escalated on the Korean peninsula. In 1952, this force was expanded and renamed the National Safety Forces. A few years later in 1954, the same year of the original film *Godzilla*, this force was reorganized and renamed the Japan Ground Self-Defense Force, which became the on-land branch of the Japan Self-Defense Forces (JSDF). (There was also a maritime branch as well.) The JSDF differs from the militaries of many other nations in that Japan's postwar constitution forbids the use of the military in an aggressive capacity. It is to be used only for self-defense.

Kachidoki Bridge: This bridge connects Tsukiji on the Tokyo mainland to Tsukishima, one of the islands artificially created in Tokyo Bay using landfill. The construction of the bridge started in 1933 and was finished in 1940 to provide access to the Japan International Exposition held that year on Tsukishima. The exhibition was to celebrate what right-wing, wartime politicians had dubbed the 2,600th anniversary of the founding of the Japanese nation. In other words, one might argue that when Godzilla attacks this bridge, he was attacking one relic produced by wartime Japanese nationalism.

kagura: A kind of sacred, ritual dance associated with Shinto, the indigenous religion of Japan. Shinto shrines were erected at places where ancient Japanese felt that gods were present; in fact, sometimes shrines were erected to ask for protection from bad weather conditions or problems at sea. The fact that the villagers of Ōdo Island gather in the woods to hold a kagura dance by their shrine suggests that such things had happened before. Perhaps the ancient villagers might have even created the shrine to protect them from Godzilla specifically.

kaiju (kaijū): This word, which literally means "scary beast" or more simply "monster," describes the kind of huge monsters that appear in Godzilla and other series. As the Godzilla movies went international, this word crept into the English language.

Kamiko Island: This island, where much of the conclusive action of the second novella takes place, is fictional. As he did with Ōdo Island (literally "big door island") near where Godzilla entered into the world, Kayama has given this island a name that suggests a deeper connection to Godzilla. The island's name is written with kanji that mean "God's child's island" (神子島 *Kamikojima*).

Kannonzaki: A cape located on the Pacific shore to the southwest of Tokyo Bay. When Godzilla passes Kannonzaki and heads north in the first novella, it is clear he is headed into Tokyo Bay.

Kōzu: In the story, this is the name of a ship. It takes its name from one of the Izu Islands closest to the Japanese mainland. Even now, the Japanese Coast Guard names many of its ships after islands and places in Japan.

Maritime Safety Agency: After World War II, the Allied powers dissolved the Japanese navy, but the Maritime Safety Agency was created in 1948 to patrol the Japanese shoreline due to concerns about illegal immigrants, disease, and piracy. In 2000, the official English name of the agency was changed to the Japan Coast Guard. In addition to the Maritime Safety Agency, the Japan Self-Defense Forces also has a maritime branch that can engage in defensive actions.

military flag showing a red sun surrounded by red, radiating rays: This is not the Japanese national flag, which shows a single red circle in the center of a white background. The Japanese military adopted the flag of an offset red sun with sixteen rays in 1870, and it became especially widespread during World War II. When Japan established the Maritime Safety Agency, it adopted a modified version of the flag with different proportions and a new shade of red.

Minato Ward: A section of the Tokyo metropolis located toward the center of the city on the northwestern part of Tokyo Bay.

Myōjin-shō: The name of an underwater volcano that erupted in the Izu Islands, far out in the Pacific, around 450 kilometers south of Tokyo in 1952. The explosion created a new island, but while the Maritime Safety Agency was surveying the site in September, a subsequent eruption destroyed the survey vessel, killing thirty-one people, including nine scientists. The following year, in 1953, the site erupted again, and the newly formed island collapsed into the sea. This memory was still fresh in the minds of people when the film came out in 1954 and the novella was published in 1955.

Namu Amida Butsu: This phrase, which means something like "All hail the Buddha Amida," is used to pray to the Buddhist deity Amida, which certain sects of Buddhists believe will escort them to paradise after death.

National Diet: The official name for the Parliament of Japan. It has two parts, the House of Representatives and the House of Councilors. The National Diet Building is located in central Tokyo in a neighborhood called Kasumigaseki. The building, which Godzilla destroys so unceremoniously in the chapter "Godzilla Attacks the Metropolitan Center," was completed in 1936 in a style that combines Japanese and Western architecture, and it is crowned with a distinctive pyramid structure at the top. It survived the Allied bombing raids of World War II, thus implying that in some ways Godzilla is just as, if not more than, disruptive as the raids that destroyed the country during the war. As historian Yoshikuni Igarashi has pointed out, it is also interesting to note that nowhere in Kayama's film (or novella) is there any mention of Godzilla trampling on the Imperial Palace, which sits not far from the National Diet Building. Perhaps the prospect of the emperor's main residence being trampled would have upset audiences in 1954, especially since so many people had died in the emperor's name during World War II, only a decade before the novellas were published.

No. 2 Battery: In the nineteenth century, several feudal lords constructed landfill islands with defensive batteries (*daiba*) to help protect Tokyo Bay after the first arrival of Western ships. The first three (including No. 2 mentioned here) were completed in 1853. Later, some of the batteries were taken down and the islands sold to the Tokyo Metropolitan government; however, eventually most of the water where the batteries were located was filled in as more land was reclaimed from the sea.

Ōdo Island: This island is fictional, but based on the other places the story mentions, it appears to be somewhere far out in the Pacific near the Izu Islands. Kayama writes it with the characters meaning "big door island" (大戸島 *Ōtojima*), a name apropos for the island where Godzilla emerges into the world. The name of the island hints that the ancient people who named the island might have been aware of their large underwater neighbor.

Ōme Kaidō: An important road that leads from central Tokyo to the west-central provinces. It was originally created in feudal times and has gone through many incarnations, but even today, it remains an important route for transportation.

Osaka Castle: This famous castle was originally created in 1586, when it was one of the biggest and most impressive castles in the nation; however, it burned down in 1868 during the armed struggles surrounding the coup d'état that brought Japan into the modern era. In 1931, the castle was re-created in concrete, but during World War II, the imperial government turned it into one of the larger armories in the country. In 1945, soon before the end of the war, Allied bombing raids destroyed much of the castle grounds, and after the war, the American military forces occupied it for three years before giving it back to the citizens of Osaka as a park. The keep of the castle again suffered serious damage from a typhoon in 1950, but as the most important symbol of the city, money was quickly raised to restore it. In short, Osaka Castle has seen many incarnations over the years and could be seen as symbol of not just the long history of the city but also the resilience of the Japanese people.

Osaka Metropolitan Police Station: The modern, Western-style building Kayama describes in the chapter "Professor Yamane" is located in the grounds of Osaka Castle Park and was created when the park was overhauled and modernized in 1931 to commemorate the enthronement of Emperor Hirohito. Through World War II, this imposing brick and stone building served as the headquarters of the Fourth Division of the Imperial Japanese Army. After serving as the headquarters of the Osaka Metropolitan Police for a short time in the postwar period, it served as the Osaka City Museum from 1960 until 2001. In 2017, it reopened as Miraiza Ōsaka-jō, which contains restaurants, lounges, bars, shopping, and small museums.

Ōta Ward: A section of the Tokyo metropolis located toward the center of the city on the northern part of Tokyo Bay.

Owarichō: A neighborhood in the Ginza. Located right by it is a department store called Matsuya Ginza, which opened in 1925 and became an icon of commerce, cosmopolitanism, and modernity in the Japanese capital. During the Allied occupation of Japan, which lasted from 1945 until 1952, it served as the post exchange store for Allied servicemen. In a sense, by destroying this building,

Godzilla is symbolically destroying the economic and military order created before and after World War II.

radioactive rain: Nuclear blasts often produce rainfall by suddenly and radically changing the level of heat in the atmosphere. This rain may be filled with highly radioactive, dangerous particles. Because this rain may travel long distances, it can spread radioactivity, harm people, and poison food.

radioactive tuna: In 1952, the American military began secretly testing hydrogen bombs in the Pacific. As the afterword in this volume describes in more detail, a fisherman's boat called *Dai-go Fukuryū-maru* (*Lucky Dragon No. 5*) was caught in American H-bomb tests near the Bikini Atoll in 1954. When their ship reached Japanese shores, it and its cargo were dangerously radioactive. Subsequent investigations showed that radioactive tuna had reached Japanese shores through other routes, and this set off a mass panic in 1954, the same year that the film *Godzilla* was written, filmed, and released.

Self-Defense Forces: See *Japan Self-Defense Forces*.

Shibaura: An area along the coast in the Minato Ward of Tokyo.

Shikine: In the story, this is the name of a ship. It takes its name from one of the Izu Islands closest to the Japanese mainland. Even now, the Japanese Coast Guard names many of its ships after islands and places in Japan.

Shinagawa Ward: A section of the Tokyo metropolis located toward the center of the city on the northwestern part of Tokyo Bay.

Shinshū: The old name for Nagano Prefecture, a beautiful area with high mountains northwest of Tokyo. This was the area to which Emiko and Shinkichi were evacuated during World War II. (See *evacuation during wartime.*)

shōji: A sliding door made of wood and paper, often used to divide a room from the corridor outside.

Sōran, sōran [**song**]: This is a local folk song from Hokkaido. The lyrics describe the experience of fishermen at sea, speaking with the natural forces around them. The words that are untranslated in the chapter titled "Celebrating the Big Catch" do not really have a specific meaning. One often finds such words in Japanese folk songs, giving lyrics to the performers to sing and adding repetition and movement to the song.

Tamachi Station: A train station located several blocks inland from the place where Godzilla first comes ashore in the chapter "Godzilla Attacks the Metropolitan Center."

Tokyo Bay Ocean Liner Piers: When Kayama mentions these piers, he seems to be referring to the piers of Tōkai Kisen Company, Ltd., located in what is now part of Minato Ward on the northwestern edge of Tokyo Bay.

zenzai: Mochi rice dumplings served in sweetened azuki-bean soup. It is an Osaka specialty, and there are numerous famous, old shops that serve it throughout town.

Shigeru Kayama (1904–1975) was a prolific Japanese novelist known for science fiction, detective stories, and adventure stories that often involve fantastic creatures and a love of nature. He worked with Tōhō Studios to produce the original scenario for the now iconic films *Godzilla* (1954) and *Godzilla Raids Again* (1955), and in 1955 he published the two novellas translated for the first time in this volume.

Jeffrey Angles is professor of Japanese and translation at Western Michigan University. He is author of *Writing the Love of Boys* (Minnesota, 2011) and translator of the Japanese modern classics *The Book of the Dead* by Shinobu Orikuchi (Minnesota, 2016) and *The Thorn Puller* by Hiromi Itō.